THE FIGHT AT THE O.K. CORRAL

First it was the Earps coming down the street, Wyatt first, flanked by Morg and Virg. Doc Holliday, using a shotgun for a cane, hobbling off to one side. . . .

In the corral itself, backed against a well, the five other outlaws, guns in hand, sweat darkening their shirts, waiting. . . .

And coming at them, now, walking in the middle of the street, the Earp brothers, Wyatt in the lead, wearing belt guns, their hands slack and easy, free and proud away from the butts.

This time nobody would go to jail. It would be hand against hand, nerve against nerve.

And the Earps marched into the corral. . . .

They still talk about that fight, they still point out where Wyatt stood, where the first man died. . . . It's history now, but then it was blood and guts and raw, sheer courage. . . .

WHO RIDES WITH WYATT

by

Will Henry

BANTAM BOOKS

NEW YORK · TORONTO · LONDON · SYDNEY · AUCKLAND

In warm memory, to the old man in the sun.
He never told me his real name.
I never asked him.

This edition contains the complete text
of the original hardcover edition.
NOT ONE WORD HAS BEEN OMITTED.

WHO RIDES WITH WYATT
A Bantam Book / published by arrangement with
Random House, Inc.

PRINTING HISTORY
Blue Book condensation published April 1954 under the title
THIS MAN WYATT

Random House edition published March 1955

Bantam edition / January 1956

2nd printing .... *January 1956*	5th printing .... *April 1979*
3rd printing .... *January 1957*	6th printing .... *March 1985*
4th printing ...... *September 1965*	7th printing .... *April 1990*

ISBN 0-553-25002-7

Published simultaneously in the United States and Canada

Bantam Books are published by Bantam Books, a division of Bantam
Doubleday Dell Publishing Group, Inc. Its trademark, consisting of the
words "Bantam Books" and the portrayal of a rooster, is Registered in U.S.
Patent and Trademark Office and in other countries. Marca Registrada.
Bantam Books, 666 Fifth Avenue, New York, New York 10103.

PRINTED IN THE UNITED STATES OF AMERICA.

RAI   15   14   13   12   11   10   9   8   7

In the beginning

He was a very old man when I talked to him the last summer of 1933 in the Pioneer's Home outside Prescott. Exactly how old I was never able to determine, for one day he would make it "ninety-three come next spring" and the following morning it would be "ninety-seven this past fall."

There were other gaps in his memory, as well. He would constantly wander and get onto other stories and had to be continually reminded of the one I wanted and the one of which I was convinced he was the sole, surviving principal. But when at last he did get started in a straight line, he never once faltered or needed to be corrected. He told it all in less than an hour, and when he was through he said that was the end of it and that he would say no more about it.

Of course, there had been no time for fact-checking while he talked, but later I was astonished at the minute accuracy with which he pictured those famous times and troubles. Because of this surprising faithfulness to an accepted history, and in grateful deference both to a rather remarkable story and to a grand old pioneer's stirring recollections of its hitherto little-known details, I determined to change not a comma of his rough speech nor a single claim of his fading memory.

Accordingly the reader will find here no highly polished professional fiction but only an unvarnished account of certain legendary happenings in southeast Arizona Territory these seventy-odd years gone. All told, without apology, in the words of a very old man sitting in the sunshine of his last afternoon and remembering, as best he could, a very old story.

W.H.

Burnt Springs Ranch
Cochise County, Arizona
1954

1 ☆

This is the way the kid himself told it to me, so many years ago now that an old man's heart aches sweet-bad with the memory of how tall and straight we all rode in those days.

The kid is gone now. And so is *he*. Him that the kid so looked up to and that he knew likely better than any man then alive or since dead. Him and the kid and all the wild rest of them, they're gone now and there's only me left to tell about it. Me that was there for the most part of it, but that never had the sand nor the speed of wrist to mix into it like the kid. And only just about sense enough to sit here in the sun and swat flies, and to maybe put all this together somewhere near as straight as the kid gave it to me.

Something you'll need to understand, right off, is that no matter if the kid thought it was himself he was telling about, the way it came out wasn't him at all but that other one. I mean him that was never beat by any gun and never bowed to any man. Him that feared only one thing in his whole life. The one thing he couldn't buffalo with a gun barrel nor find the courage to face up to. The only thing that ever backed him flat-down, and that broke off the piece of his iron heart he left behind him when he put his big red gelding up over the Dragoons for the last time and went out of the San Pedro Valley for final keeps.

Yes, him and Evvie Cushman. Those two, and then Lilly Belloit. That's the real story the kid told me. But he never saw it that way.

The way he saw it, it was all guns and raw guts. All stage stick-ups and cattle run-offs and posse dust building over the far hill. All deputies' badges and sawed-off shot-guns and sudden blood on Allen Street. But he was young then, remember that.

3

An old man sees things different.

If the kid's story wobbles some and doesn't seem to hang together all of a piece like it should, keep in mind it's being laid out by a toothless old coot waiting in the sun for his noon baby food. And doing his dim-minded best to put down a yarn he was given and told and took some small part in more years ago than a man likes to remember or wants to admit to.

It lay way down there in the southeast corner of the old territory, setting up on a 4,500-foot bench that fanned down out of the Dragoons without a solitary tree on it big enough for a horned toad to bother hunching up under. Cross-valley you could see the Whetstones pushing up their busted backbones, and north, up past Benson and the S.P. tracks, the Limestones and the Dos Cabezos doing the same thing.

To start off, there wasn't anything there but good grass and water and some few Chiricahua Apaches. Then old Cochise up and died peaceful in '74 and there wasn't even any Apaches there any more. There wasn't really anything there any more after that. Nothing excepting that good grass and that year-around water in the San Pedro, and maybe plenty of quiet nights and hat-size stars and a handful of lonesome, arguey coyotes.

Those things, likely, and then just one other.

More high-grade silver ore than God Almighty ever crammed in under any other piece of greasewood real estate south of Virgina City and the old Nevada Comstock.

Johnny—that was the kid's name—he wasn't there in the beginning. He didn't even hear about it until two years after Schieffelin hit the Lucky Cuss and pulled that first ton of payrock out of the surface porphyry. That was the ton that assayed $15,000 in raw silver and started the whole thing. By the time Johnny got there they were through the limestone caprock, into the quartzite. The Lucky Cuss was down 300 feet, the Contention 550, the Tough Nut and the Grand Central somewhere in between, and better than ten miles of shored-up stopes were drifting under the town itself. They had already shipped $12,000,000 worth of bullion and they weren't calling the place Watervale or Goose Flats any more.

They were calling it Tombstone.

That was the winter young Johnny turned twenty-one, and the same one in which he felt his first urge to look for a cooler climate. And in which he rightly ran for his reins-tied pony in front of the Hairy Dog Saloon, fully sold on following Mr. Greeley's good advice to point his prospects west.

This offhand migration of the kid's began clear back in southwest Texas, and in some pretty salty company. Accordingly, if a man were to back up about here to lay out how it happened, it doesn't seem he could rightly be called for stalling a hand that was mostly played-out, off in Cochise County, Arizona. A boy's got to get his start somewhere, and Johnny got his in San Angelo, Texas.

He was a ranch kid from down in the corner of Crockett County, where the Rio Pecos crosses into Val Verde County and the Mexican border country.

To begin with, his folks were from Missouri, kin to a couple of clans up there that wouldn't need any introductions if a man were to tell you their names. But the kid's side of the family didn't hold with busting banks and hoisting Railway Express Company safes, and didn't cotton to the way the Clay County Vigilantes and the Pinkerton detectives were cleaning out the better-known branches of the clan up north. So they pulled out and shoved on down into Texas.

Well, in this winter I'm telling about, the kid was up in San Angelo with a piece of one of the last big trail herds. This piece he was riding drag for, was to pick up the main herd south of San Angelo. Then the whole bunch was to lay over on the good grass up there waiting for the snow to go out and figuring to hit on north for Wyoming right back of the first decent thaw.

Now, at the time, this boy was a long day's drive from being dusty behind the ears. He hadn't ever been up into Tom Green County or San Angelo before, nor for that matter more than fifty miles from the Pecos or into any town bigger than Langtry. Which is to say one with more than five shacks and fifteen year-around voters. He had about $300 saved up from four years of brush-popping the Pecos pear thickets, and when he saw the city lights of San Angelo he figured he had spotted himself a pretty prime hog. Naturally, he aimed to cut that hog right

5

proper before some other sharp boy from south Texas should lope into town and beat him to the butchering.

As said, he was some green.

They've got a saying down in Crockett County that a fool shows his money and a monkey shows his backside. Young Johnny wasn't in town two hours before his Levis were clean down around his ankles. Shortly, the man-grown customers in Emmett Slattery's Hairy Dog Saloon were advising him to shorten up his cinch and hit for home. It was pretty good advice but it came a little late in the game. By that time he was $275 in the hole with his last twenty-five riding on the case ace. Also, by that time, he was tolerably convinced the dealer stunk as bad as that stuff on a sheepherder's boots.

In those days faro was still being dealt by hand in most places, the Hairy Dog Saloon being for sure one of those places. Likely, had he come along a couple of years later when they were pulling the cards out of that new-fangled box with the slot in the side, and they couldn't be palmed —not even on a country boy—Johnny would have gone on up to Wyoming and started his own spread like he intended to do in the first place. He would have been known by his own good name—and decently forgotten long ago —instead of by that other bogus name he picked up and by which he'll be remembered as long as western talk winds up, like it always does, on bad hombres.

But then, hell. If the dog hadn't stopped to hunker down, he'd have caught the rabbit.

The way it was, this kid, Johnny, was bucking the tiger with the last nickel in his jeans when he finally saw the house slicker shifting the pasteboards on him.

He had on a gun, like any fool kid. And like most of them he had some far-fetched ideas about how fast he could get to it in case any tinhorn sport should get to crowding him. Right at the time, he didn't even wait for the play or the call on that last spade, but went digging, hog-wild, for his kicker.

Well, a couple of things happened then.

First off, he got his own hardware into action quick enough for it to be clear there was maybe some small justification for a man to allow the kid's notions on his natural gun gait weren't *too* long-fetched after all.

Second to that, the dealer was close to being as clumsy

6

with his Colt as he was with his cards. For a man making his living at faro, being slow with his kicker is one talent he ought not to go into business with. Leastways, not if he can't palm an ace so that a twenty-year-old kid can't catch him at it.

Johnny bucked two slugs in under his shoestring tie before the sharper got halfway out of his chair. Mr. Dealer fumbled around with his shirt front like he couldn't believe the bullet holes were really there, slid under the table and was out of the play for keeps.

Along about then two tough-looking housemen were moving in on the table. Players and onlookers, alike, were fanning out to give them all the room they might figure they would need to down this fresh kid. Ordinarily the boy's next play would have been out the swinging doors, feet first and sagging in the middle like a sack of wet oats. But where card luck wasn't with him, the good Lord was.

The good Lord and a tall, quiet fellow who had been standing back away from the table layout, watching him get cleaned.

Johnny had seen this big cuss with the straw-yellow mustache move up slow on his right side as he was dropping his next to last chunk. But he hadn't paid him any particular mind save to notice he was powerful wide and tall, and easy on his feet, and maybe dressed some shades too natty to be a cowhand or a rancher. Past that, there wasn't time for much noticing. He was still climbing out of his chair, flustered plenty by having just drilled his first man and doing nothing with his gun but letting it dangle while he eyed the blood on the dealer's shirt, when the first houseman went for his shoulder holster.

2 ☆

The kid should have died quick, then and there. That first houseman had his iron out and was lining him up, dead center. He wasn't hurrying any, either, because he could see he didn't have to, and he was taking his sweet time swinging his barrel onto where the boy's rib bones left off and his belly began. A man could guess that house tough had been there lots of times before, and that he didn't aim to take more than one shot to make sure the reputation of the Hairy Dog's faro layout didn't get run down by any short yearling from Crockett County.

He was just letting his thumb up off the hammer spur when he happened to shift his eyes from the kid onto the big quiet fellow who had moved up to side him.

There wasn't any doubt about the way that houseman's thumb clamped back down on that hammer and eased it off-cock. Nor about the way his eyes opened up at the same time his color got bad. Nor yet about the hot-handled way he let go of his Smith & Wesson Banker's Special when the big man just nodded at him without saying a word. He didn't bother talking back. He just dropped that short-barreled Smith like he'd fished it out of a pot-bellied stove. That was all there was to it.

The big man looked real pleasant at the houseman and nodded to where the dealer's boots were sticking out from under the table. "I see Cherokee is still as big-fingered as ever," he observed thoughtfully. "I'm surprised at you though, Pete. Wouldn't have thought you'd work a layout with such trash."

"Beggars cain't be choosers," scowled the other, getting a little of his color back. "I bin down on my luck since leaving Dodge. Besides"—he said it in a way that told he didn't like this big blond devil and was mortally afraid of him—"we cain't all be in your class when it comes to dealing a layout."

"An unhappy truth," agreed the tall stranger. "I admit I limit my game to men."

Pete ignored the reference to the white-faced kid.

"Where's your play in this?" he asked nervously. "The kid got a good shake. Cherokee carried him along better'n two hours. What's your call in it, anyhow?" he repeated uncertainly.

By now the other houseman had sidled up to back Pete. There was no mistaking the way he eased his coat back to clear the two beltguns he had on. It was equally plain he had never laid eye on the stranger before. "What the hell's going on, Pete?" he challenged. He eyed the gun on the floor, then the obviously shaken Pete. "You got the dropsy or something? This bird ain't even touched his artillery. Who the hell is he, anyhow?"

8

Pete started to speak but the big man broke in on him, still pleasant about it and still standing easy, his right thumb hooked in the armhole of his vest, his other hand sort of currying and twisting up the left end of his mustache as though he was thinking about something real serious—like should he have steak or pork chops for noon dinner.

"Old Bill Shakespeare had it about right on names," he drawled quietly. "He always allowed there wasn't anything much in them, one way or the other. It's what a man's got in his mind that counts," he continued gently. "Now what is it that you boys have got in yours?"

"What I got in mine," growled the second houseman quick enough, "is that you talk too much."

As he said it, the kid saw the gambler start for his two tied-down Colts. Neither the kid nor any of the other onlookers saw the blond giant move for his gun. But the plain fact was, he was one minute standing there with his hands empty and the next he had a long-barreled Cavalry Colt just sort of laying in his right hind. That was it. It was just sort of laying there, not pointing at the houseman, nor his pal, Pete, nor anybody. But only kind of wandering around, aimless-like, while he went on talking.

"A minute ago, Pete, you were asking me where I stood here. That depends." He turned to young Johnny, eyeing him slowly. "How much did you drop, boy?"

"Three hundred," blurted Johnny, and had sense enough just to give the rough count, not beefing it up with any bad loser's tallow.

The big man chucked his head. "You want it back?" he asked softly. "You figure you got it coming?"

The kid had always had to sit back on his temper with a spade bit. Right now, with the big cuss crowding him soft and quiet, not tipping his hand either way, he felt his dander go over the bank and into the willows. "No, goddamn it!" He backed off a step, got up on his hind legs and began to paw a little ground. "I set here and watched the damn stuff go without any help from you. I reckon I don't need any dude-dressed wetnurse to bottle-feed it back to me!"

Like any kid in a bad tight, where he knows he's been a tom fool and isn't improving the condition a cussed bit, he began to try to make up for short years by long talk.

9

He was fair yelling when he got around to the two house-men.

"As for you lousy bastards, you see me again you'd best scratch leather without waiting for any invitations. By Christ, I'll . . ."

"Big talk boy," said the tall man, easily.

He made the break-in very soft, but he wasn't half-smiling any more, nor looking pleasant like before. "Shut your damn mouth and get outside."

He waited a spell and when the kid didn't answer, gave it to him again. "You hear me, boy? I said get out."

"By God, I heard you the first time! But neither you nor any of these other sons of . . ."

"Get out."

He made that last call plenty flat and ugly. Johnny could see it was him he was mad at, now. Still he didn't know who this big ranny was, didn't rightly give a damn anyways. He hadn't sense enough to know how close he'd been to six foot of San Angelo sod two minutes ago. Nor how close he still might be to the same measurement. He was mad clean through, that miserable temper of his that was the cause of so much of the hell he got himself into later, clean out of hand. He was embarrassed, too, having that rotten, high pride of the kind that nearly always runs with thin temperament and quirky nerves.

Accordingly, he bellied up to his quiet-talking backer, making the most of the fact that he was a six-foot-and-then-some boy, himself, and could do a little better than look the big man in the eye on even terms.

"And just who in hell you think is going to put me out, little man?" he yelled.

The stranger didn't raise his own voice a hair. But anybody other than a paint-green kid could see he didn't cotton to twenty-year-old cowhands bracing him spit-close like that.

"I reckon you're nominating me, son," he nodded.

With the self-preserving genius of riled kids for talking a big fight right up to the last possible second short of actually getting caught in the middle of one, Johnny backed off another step. He was still talking loud and big but the fartherest man in the room could smell the stall now. He bellowed like a steer that has already dropped

10

his tail and knows full well he isn't going to put his head down to go on in.

"And who the hell are you?"

The big man looked at him a long five seconds, not saying anything nor moving a finger. Then, so slick and easy that only the old hands in the crowd followed it, he palmed his Colt back into its leather. In the same motion he hooked his thumb back into his vest and let the kid have it right between the eyes.

"Name's Earp," he grunted softly. "Might be you've heard of me."

It was Johnny's five seconds then. He took all of them before he could get his throat to working.

Nor was he the only one in the Hairy Dog having trouble with his swallowing apparatus. The whole crowd of toughs melted back as though somebody had just dumped a gunnysack of diamondbacks on the floor, the hard-boiled houseman previously siding the white-faced Pete dissolving farther and faster back than the simplest-minded ranchhand in the place.

When the pride of Crockett County finally did get his Adam's apple to go down, he took the first swallow to get his wind back, the second to gulp out, *"Jesus Christ A'mighty!"* Then, with what little strength and horse sense he had left, he crawfished around and backed all the way out the swinging doors, the sudden water in his knees making him stumble and feel around for his footing like a payday drunk.

Young Johnny might be all shades of green. He might be one hundred miles from the Pecos River for the first time in his life. San Angelo might be the biggest town by several hundred he'd ever seen. But the name the tall blond gunman had just given him was as well known in Langtry as it was in St. Louie. Or in Baxter Springs, Abilene, Ellsworth, Dodge City or Fort Hays.

No kid of ten, let alone twenty, living south of the Santa Fe tracks and west of Fort Worth, needed to be told what first name initial went in front of the Earp part of the pale-eyed stranger's answer.

It was a big, black W.

This was *Wyatt Earp,* mister.

11

3

When Wyatt came out of the Hairy Dog it wasn't anything like you read about his kind doing in these johnny-come-lately cowboy books. There wasn't any of that cautiously moving out backward through the slat doors with two big .45's trained on the local villains inside. He just walked out, frontwards. Like he'd no more than sashayed in for his morning snort of forty rod and was ready to mount up and ride on.

But the way he looked the kid over when he found him waiting outside by his crowbait cowhorse, was something else again. The kid remembered that he'd never seen such a scarey pair of fish-blue eyes in his life. They cut into him like two chips of ax-blade iron flying off a ten-pound grindstone. Still the big man didn't say a word. He just swung up on his outsize red gelding as though he'd said all he intended to, inside, and meant to move right along without any good-byes.

Johnny was some little subdued by this time. The jolt was wearing off of him and he was beginning to suspect he'd just killed a man and that Tom Green County wasn't going to be near big enough to hide him out.

He moved quick, stepping over to Wyatt's stirrup, hat in hand and having trouble getting his words out.

He was wanting to say something that added up to thanks, but the way the big gunman was staring down at him, he couldn't make it. Wyatt let him sweat a minute, then chucked his head at him like he had inside.

"Crawl that roan, boy," he advised, nodding toward Johnny's scrub. "You'd best ride along with me a spell."

Johnny knew what he meant. He jammed his hat back on and crawled.

They rode slowly up Main Street, Johnny saying nothing, Wyatt tugging at the left side of his mustache and maybe thinking some. Whatever he had on his mind, it was in front of him, not behind. He didn't look back the whole of the way out of town. Johnny naturally took care of that department. By the time they were past the last building and into the sagebrush, his neck was stiff from swiveling back toward the Hairy Dog and he couldn't keep his concern tied down any longer.

"Why you reckon they aren't coming after us?" he blurted out. "There hasn't anybody even stepped out the doors yet!"

Wyatt glanced back. "Figures," he shrugged.

"How come?" demanded Johnny, still with not too much color around his gills.

"I told them it made me nervous to have anybody looking over my shoulder."

His wide mouth didn't lift a muscle when he said it, but Johnny could see the smile way back inside those pale eyes.

It somehow made him feel all at once warm and good down in his belly. And like if he should have the chance about now, he'd gladly lay right down and die for Wyatt Earp. It was the first taproot of a feeling that was to keep growing in him until that long-away twilight when Wyatt came to put his big hand on his shoulder for the last time. But for now the kid could only sense the twinge of it inside him, and couldn't in any way begin to know what it was going to turn into.

After a long minute of cutting through the flats west of town, he got his thoughts working back onto where he was.

"What are we going to do now?" he asked anxiously.

"We?" said Wyatt deliberately.

Johnny flushed. "I mean, what you aim *I* should do?" he corrected. Then, the words tumbling out suddenly. "He was dead, wasn't he? I never looked at him after he slid under the table. You've shot lots of them. You sure he was . . ."

"He was dead, boy," interrupted Wyatt harshly. Then, voice softening a little, "A man can tell without he has to look twice. It's the way their eyes go dumb and straight, and the way they sag when the slugs hit into them." Again he paused, catching Johnny's glance and holding it as he eased the rest of it to him.

"You're a killer, boy."

Johnny felt sick and cold inside then, the warmth and the glow of the minute before gone out of him like a guttered lamp. If he had had any doubts about where he

13

was, Wyatt Earp had just spelled it out for him. And to make doubly sure he didn't get it wrong, the tall Dodge gunman went ahead and totted it up for him, slow and careful.

"If you look at the law like it's a fence line, boy, running say due north and south, you can see it splits the grass into two pastures. On this side, in the east pasture, is the registered stock, legally branded, grazing peaceful and putting on tallow. Over yonder, on the far side of the wire, the grass gets mean and thin. What few head are cropping it look pretty tick-sore and fly-blown. They're all ribs and horns and loose hide. And all spooked and hoof-split from grabbing their feed in the rocks and on the run. You see that, boy?"

Johnny looked at it, and he saw it.

"I reckon," he said at last and only half-aloud, "that crimping that crooked faro dealer puts me somewhat west of that line fence."

"Somewhat," was all that Wyatt said.

Johnny thought that over, but it only brought him back around to where he'd been before.

"I got to ask you again, Mr. Earp," he muttered. "What's a man to do?"

"You calling yourself a man now?" asked the big rider quietly.

Johnny looked at him and thought he saw that back-of-the-eyes grin once more. For the first time since stumbling out of the Hairy Dog, he got back a little of his natural brass. "Likely I just shot myself out of the boy class, back yonder. I don't feel too hairy-chested right now, but I reckon Colonel Colt and the calendar are both against me."

"Meaning?" said Wyatt.

"I was born January 15th, in '59."

Wyatt nodded. "If I've not lost count since leaving Kansas, this is January and today's the 15th."

"You ain't lost count, Mr. Earp."

"Happy birthday," grunted the big man expressionlessly.

"It makes me twenty-one," said Johnny unhappily.

Wyatt Earp looked at him. He reached across between the loping horses, just for a second putting his hand to Johnny's shoulder. When he took it away and shook

14

his huge head, the warm backlight was behind his eyes for sure.

"*It makes you a man*," he corrected softly.

They rode for two hours without another word.

Then, suddenly, Wyatt pulled his horse up and turned to Johnny. "You know anything about laying tracks, boy? And about covering them up?"

"Learned a little," said Johnny, puzzled. "Our ranch set in the brisket of Comanche country."

Wyatt watched him a minute, nodded abruptly. "Don't turn around, keep looking west. Now tell me—what kind of prints does this Big Red of mine leave?"

"Clean in front, saving for a calk that marks extra-deep on the inside of the right shoe. Goes medium wide behind. Left shoe twists a mite when he pushes off on it. Leaves a kind of smudge." Johnny didn't even think about it, just answered up like he'd been asked for the time of day or the loan of a light.

Wyatt narrowed his eyes. "You'll do," he said. Then, quickly, "You can look back now."

Johnny took his look. When he did he lost a little of the color that had been building back into his face over the past couple of hours. It was low on the skyline, yet a long ways off and hazy, but it was dust all right.

"Don't get jumpy now," advised his companion drily. "It's not much of a posse and they're a far piece back. You see that line of rocks down south there, boy?"

Johnny nodded and the big man rattled it to him.

"Well, you hit out for that ridge. You'll see it bends around north again and that it tails out in that mesa country up ahead. Counting from our left you'll see five main buttes. I'll be camped back of number five, last to the north. You got that?"

"Got it," said Johnny, gulping hard.

"That bunch back there will be up to the split in our tracks along about dark," continued Wyatt. "When they are you can lay ten to one they'll turn off after you." He broke off, nodding thoughtfully, and Johnny saw the shadow of the eye-smile again. "You can make it twenty to nothing they won't trouble to tail *my* prints," he finished quietly.

"No bet," grinned Johnny, beginning to feel immensely better but at the same time still understandably concerned about his own immediate future. "How do you figure *my* play from here?" he asked nervously.

"You ride it right and proper, boy, you ought to be able to lose them along that ridge sometime after dark. Providing you've learned anything at all from those Indians back home."

"Well, all right," agreed Johnny uncertainly, "but where do we stand when the sun comes up?" It was the big question. The kid knew it and the way he asked it let Wyatt know he did.

"Depends," said the latter slowly. "If there's still posse dust between us and San Angelo come daylight, we split up for good."

"Otherwise . . . ?" Just asking it, Johnny felt the cold of the fear and the loneliness beginning to get back into his belly.

"Otherwise," answered the big gunman, eyeing him, "I reckon you can ride along with me yet a spell."

Johnny's heart jumped at the words. As what green ranch kid's wouldn't?

Ride along "yet a spell" with the greatest gunfighter of them all? Head on west with the man who had pistol-whipped Ben Thompson? Took the guns off Henry Plummer and elbowed him into the Dodge City hoosegow, all by himself? Side up with him that the likes of Luke Short and Bat Masterson had been glad to wear a badge under? Well! Just a little bit more than *maybe,* by God! You could bet into that hand all night, mister!

He swung his pony. His throat went a shade tight on him, and he tried to hold his voice down to where the other wouldn't notice the choke in it. "I'm beholden to you, Mr. Earp. I'll do my best."

"Boy!" The big man's hand shot out and clamped the roan's headstall. "Out here a man doesn't 'mister' his friends. You ought to know that."

"Yes, sir!" stammered Johnny, already bogged to his belt buckle in gratitude and now up to his armpits in embarrassment. "Ugh—so long—*Wyatt!*"

For the first time, the Kansas gunman brought the grin out from behind his eyes. He swung his dusty hat, whacking Johnny's roan across the haunches. "So long, boy," he called after him. "Look sharp and stay off the skyline."

He sat and watched the roan grow small with distance, his left hand tugging at his sun-gold mustache. He looked back, squinting thoughtfully at the far-off dust cloud to the east. He brought his eyes back to the kid and the southward sweep of the rocky country into which he was riding.

They were all alike, these halter-broke stud colts, crazy for a gun and worshipping anybody that had to use one for a living. Take this kid, now. Riding his heart out, yonder. Tearing along into those rocks not thinking about the man he had just killed nor the posse that was after him nor a blessed thing in the wide world but getting the chance to share a little trail with Wyatt Earp.

Wyatt shook his head, quit tugging at his mustache, heeled Big Red into a lope. The brief nod of the massive head was for young Johnny, but the words that came with it were for somebody else.

"If we get joined up by the company that generally rides along with me, boy," he muttered into the rising wind, "you'd likely be better off if that posse caught up to you."

Ordinarily, Wyatt wasn't overlong on imagination. Nor was he one for fancy words or thoughts. But he knew the shape and shadow of that other horseman who never left his side, who forever followed where he led, one step off the trail and always waiting. He knew him and he knew him well. There was nothing fancy about it. You saw him there and you nodded to him like to an old friend and you knew why he was there and what his being there meant to anybody who shared your trail.

Who rode with Wyatt, rode with death.

It was that simple.

4   ☆

Johnny got every break a first-time killer had coming to him. And maybe then some.

Along about mid-afternoon it clouded up and began to

sprinkle, laying the dust so the San Angelo posse couldn't sight-trail him. After dark, the clouds came down low, making a murk of broken moonlight that would have set it up tough to spot a white coyote forty yards out. To cinch it, the rain came on for sure just before midnight, licking the roan's tracks as clean off the rocky sand as top cream from a ranch cat's whiskers. By the first gray of false dawn, an hour ahead of real daylight, he was skirting the fifth butte, squinting through the dark for Wyatt's camp sign.

Pretty quick he caught it, a whisper of cottonwood smoke sneaking out of a cluster of creek willow at the base of the bluff ahead.

When he had told Wyatt he'd picked up a pointer or three from the Comanches, he'd been putting it modest enough. Johnny, for all his lack of broad travel and big birthdays, understood how to take care of himself in the brush. Seeing Wyatt's smoke now, he wondered that the famous lawman would be so careless. He allowed, in the same superior eye squint, that he saw up yonder a good chance to steal a march on his betters, and maybe play it so cute the big man would have to figure he hadn't made any mistake giving a green kid the chance to side him.

About one hundred yards short of the willows he slid off the roan, leaving him in a pile of rocks, reins trailing.

He went the rest of the way in with his boots in his hand and a big grin on his face, walking up wide and easy across the creek-bottom loam. He didn't scrape a twig getting through the willows. Five minutes after leaving the roan he was standing across the campfire smoke from Wyatt's blanketed form, smirking fat and happy and figuring how he'd best handle the rest of it.

First off, he knew better than to jump a man like Wyatt out of his blankets cold. A little joke was one thing. Getting yourself killed having your laugh on a famous man-hunter, was another.

No, best thing was to just work into the fire, squat down to it like you'd been there all night, then go to fussing with the coffee tin, pretty soon making just enough noise to wake Wyatt up, easy.

Still grinning, he stepped out of the willows.

That was all he remembered.

18

Well, that and the few thousand stars that exploded somewhere behind his left ear, flared up in a chain lightning flash, then went black as a hibernating bear's den.

Wyatt pulled the .44 barrel gently away from the boy's skull, stepped to one side to give him room to fall, face forward, into the campfire soot.

He didn't hurry pulling the kid out of the ashes, knowing they were long-banked and not hot enough to more than blister him so he'd remember it. When he did reach down and drag him back, he walked on over to the creek, dipped a hatful of water, poured it down on the kid in a long stream. After that, he threw a few fresh chunks of bark on the fire, sat down on the log he had rigged up for a dummy under his blankets, eased back to wait for strong young nature to take its bull-headed course.

Pretty quick the kid sputtered, sat up, had himself a look around.

Just before he found Wyatt across the fire, he found the duck egg that was hatching back of his ear. When Wyatt saw him go to fingering the lump, he cleared his throat, nodded to him, tapped the seven-inch barrel of the Colt he still held laid across his knee.

As has been indicated, Johnny was only young, not downright stupid.

He grinned, half-foolish, and started in, going a little lame in the offhind foot about it, to make his apologies. "Reckon I've been a damn fool, Wyatt. Might have got myself killed coming up on you like that—you not knowing it was me and all."

"Correct," agreed the latter, unsmilingly. "Save for one small item."

"Such as?" grinned Johnny, still trying to smirk it off as best he could, especially seeing that his big friend was a long rope-toss from laughing himself sick over it.

"Such as I *did* know it was you, boy."

Johnny took that. He thought it over a considerable spell. He added it up with another tender feel of the lump back of his ear—which same was now getting out of the mallard grade and pretty well up into he-goose class—and decided that, big-wheel cowtown marshal or not, he didn't like it.

"Knowing it was me," he complained, his bad temper

19

showing in the sulky way he said it, "I don't see you had any call to lay a man out thataway."

"A *man,* no," said Wyatt Earp, real slow.

"Now what the hell you mean by that?" Johnny was getting his tail up for sure now. And that goose egg was pounding away fit to bust his head open.

"A *mule,*" said Wyatt, still in that deliberate, thoughtful way of his, "never learns anything through mother love nor gentle discourse. You've got a thick skull, boy. Better that I put a dent in it right now, than that the next man along drills a hole clean through it. You follow me?"

Johnny dropped his head. He hadn't missed the peculiar, soft way Wyatt had said it. Nor the unsettling, direct look he had put back of it. While he reached around for something to say, he felt the thrill of it grow inside him. It was hard enough to believe, but it was almost as though the biggest man west of Abilene, Kansas wanted powerful bad to be friends with a dumb kid from Crockett County, Texas. To have somebody he liked and could trust, to talk to. And as though if you had the good sense to say the proper thing right now, he was thinking of maybe letting you be that somebody.

He brought his head back up, awkward and slow about it. "Yes, sir," he managed humbly, "I follow you. And I mean to keep following you, just so long as you'll leave me do it."

"All right." Wyatt chucked his head in that short way Johnny was beginning to know. "What's your name?"

"Ringgold. Johnny Ringgold. Spelled with two g's."

As had any man living up on the Kansas-Missouri border a few years back, Wyatt had heard that name. And those other names hooked up with it, clanwise.

"Don't care how you spell it, boy," he said, wagging his big head doubtfully, "it won't do. Too off-color. Too easy to remember. Too well-known in these parts, as well as up yonder. You'll need a new one where we're going." He hesitated, thinking it over. "What you got in your family tree outside of Ringgolds and Youngers and Daltons?"

"Ma was a James," the kid said, quick and proud. "Third cousin to Jess's pap, back on the Kentucky side."

"That's one hell of a big help," nodded Wyatt acidly.

20

"Tell you what, boy, we'd better go back to the Ringgold. Shorten it up somewhat, knocking about three spots off of it and having it to come out more like Ringel, or Ringo, something on that order. Take Ringo. That's a name nobody ever heard of either in Texas or Arizona, let alone up yonder on the border."

"Sounds good," said the kid, fliplike. "Got a nice roll to it. I'll take it. How about the rest of it? The front-handle part?"

"You got any natural preference?"

"Always favored John, somehow."

"Keep it then," said Wyatt, and stood up. "Just remember it, that's all. From now on you can call yourself free, wild and twenty-one. But your name's not Johnny Ringgold any more."

He looked at the young Texan a long ten seconds. When he finished there was a faraway frown back of his light-colored eyes, and the smile was long gone from them. "See that you don't ever forget that fact, boy. From now on you got a brand-new name. One you can make as bad or as good as you want."

"Ringo . . ." said the kid softly, not even hearing him. Then, even lower voiced, and looking clear off west to where the last morning stars were winking out over the distant Pinals and Old Cochise County, "*Johnny Ringo!*"

5 ☆

They were on the trail three weeks, making south and west the whole of the time, just plain enjoying the country and themselves as they went along. Wyatt didn't appear in any hurry, nor even to be going any place special. Naturally Johnny didn't press him any. The new Mr. Ringo had no reason to fret about their direction or destination, so long as both were wide out and far away from San Angelo, Texas.

Along the way they camped where the water and grass were good and where high country gave them a long look at their pony tracks, coming and going. That thing of sticking to the ridges was just one of many little pieces of out-

21

law information young Ringo picked up on that trip. No matter that most who've written about him have put Wyatt down for a surly man with a tight mouth and a short trigger finger, he showed himself anything but close-worded with the Crockett County lad.

When he was alone with a man he trusted, the simple truth was that nobody liked to talk better than Wyatt Earp. He was an odd one, too, for his day, for he'd had some schooling somewhere back in the settlements and didn't use the broken-down English that most in that country got by on. He could spin words together mighty easy, had a quiet, salty sense of humor, was anything but mean or poor in his ways and outlooks on frontier life and lawbreakers.

Maybe that's one reason they got along at first, for young John came from educated folks himself and could hold up his end of a civilized conversation without fracturing too many of McGuffey's third-grade grammar rules. Providing, always, that he was of a mind to want to talk decent.

Wyatt seemed to have plenty of money, staking his youthful partner to the best of everything in the few towns they rode through. Among the things he bought plenty of was pistol ammunition. By the time they crossed into Arizona, following Railroad Pass between the Graham and Chiricahua Mountains, he and the ex-Johnny Ringgold had burned the better part of a case of hulls in off-hand six-gun practice.

This would hardly be worth mentioning except that it was Wyatt's way to try the boy out. More than that, which Wyatt never realized, it was the boy's way of sizing up the old Kansas Coltmaster himself. How far apart they were in their separate opinions of one another—and neither one of them ever peeped to the other on that score—probably told quicker than anything else just how sure it was they were never made to trot in double harness.

Ringo watched Wyatt handle his gun like a city kid would eye old Grover Cleveland Alexander burning them in across the plate, belt-high and whistling every time. But with Ringo that's as far as the kid part of it went. Instead of gulping hopelessly at his chewing wax and allowing he would never be able to pitch like that, Ringo shifted his cud of long-leaf Burley, spit into the sage-

22

brush and began to wonder if maybe he wasn't just a shadow faster than the old man, himself.

That way Ringo had of thinking of Wyatt as "the old man" was sort of funny, incidentally. At the time Wyatt couldn't have been more than twenty-eight, twenty-nine at the outside. And Ringo was going on twenty-two, himself. But there was something to it, just the same. Maybe Wyatt pegged it best himself when he thought it over years later. "I don't really remember being a boy," he said. "I was born, I guess; then all of a sudden I was fifteen and they handed me a Sharps' bullgun and I was market-hunting buffalo with the rest of the men."

But back to that six-gun practice, and the way Wyatt saw it. That's to say, the way it let him see Ringo.

He'd watch the youngster jump his old Confederate-issue cap-and-ball Colt out of its homemade leather so fast there weren't probably six sets of eyes in the southwest could follow it. Then he'd watch him go ahead and smoke his lead into whatever targets they were blasting at, usually an empty condensed milk can or Arbuckle's coffee bag propped up on a mesquite bush, in not more than half the next eye wink. He never said anything other than, "That's pretty good, boy. Likely you'll do." Then the two of them would mount up and ride on with no more said on the subject.

But what Wyatt said and what he was thinking were off-brand horses.

The raw kid he'd chaperoned out of San Angelo and renamed Johnny Ringo was, without any solitary exception Wyatt could remember, the fastest natural and dead-center shot he had ever seen. More than that, his bad temper and thin pride put him in a bad-touchy class. Nobody knew that better than Wyatt Earp.

There were two main breeds of dangerous gunmen, the man-grown professionals like Wyatt himself and like his old friends Luke Short and Bat Masterson, and then the amateurs, the crazy, hot-headed, cold-jawed kids who never grew up. These last were the ones like young Wes Hardin and Clay Allison, wild, no-good kids who bucked a gun out just for the pure hell of hearing it go off and seeing a man grab his guts and go down. Who, once they'd killed their first man, found the rest to come as easy as live pigeons at a county-fair trapshoot—just so

23

many target birds sprung out of a field box, with the main idea to see how many you could run out before you broke your string.

Unless thirteen years as a working peace officer on the firing line with both kinds didn't qualify him to separate the *professional men* from the *amateur boys,* Wyatt figured he already knew where this Ringo kid fitted. He was a simon-pure bad one, as young and crazy as they came. Unless he got the right education, and got it quick, he wasn't going to have to *worry* about growing up. As the twenty-third day on the trail brought them at last across the Pima County line and down onto Tucson, there was only one question still waiting in Wyatt's mind: *was there yet time, or any real chance remaining, to make a man of Johnny Ringo?*

Tucson was the old Pima County seat before they broke the county up to make Pima out of the west half and Cochise out of the east, and it was a pretty quiet town for the day and time.

Wyatt left Johnny in the first saloon they hit, knowing his own errand would be quick enough done and that he'd be back before the kid could get oiled up to the trouble mark. Wyatt himself never touched the stuff— he was over forty before he took more than a social beer or light wine—and besides, he had a man to see about a badge.

Down the street, he found the county jailhouse. He legged wearily down off of Big Red, eased in through the open door, and casually introduced himself to Sheriff Charles Shibell.

Shibell was a little man, too big in the belly and small in the eye to suit Wyatt. But he clapped the big Dodge gunman on the back friendly enough, offered him a good Habana cheroot, kept his greeting admirably short and to the point.

"Glad you could come, Earp. You was that long about it I thought maybe you hadn't got my letter."

Wyatt patted his vest pocket. "I got it all right. What's the deal? Must be a pretty ring-tailed police job to pay what you say it will."

Shibell returned his look, squinting shrewdly.

"It'll pay what you make it pay." He put a sly wink

back of the nod, as much as to say that Wyatt could guess what he meant. For the record, Wyatt wasn't in a guessing mood.

"I can gamble on my own time," he said shortly. "I didn't ride nine hundred miles to sit in on a speculation. What's the deal, Shibell?"

"The deal," said the little sheriff, "is cut and dried. Providing," he added, throwing Wyatt another of his wise winks, "you're man enough to slice it and string it up to cure."

Wyatt reached over and got a match out of the sheriff's shirt pocket. He took his time lighting up his cheroot. When he'd got a half inch of hot ash growing on it, he held it up and looked at it, absentlike. "This is a good seegar," he observed. "Burns even, leaves a tight ash. Now, if you don't want it stumped out in your mustache, Mr. Shibell, you'd best leave off riddling me."

Shibell laughed a little too loud and quick.

"Got a sense of humor, eh, Earp? That's good, that's good. Come in handy where you're bound for."

"Which might be where?" growled Wyatt.

"*Tombstone!*" rasped Shibell.

"I've heard of it," shrugged Wyatt. "What's there?"

"Trouble," frowned Shibell, "and twelve months of back taxes."

Wyatt scowled back at him, nodded abruptly, got to his feet.

"What you need isn't a deputy, Mr. Shibell. It's a tax collector."

He leaned over the desk.

"Let me give you a little advice, friend. In the future, you got a job for a boy, don't send for a man. And don't ever send for *this man*. You understand?"

Shibell understood. He quit winking and grinning, got right down to bedrock.

"Earp, I bin a long term in this office. When I send for somebody, I ain't mixing my age groups. I'd hate to be the 'boy' that tried riding the county tax route down to Tombstone. When they got all through making tough towns they threw away the mold and poured what was left of the mix out into the sagebrush down yonder on Goose Flats. What cooled out and set up was Tombstone."

Wyatt started paying attention. "Tell me more, Mr.

25

Shibell. Could be I've touched you with the wrong spur."

"First off," said Shibell, "from all I hear you're square. You take your job serious and a badge means something to you."

"Skip the posies," grunted Wyatt. "I'm hired to do a piece of work, I do it. Get on."

"I'm not throwing kisses at you," scowled Shibell. "But this ain't strictly a law-and-order job. Unless you got that straight to begin with, don't take the badge."

"You wrote the wrong man."

The Pima Sheriff didn't like the look in the Kansas lawman's eyes, as Wyatt went on.

"I wanted to be crooked, I'd be rich by now. I pin a star on, I pin it proper. It don't come loose and it stays on straight."

"Nobody's asking you to be crooked!" gestured Shibell testily. "Ease off, Earp. Damn it all, you're the man for the job, or I wouldn't have sent for you. Now set still and listen."

Something in the way he said it got to Wyatt. "Make it short," he nodded. "I got a kid up the street in a saloon. He's some dry and soaks up fast."

Shibell made it short.

Tombstone was the richest district in Pima County. Not a nickel in taxes had come out of it since Schieffelin struck the first ledge, and for a good and simple reason. No local deputy was tired enough of pulling good Arizona air into his lungs to go down into the San Pedro. Result was, Tombstone was the third biggest town in the territory and no representative of the duly elected law enforcement offices of Pima County had ever set foot in it. The camp was running wild and its four thousand legitimate citizens were beginning to squawk loud enough to be heard in Prescott. Next thing would be the territorial legislature starting to poke around in Pima County likely to wind up with their noses on Sheriff Charley Shibell's trail.

That wouldn't do at all, naturally.

What *would do,* would be if Shibell could get a good man down there to start pulling in all those back taxes, which same money—politics being no different in Arizona Territory than any place else—would go a long ways toward plugging up the nostrils of the boys from

26

Prescott. As well as keeping everybody in Pima County in office and fat and happy.

The idea for the man who went down there was definitely *not* law and order. The hell with that. That was the sheriff's job, and the sheriff was good old Charley Shibell.

When he finished and sat back to look at Wyatt, the latter had to admit that the little Pima County officer had laid it on the line. You could take it or leave it. But if you took it you knew where you would stand, which would be some west of that north-south line fence of the law that you'd long ago built down the middle of your own mind.

But there was perhaps one small pair of wirecutters left in your back pocket. Once a good man got his star, it took a better man to take it away from him. Looking now at Sheriff Charley Shibell, Wyatt got ready to step over the fence.

"What's the badge rate?" he asked slowly.

"First Deputy, Pima County, District of Tombstone," said Shibell quickly. "Due and legal and swore right now."

"Pin it on," said Wyatt Earp. "Tombstone's got a tax collector."

6 ☆

It was Wednesday, the 19th of February, when Wyatt Earp took the stage out of Benson, for Tombstone.

If he had taken the one on the 18th, or the 20th, or any one that week saving that one on the 19th, chances are good that a fair part of this story would have tailed out some different, which is to say, some considerable quieter.

But the way it was, him and Ringo had ridden their tuckered-out ponies on down to Benson, from Tucson, Wyatt not wanting to part with Big Red even though the tall sorrel was trail-shot and should have been left behind. They got into Benson at noon, Tuesday, but couldn't ride on because Big Red had picked up a stone bruise in his left front frog and was going lame on it. Wyatt knew the horse would never last it on into Tomb-

27

stone, packing his two hundred and ten pounds, so he called it a day and hunted up the stage office, figuring Big Red and Johnny's roan scrub could trot down behind the coach, tied to the boot. That way, not carrying anything but their saddles, both horses could make it on down to Tombstone at the same time him and the kid did, and be ready to hand when they might be needed down there.

And that's how come him to find out the next stage was the Wednesday morning run.

What he didn't find out until he checked the Wells Fargo freight dock just ahead of stage time the following A.M., was that the Wednesday run was the one that took the Wells Fargo box down to the diggings each week, with the Contention Mine payroll in it.

The Contention was a fair fat hole in the ground by that time. The little rawhide trunk that the regular messenger was boosting up to the driver as Wyatt sauntered up to the Company dock, was busting its straps with $15,000 in cash money.

It's little things like that which file off history's triggers and keep deputy sheriffs from dying of old age in office.

Of course, Wyatt hadn't come down to the express office fretting about any cash boxes or mine outfit payrolls. It was just that he'd worked some for Wells Fargo in his time and was only wondering if by chance he knew the Agent there in Benson.

It turned out that not only did he knew the Agent, the Agent for sure knew him.

"Well, Good Gawd A'mighty! If it ain't . . ."

"It ain't nobody," broke in Wyatt, quiet-like and giving him the nod. "You understand?" Then, grinning, "How you been, Bill?"

Taking his cue, Bill dropped his own voice and moved away from the loading platform. He dug an elbow into the big gunman's ribs, like nobody but a mighty old friend would think of doing.

"I bin great, but the Company's catching hell. How you bin, Wyatt?"

"Tolerable. What's this about Company trouble? Mean to tell me the road agents have moved west ahead of the sheriffs again?"

"Wyatt, I wouldn't horse you, you know that. I bin with the Company twenty years now. But I never seen a thieves' road to beat the one between here and the mines. We've hit the insurance companies for $40,000 in losses just this year a'ready. And we got ten months to go! Man alive, you wouldn't be looking for a shotgun ride, would you, old salt?"

"Not much, Bill. I've had my day up on top. From now on I ride inside."

"Well, by Gawd, you got a free pass so long as I'm running this station. Say, what in hell's name you doing down in this gawd-forsaken desert anyways? Running out a Jayhawk murder warrant?"

Wyatt shook his head. "Nope, I'm done with Kansas, Bill. Down here for my health. Doctor said I needed a climate with less lead in the air."

"You picked it," said his companion, forcing the laugh. "Even the bullets are cast out of pure silver down here!" Then, nervously watching his messenger follow the Contention payroll box up onto the driver's seat, "Say, Wyatt, you sure you wouldn't ride shotgun for me just this once? For old times sake? If they hoist one more payroll out of my station the Company will jerk me for good. I can't pay you none, but . . ."

"I'll set your box, Bill," said Wyatt softly. "I'm not so old that I can't remember who gave me my first shotgun job back in Kansas."

"You sure looked gawky squatting up there with the scattergun in them days," reminisced Bill. "But I can recollect one thing, no matter."

"How's that?" asked Wyatt, thinking back himself.

"We never lost a dollar on the Leavenworth run that fall!"

Wyatt grinned. "I'll bring you up to date, old horse. You're not going to lose one on the Tombstone run this morning, either." Then, quickly, the grin long gone, "Pull that messenger off the box."

Thus it was that the paying passengers waiting in front of Wells Fargo's Front Street Station in Benson were treated to the sight of the greatest shotgun rider of them all sitting the box of a four-bit coach pulling up to the stage stop of a penny-ante Arizona railhead town. None

29

among them, save the surprised Johnny—and him shut up by a warning wave from Wyatt—had the least idea of the rare privilege being granted them that fine winter midday. But where Wyatt by his own short instructions to Shibell and Bill Gray, the Fargo Agent, was unknown in Tucson and unannounced in Benson, the picture of him sitting up on that driver's box was one calculated to grab any eye, forewarned or otherwise.

Still, while all the passengers on that stage took the same look at him, each one of them saw him different, which was one of the strange things about Wyatt and which was nearly always true about the way he hit people.

The funny thing was that not one in a hundred ever saw him the way he really was.

To Mrs. Ah Chum, better known in Tombstone as China Mary, slant-eyed boss of that city's notorious Hop Town and one of the town's foremost importers of high class white girls, he looked like money in the bank. To the two new rose-light recruits China Mary was chaperoning back to Tombstone, he looked like what all their kind hoped to get with the luck of the evening's draw. And seldom did. A real gentleman, well-heeled, easy in manner, clean in dress and mouth and person.

To sharp-eyed J. P. Clum, renowned first captor of the renegade Geronimo, present mayor of Tombstone and editor of the daily *Epitaph,* he looked like another undesirable citizen of the gun-toting persuasion to be added to the town's already overcrowded collection of same.

To heavy-set, smooth-shaven, ex-territorial legislator and rising Pima County political power, Johnny Behan, presently bound for Tombstone on a mission fatefully tied up with Wyatt's own, he had the look of just the sort of professional gun Mr. Behan could use in his coming plans—and which he made immediate decision to contact on arrival in Tombstone.

To shabbily elegant Lilith Belloit, the faded "Tombstone Lilly" of subsequent dance-hall legend and currently the second-lead star of the Bird Cage Theatre's stage show, he looked most nearly like what he was: a stark, still-eyed, compellingly lonely figure of a man; fierce and kind and gentle and terrible, all in the same breathless eyeful.

But in the end, the one that couldn't get her eyes off of
30

him was the tall girl in the quality, store-bought clothes; the one that stood back and sort of away from the others; not so much snooty or anything like that, but more like she was maybe higher-bred and just naturally stepped daintier.

What this girl saw was a better than 200 pound man, six foot and one inch tall. He was big all over; size twelve boot; broad through the back as a white-face bull; long and thick in the arm, with hands big enough to fold around a twelve gauge Parker shotgun like it was a pocket pistol. His head was huge, his hair ash-yellow and thick and growing with a stiff sweep and heaviness to it that put you in mind of a circus lion's mane. His face went right with the head and hair. It was broadly massive, square in the chin, high-boned under the eyes, the nose big and sharply hawked. His mouth, while not actually narrow or mean of lip at all, was that wide and straight and its grim line so chopped off by the fall of that famous, fierce mustache of his, that when put together with those stary, light blue eyes it gave his whole normal expression a look about as warm as a water hole full of scum ice in October.

But if this classy brunette was some unsettled by the new shotgun rider, she was a long ways from alone in her trouble.

Wyatt locked eyes with her and stiffened up like somebody had slapped him on the haunch with a hot iron.

She was a right tall girl, five-six anyways, and black-haired as a Kiowa squaw. Her eyes were set wide and colored deeper than burnt charcoal, but, all the same, hot with the fire of the life and the strength in her. She was full-lipped and clean in the mouth, with an oval face, creamy skin and cheeks rich-flushed with natural high color.

This was a real woman!

Wyatt turned away first, clumsy and awkward as a cub bear caught up a slick-bark sycamore. In turn the girl colored angrily and broke her own glance away in sudden shame. It was not in her kind to look at men that way. Particularly big men, like that great hulk of a brute on the box with the driver. The boldness and the maleness of that kind had always frightened her. She was mighty relieved and grateful to accept the arm of the slim, good-

31

mannered boy who stepped forward to hand her politely into the coach.

The others piled in after her, Behan helping Lilly Belloit in, and eager Johnny Ringo, still holding the door and playing the natural-born lady-killer to the hilt, eyeing the dance-hall girl's ripe form with an interest far more grown-up than the boyish charm he had put on for the previous, and very proper, young lady.

The stage was an old eight-passenger Concord and could have held Johnny without any trouble, but seeing Wyatt up on top and getting the play from the girls because he *was* up there, nothing would do but that he had to slam the door and scramble for the luggage rack himself.

Wyatt put a fatherly boot in his face, leaned down and advised him off. "Inside, boy," he grunted, holding his voice down. "I understand they figure there'll be some fun down the road a piece. If so, we don't want all the artillery on top the hill." He paused, finger-pointing his instructions. "Now, if we *are* jumped, I look to you to get those women on the floor, down below the window sills. You got any time left after that, you can open up with your popgun and show me if I've taught you anything on the way over from San Angelo."

Johnny looked for a minute like he meant to argue the matter, not cottoning to the man-to-boy way Wyatt was putting it. But then he finally grinned, dropped off the wheel hub, climbed into the cab, latched the door, waved up and hollered the "All set!" to the driver.

The latter hawked at his cud of long-leaf, kicked off the brake, clucked to the wheelers, cussed the leaders, spanked the swing team with the lines, spit three ounces of Burley juice over his left shoulder and considered the run under way.

The big Concord settled back on its leather thoroughbraces, shook itself to settle the luggage in the top rack and unseat the passengers in the tonneau, lurched forward into the rumps of the wheelers, and eased off into the wallowing sideway of its regular road gait. Twenty wheel turns later, it was out of town and into the sagebrush.

You'll say it doesn't sound like much, but that's the way that Wyatt Earp took the stage for Tombstone. And that Johnny Ringo eyed Lilly Belloit and held the door for Evvie Cushman. And that all hell started rolling down onto old Ed Schieffelin's silver strike at Goose Flats that long gone February morning.

You'd better believe it, too, mister.

It was rolling at a six-horse, stage-line gallop!

7 ☆

It was a near daylong pull up the treeless valley of the south San Pedro, and a stiff climb every trace-chain jingle of the way. Even with the team change at Coyote Wells, halfway along, the stage was an hour late into Fairbank, the last stop. The early winter twilight was crowding in fast, as old Monk Wilson, senior Fargo driver on the Tombstone division, headed his horses east for the final grade up to Goose Flats.

Wyatt had hours ago had his talk with Monk and was convinced he could expect his trouble somewhere between Boquilla Springs and Watervale—providing there was going to be any trouble. That piece of road seemed to be the favorite haunt of the local road agents and, studying it carefully through the fading light, Wyatt had no difficulty seeing why.

It was a lonesome stretch of country, and no two ways about that.

But twenty minutes past Boquilla Springs, right in a coach-high jumble of bedrock, it got considerable less lonesome. That is, if the hand-close company of eight masked horseman could be said to make it that way.

They seemed to melt right out of the rocks, three in front of the stage, five behind it.

Of the three in front, two had the slight, slender look of youngsters. The man between the young pair bulked older and heavier. Wyatt gave no look or thought to the five behind, his whole attention hanging on the heavy-set leader of the front three. He thought he recognized him, mask or no mask, and when he spoke he knew he did.

"Ease off, Monk!" The bandit leader's call went familiarly to the old driver. He pushed his horse forward, peering uncertainly up at the box. "If that's a new man up there with you, you'd best advise him to toss that Parker down, peaceful."

33

"I got you," Monk called back. Then, out of the side of his mouth to Wyatt, "Go ahead, drop it, boy. These fellers don't play fer fun."

Wyatt didn't move. He knew where he was now and for the first time since leaving Benson he felt at home and comfortable. The thick-set bandit was clearly sure of himself, hadn't even unholstered his guns or unbooted his Winchester. His two companions, not so old at the game, both had their saddleguns out and swung up onto Wyatt.

"You hear me, mister?" the heavy man asked pleasantly of Wyatt. "Throw down that shotgun."

"*I hear you, Curly,*" said Wyatt evenly, and threw down the Parker.

That is, he threw it down in the western sense, by dropping its worn butt to his hip and firing point-blank from there; the right-hand barrel taking the young horseman to Curly's left, the left-hand tube blasting the one to his right.

The gun was a cylinder bore, loaded with No. 2 gooseshot. The range was not over ten yards. The first boy was dead before he hit the ground. The second, nearly cut in two at the waist, was still alive and on his horse.

By this time Wyatt had shifted to his Winchester and Curly had found his voice.

"Hold off!" he yelled hurriedly to his five-riders beyond the coach. "Don't nobody move!"

Even while advising his followers, he was taking his own instructions literally. He didn't shift a muscle toward any of the three guns he had within arm's reach, but instead carefully raised his palms starward to show his good intentions, and talked up to Wyatt as easy and irritable as though they were sitting to a coffee-fire argument over old times.

"Goddamnit, why didn't you say it was you in the first place?" he complained with honest indignation. "You didn't need to gun those two kids down."

"You didn't give me a chance," said Wyatt, with no return of the easy feeling. "But I'm going to give you one, right now. Order the rest of your boys on around front, here."

"Come on around, boys," directed Curly. "He's got me, cold."

The five moved their horses up through the gathering

34

dark, none of them saying a thing nor moving for his gun. Wyatt kept his Winchester centered on their leader's Bull Durham sack, while he slowly and carefully read him out.

"Now, you take your boys and get. I'm leaving you go with fair warning this time, but here's something you'd better see gets heard by all your friends hereabouts. You're all through in this end of Pima County. The law's come to Tombstone, boys, and I'm it. Move along. Don't bother looking back."

There was no answer from the bandit group. There was nothing wrong with their ears even if the full dark was down now and they couldn't see the big new shotgun rider too well. They moved. Quick and quiet and all together. Nobody looked back. The last clink of their ponies' hoofs on the bedrock died away thirty seconds later.

The spot inquiry, headed by Wyatt easing down off the driver's box to catch up the bandit pony that was still packing the wounded boy, was short and sharp.

The passengers, with Ringo in the lead and running to join Wyatt, tumbled out of the coach. They moved up through the dark to mill around the latter as he gentled the pony and had a quick look at what was slumped, unconscious, in its saddle. "Don't bother with him just now," he warned, waving them back. "He'll keep. I got a question that won't."

"But he's hurt," cried Evvie Cushman, starting to push past Wyatt, "terribly hurt! We've got to help him."

Wyatt grabbed her by an arm, none too gentle, and shoved her back. "Leave him be," he grunted. "He's well past any help of yours, miss."

Before the indignant girl could reply, he wheeled on the others. "You, Monk!" he barked at the wizened driver. "That big bird called you by name. He seemed to know you. Who was he?"

Monk shrugged, dropping his eyes. "Dunno, mister. He had on a mask, didn't he? Could have bin anybody."

"Could have," nodded Wyatt, eyeing him hard and straight. "Only he wasn't." He turned disgustedly from Monk. "Anybody else recognize the big man? I mean," he added deliberately, "anybody that wouldn't mind ad-

35

mitting it?" He looked at Behan, who had been at the window nearest the outlaw leader.

Behan returned the look, spoke quick. "Never saw him before in my life that I could swear to. It was pretty dark, you know."

Clum said simply, "I can't help you. I was on the far side of the coach."

"Ma'am?" said Wyatt, turning to Lilly Belloit, who had been with Behan on the action side.

"Could be, mister. But a girl's got her future to think of."

"Thanks," said Wyatt. "At least you don't bother to lie about it."

"What does that mean?" Behan pushed forward belligerently. "Are you saying the others of us have?"

"I'm not saying a thing," Wyatt answered him. "Just thinking. Little habit of mine."

"It's a bad one," nodded Behan, not dropping his gaze. "In these parts you can think yourself into a lot of trouble." He paused, looking pointedly at the dead boy on the ground. "Offhand," he said quietly, "I'd say you'd better use any excess brains you've got to think yourself *out of* trouble, not into it."

"Meaning?" asked Wyatt lazily.

"You had no call to shoot these two boys. That was pretty close to murder, mister. You didn't even wait to find out what it was they wanted."

Wyatt eyed him. "When a man," he said slowly, "asks for my gun, I never question his intentions. It's what you might call an extra-legal assumption. What makes it binding is whether I give it to him faster than he can take it away from me."

"And who are *you*," demanded Evelyn Cushman, highflushed, "to set yourself up as a judge and jury?"

She flung a slender hand toward the youth in the saddle. "I know that boy!" she cried. "Look at him, Mr. Clum," she appealed. "Isn't that Lennie Watrous?"

The mayor had his look, nodded back to the angry girl. "It's young Watrous, all right, Miss Evvie. But I'm afraid that isn't going to help him any. He had a gun in his hand."

"Every man in Tombstone has a gun in his hand!" said the girl bitterly. "There was no reason to shoot him down in cold blood like that. I agree with Mr. Behan. It was outright murder, and I'll testify to that!"

"You'll have quite a long ride, Miss Evvie." Clum simply stated the fact of Pima County's lack of judicial machinery. "There's no court of constituted law nearer than Tucson. You know that. I suggest we don't try to convene one here, not on either side of the argument."

"Mayor Clum's right, ma'am," interrupted Johnny Behan smoothly. "We can all have our say in town tomorrow at the coroner's inquest. Right now I sure do agree with you that our first duty is to this poor wounded boy!"

"First duty," disagreed Wyatt softly, "is to the law. I'm still asking all of you about that hefty outlaw on the bay gelding. Who was he?"

Nobody answered, nor even started to answer. He let them stand a minute. "All right," he said slowly. "Then I'll tell you." He was watching Behan when he said it. He saw the politician's eyes flick.

"That was William Brocius Graham, alias William Brocius, age twenty-eight, blue eyes, black hair, height five foot ten, weight about 215 pounds. Is very fast with a gun, will not submit to arrest willingly, and must be regarded as extremely dangerous."

"You got that written on your cuff somewheres?" suggested Behan, narrow-eyeing him. "You're pretty pat with the law talk for a shotgun rider. Who are you, mister?"

"Coming to that in a minute," grunted Wyatt. "Now, how about that description? Anybody recognize it?"

"Not I," said Clum seriously. "Should we?"

"You should," said Wyatt. "That was Curly Bill."

"Curly Bill!" gasped Clum, and if he was faking it he was faking it solid. "Man, you can't mean it. Why I know Curly Bill as well as I know anyone in this coach. I'm sure I'd have recognized his voice."

"Witnesses are always sure," agreed Wyatt grimly.

"You're crazy," broke in Behan heatedly. "We all know Curly Bill. Naturally. Know him well. That couldn't have been him!"

"You're one-half right anyway." Wyatt was still easy and still agreeing. "You know him well, all right."

Behan started to light his fuse and sputter it, but Wyatt cut it off and tamped it out for him.

"You and Mr. Clum can pull that kid off his horse now

37

and get him into the coach. Don't bother being slow about it, he won't know the difference. Back on the box, Monk. Inquest's closed."

Evelyn Cushman, still pale with the shock of the double shooting, refused to budge.

"I'm not moving a foot," she declared to her fellow passengers, "until this murderer identifies himself. Anyone can see he's no regular company messenger. Just who are you, mister," she demanded of Wyatt acidly, "a Wells Fargo detective?"

The way she put that last let Wyatt know not only where he stood with the girl but where the Fargo secret agents stood with the local citizenry. He filed the latter away for future reference.

"Not quite, ma'am," he answered softly. Ringo, watching him say it, knew by the way it was put that the shadow-smile was back of his eyes. "But you're getting warm." He opened his sheepskin winter coat to show the dull wink of the star against the dark broadcloth of his gambler's vest. "I'm a deputy sheriff, Miss Evvie."

He wasn't watching the girl when he said it, but rather Behan and Clum. The latter handled it easy enough but Behan didn't like it a little bit and a man could see that before ever the smooth-shaven politician opened his mouth.

"You're *what?*" he challenged incredulously.

"You heard me," was all Wyatt answered.

"Deputy sheriff of *what?*" snorted Behan belligerently.

"Pima County," said Wyatt evenly. "Tombstone District."

"Tombstone District!"

There was no mistaking the way that Behan gasped out the repeat. He couldn't have been any more belly-struck if he'd been belted in the brisket with a whiffletree.

"Either you got bad ears, Mr. Behan," observed Wyatt calmly, "or you're not quite smart."

The Cushman girl got back into it before Behan could make up his mind what to do about the insult. "Well, there's nothing wrong with *my* ears, sir," she snapped, "and you still haven't told us your name!"

Along about this time, Ringo, who'd been pretty well shoved out by all the talk, saw his opportunity. The kid always did have a flair for hogging the middle of the road, not cottoning to taking a side track for anybody. Not, particularly, where there were two well-set-up women standing by and somebody else getting all their play.

"Allow me, ladies!" he grinned, stepping forward and overdoing the way he pulled off his hat and bowed.

"Miss Cushman, Miss Lilly, gentlemen . . ."

The grin got wider as he paused, but Wyatt, never the one to miss a shadow on any man's face, saw instantly behind it to the sarcasm and green envy of it. It was the first hint he'd had of jealousy from the boy and instead of heeding it like he should, he shook it off while Johnny finished his flourish.

"Mr. Wyatt Earp, late of Dodge City, Kansas, and other points well past the law."

Wyatt watched them take it. To the women it wasn't anything special. Neither of them rose to it. Monk Wilson swallowed it like a man who'd felt its hook before. But he was very busy sorting out his lines and knew when he was well out of a bad bargain. Behan just grabbed it in his stumpy teeth, clamped down on it and said nothing. It was J. P. Clum, the cocky little Tombstone mayor, who bolted it in stride. That stride, quick and crisp, was toward Wyatt and came backed by his outstretched hand.

"Mr. Earp," he just said it without any fancy trimmings or any fooling, "I'm sure we all heard you a few minutes ago when you told that outlaw the law had come to Tombstone. I'm equally sure, sir, that at the time none of us had any real idea what you meant."

"And now . . . ?" said Wyatt slowly, letting his pale eyes drift the whole awkward bunch of them while he waited.

"You've already said it," replied Clum, dropping the big gunman's hand and stepping back to face his companions. "Friends," he said simply, "the law *has* come to Tombstone. Thank God, and at last."

None of the others moved until Lilly Belloit pushed past Wyatt to head toward the wounded boy on the pony.

"There's only one thing to add to that," said the dancehall girl. She caught Wyatt's eye with a look he felt clean to his saddlebones. And she said it in a good clear voice that reached everybody, equal, but seemed aimed straight at Johnny Behan.

"Amen . . . !"

They pulled the dead boy out of the wagon ruts, leaving him clear of the siding brush, where he could be easy found and packed in next morning. Wyatt lifted the injured one off his horse, mighty gentle about it despite the way he'd talked about him, carried him over and put him in the coach. Mayor Clum and Lilly Belloit, without being told, got inside to tend him. Responding to Wyatt's sharp order, Ringo and Behan swung up on top and rode the boot the balance of the way in, watching and waiting with drawn beltguns for any return of the bandits.

Inside the jolt and sway of the stage, on the seat across from the dying boy, Evvie Cushman crouched back in the shadows fighting down the nausea and the tears that rose up in her. By the time the youth had drowned in his own blood, welling thick up inside his punctured lungs, and had died clinging to Lilly Belloit's cool hand and crying like a lost, scared kid, the tall brunette had but one feeling left for Tombstone's new deputy sheriff.

He was a cold-blooded, hired, professional killer.

And as she hated all he was, and all he stood for, so she hated Wyatt Earp.

8 ☆

Even Wyatt's experienced eyes widened a bit when the stage topped the Watervale Grade an hour later to show Tombstone, blazing in all its gaslit glory, a quarter-mile away across Goose Flats. Natural gas had been brought in just the month before and the citizens of "Sodom in the Sagebrush" were burning the pipeline, both ends against the middle. At eight o'clock of a fine winter night its glary blue light let an old, tough-town hand like Wyatt see plenty. And as Monk cussed his six-horse hitch through the hardened artery of Allen Street, he was *looking* plenty.

Experienced professional that he was, Wyatt always mapped a place in his mind as he rode into it. Once in a Comanche moon he might miss a corner line that would have to be redrawn next day, but mostly he got it right the first time around and could quote you chapter and verse on any detail within 320 acres of the town square. Since half a section of flat land would cover the whole bench that Tombstone squatted on, with 120 acres left over to put into back pasture, you can lay he didn't miss much on that short trot up Allen Street.

What he couldn't see for himself, he dug out of Monk between the old man's gees and haws and whipcracks at his lathered lead team.

The town lay quartered across the compass a little slanchwise of due east and west. But the four main drags of Safford, Frémont, Allen and Toughnut still ran near enough to true to be called east and west. The north-south streets were named by numbers, beginning on the west. Starting with Second and going uptown through Seventh, you just forgot about the rest of those streets because they weren't anything but Mexicans and mud-holes and dead dogs and sun-blown burros, anyways, so that you came out with a town barely four blocks by six in its main-building size.

Coming in from the north like they were, down Sixth to swing west up Allen Street, Wyatt got to see the most of the names and places that were to give him the best part of the hell he was heading into—the Bird Cage Theatre, Cosmopolitan Hotel, Oriental Saloon, Crystal Palace, Campbell and Hatch's Pool Hall, Hafford's Saloon—before Monk pulled up at the station by the O.K. Corral Stable between Third and Fourth.

The one place he didn't see was the one where *all* his hell was going to head up. But then the O.K. Corral Yard wasn't on Allen with the Stable, but back over on Frémont just down the street from the jail. A man sure couldn't be blamed for not being able to see it from the stage stop.

At the time that Wednesday stage from Benson brought Wyatt Earp into Tombstone, the mines were running open twenty-four hours a day. And Tombstone was damned if it was going to miss a cussed minute of any of those twenty-four hours. Add to that the fact the miners were getting four dollars a day, seven days a week, and that the camp's total population was over 6,000, with better than ninety percent of that being muckers and bullprod drillers, you got a fair idea of what Wyatt had got himself tagged deputy sheriff for.

But only just a fair one.

The big part of the idea, and the dirty part of it, hung

41

with the ten percent that took such loving care of the ninety. And of their payrolls.

Wyatt got his visit from the official representative of that top dog ten percent less than an hour after he climbed down off the box of the Benson stage.

He was a shortish, brown-haired, clean-shaved man, with a bad shift of eye and a face as dim and hard to read as the fine print in a fire insurance policy. He didn't have to introduce himself, for him and Wyatt had already met. And would many times again.

It was Johnny Behan.

Mayor Clum chased after Wyatt in the crowd gathering around the stage, offering to take him around the block to show him the city jail and introduce him to the present town marshal. Wyatt agreed, and after instructing Ringo to look to Big Red and his roan, and to meet him later at the Bird Cage, walked on over to Frémont with the mayor. He met the marshal, a Citizen's Safety Committee man, with no legal standing in the county whatever. He was a weak duck in Tombstone's plenty bad water and was only too glad to hand in the resignation which Wyatt asked for on the spot.

He next inspected the one-story adobe that was to be his office and jailhouse, turned down Clum's invite to spend the first night at his house, bid the mayor a short good night, closed the door after him and turned up the wall jet on the front office's gas lamp. Then he sat down at the little oak desk to do himself a little Earp-style calculating.

He hadn't got well started when the plank door opened up and Johnny Behan walked in.

To his credit, the Tucson man made his point right off.

"You're away to a shaky start, Earp," he nodded to Wyatt. "If that *was* Curly Bill, you've made yourself the worst enemy you could have picked in Pima County."

"I don't think so," said Wyatt bluntly.

"You don't think what?" countered Behan, puzzled.

"That Brocius is the big trouble in Pima County, Mr. Behan."

"You've already got other ideas, eh?"

"I reckon. A man's got eyes."

Behan's second nod agreed. "You'd better not keep yours so open, my friend."

"You're talking."

"All right. This place isn't ready for the law yet."

"I never rush things," said Wyatt evenly. "It'll have till daybreak tomorrow to *get* ready."

Behan watched him a minute, abruptly changed the subject. "Who appointed you?" he asked.

"Mr. Shibell, up to Tucson."

"I don't believe it." It was flat. "He didn't say anything to me. He'd know better than to send a man in here, cold."

"I noticed a new telegraph office uptown," offered Wyatt. "For a dollar you can make me out a liar."

"I will, don't worry," threatened his visitor, "but if Charley Shibell was simple-minded enough not to warn you, I will. This town is running just right the way it is. It doesn't need any gun-tough from Kansas." Not liking the way Wyatt looked at him when he said it, he oiled it up a little. "Now, don't misunderstand me, Earp. I don't see any reason for trouble between you and me. More than likely, we'll get on. I'm just here to make sure that we do." He paused, taking Wyatt's silence for encouragement. "Now, I'm down here from Tucson to make certain investments of my own, investments that won't stand any meddling from the law, you understand?"

"Your investments are your own business, Mr. Behan, but this is the Sheriff's office, not the Chamber of Commerce. What do you want of me?"

"Co-operation," said Behan quickly.

"All right. Go on."

Taking Wyatt's easy attitude for continuing agreement, Behan figured to read him off his orders, blunt and clear. And to plaster them down with a little hard cement.

"Good enough. Now get this, Earp. Neither you, nor anybody else, walks the middle of the road in this town. There's just two sides to Allen Street, ours and theirs."

"Who's on *our* side of the street?" asked Wyatt pleasantly.

Behan couldn't be sure from the way he said it whether he meant it like it sounded or not. "*You,* if you're smart," he said carefully, "along with me and Shibell for sure, and maybe a few others here and there."

43

"Such as Bill Brocius?" Wyatt wanted to know.

"You'll get that answered no matter which side you take," nodded Behan darkly.

"I suppose Clum and his Citizen's Safety Committee holds down *their* side of the drag," ventured Wyatt.

Behan answered quickly and as though he was sure where the big deputy stood now. "They're a shade ahead of themselves, that's all, Earp. We're just not ready for wide sidewalks and church suppers. You follow me?"

"Not very far," said Wyatt, and got up.

He moved to the door, held it open. "Good night, Mr. Behan. I've a stomach to fill and lodgings to find. You'll know where to locate me should you need *the law* some dark night."

Behan, who had not sat down the whole of the time, nor been asked to, just blinked and stared, and stood stock-still. Johnny Behan never did prove quite bright enough to cut the hog that history had hung up for him. Right now he was needing a little time to chew up Wyatt's answer, and he took it. But, bright or not, he wasn't so slow it didn't finally soak in on him.

He started for the door, stopped just inside it.

"I suppose you know where this leaves you standing, Earp." The threat in it wasn't implied. It was advertised. In foot-high letters.

"I do," replied Wyatt politely, moving easily in on him with the acknowledgment. "I'd say right square in the *middle* of Allen Street."

He paused, not a foot from Behan, treating the Tucson politician to his first look at the famous, frostbit grin. "And do you know where it leaves you, Mr. Behan . . . ?"

He moved too quick for the startled Behan. One big hand grabbed his coat collar, the other, the seat of his pinstripe pants. He was still strangling and treading air when Wyatt, ten strides out the door, into the dirt of the road, dumped him to the ground. *"Sitting, Mr. Behan,"* he finished quietly, not even breathing hard, *"right in the middle of Frémont Street."*

He paused, tugging at the left side of his mustache. "But if you want my professional advice, mister, I'd suggest you don't spend the winter there."

He stepped back, as the white-faced Behan stumbled

to his feet. "Whatever way you were going," Wyatt continued, "let me recommend you keep at it. If you're not out of reach down Third Street in sixty seconds, I'll lay you out for the evening."

It was the first and last time he put actual hands to Johnny Behan. Nobody saw him do it, and he never told anybody about it until years later. But for the record, and in somewhat less than the time it allowed, he was standing alone in the middle of Frémont Street. Mr. John Behan was long gone down the gaslit stretch of the boardwalk toward Third and Allen.

9 ☆

Johnny Behan wasn't the kind you put off on and got away with it. He was a man that went to bed late, slept light, got up early in the morning, used what brains he had, right on around the town clock.

When he came around the corner of Third, onto Allen, he was thinking plenty. He was still doing likewise when he got across Fourth and spotted Johnny Ringo coming out of Campbell and Hatch's Pool Hall. When he saw the kid, something clicked into place in his mind and he went after him. He caught him just outside the Crystal Palace.

He bumped him, deliberate, in the crowd and after letting on he was surprised it was him, invited him into the Palace to "have one on me, and meet the boys."

The Palace was something to see in those days, and to be seen in. Pretty soon, what between the dazzle of the rock-crystal chandeliers, the hip-short skirts on the housegirls and the 100-plus proof of the bar's sourmash, Johnny was thinking Behan and his friends were some local potatoes. Especially when Lilly Belloit showed up to bolster the fifth round of bourbons before she sauntered across Allen Street to do her nine o'clock turn at the Bird Cage. Most especially when, as she was leaving, Behan suggested Johnny join her on that saunter and escort her to the stage door, before rejoining him and the rest of the boys in the pit audience to watch the Tombstone Lilly strut her considerable stuff.

If Ringo had on purpose set about picking the right crowd for the wrong start in Tombstone, he couldn't have done better. In his half-hour at Behan's back-table in the Crystal Palace he met and shook hands with a baker's bad dozen of the town's less kindly lights, including the likes of Phin Clanton, Frank Stilwell, Pete Spence and young Billy Claiborne, for but a part of them. More to the point, he reckoned they were all grand fellows, cut right to his own straight-whiskey-and-no-water pattern.

By the time he swaggered out of the Palace's cut-crystal doors with Lilly Belloit on his arm and the best part of a quart under his belt, he was sold on Johnny Behan and his Allen Street boys.

Meantime, Wyatt was elsewhere in town, trying his own luck and finding it not too good.

After locking the jail, he followed Behan's course down Third to Allen. At the corner, he collared the first sober citizen and asked him where was the best available boarding house.

The citizen turned out to be high on a place called the Miner's Rest, run by a right decent young maiden lady over on the northwest, respectable, side of town. Wyatt thanked him, got Big Red out of the O.K. Corral Stable and headed uptown, following directions. He soon enough found the place, a nice, white-painted frame house with a picket fence and all the proper trimmings. Tying Big Red to the iron jockey out front, he moved up the boardwalk and knocked at the door.

He was in for a passel of good jolts that evening. He got the first one of them when Evvie Cushman answered the door.

"Why, evening, Miss Evvie." Wyatt was no fool with women. He always had his own quiet way with them, though he never was a chippie-chaser like Ringo and some of the others. "I didn't rightly expect the pleasure of seeing you again so soon. Is the landlady in, ma'am?"

"Not to you, Mr. Earp."

Wyatt looked at her, not quite knowing how to take it. "Beg pardon, miss?" He left off the Evvie, not even realizing that he did.

"What was it you wanted, Mr. Earp?"

"Well, I wanted the landlady." Wyatt was too taken up with the haughty, fine look of her there in the lamplight to feel the frost in the air. "But I reckon you'll be able to tell me if . . ."

"I *am* the landlady," she interrupted bluntly.

This being the kind of shock any man could enjoy suffering, Wyatt bore up under it real brave. "My luck was due to change, ma'am. I'd like a room for two, please."

"My last room was let an hour ago. To that nice young man on the stage, Mr. Ringo." The frost was on for sure, now. "It was a single room in any event, Mr. Earp, so you'll simply have to look elsewhere. My suggestion for *you* would be the Cosmopolitan Hotel."

Wyatt's face set up. "What do you mean, 'for me,' Miss Evvie?" Watching her, he saw her stiffen as she said it.

"I simply don't take in hired killers. Good night, sir!"

He saw the angry flash of the black eyes but the deal had suddenly gone too far down in the deck to just back off and call it a pleasant evening.

"Just a minute, Miss Evvie." She hadn't seen his boot slide into the door, but the jolt of its stop tore the knob from her hand, leaving her facing him high-flushed and breathing hard. "There's one thing you and a lot of other people in this town better get straight right from the beginning. I am an officer of the law, not a *hired killer.*"

"Good night, sir . . . !"

"I'm not through talking, miss, and you're not through listening." His pale eyes stared her down. It was the first time in her fine lady's life that any man had used that tone on her. The pure surprise of it stopped her.

"I've been in many towns," said Wyatt Earp slowly, "and worn many stars. In all that time, no outlaw has made my real trouble. It's always the *good* people who have. People like *you,* Miss Evvie," he finished softly.

"Are you quite done, Mr. Earp . . . ?" she was still angry but, watching her, he knew she had been listening. And was starting to think.

"Not quite, Miss Cushman." The soft part was out of his voice, the iron back in it. "I'll tell you something now, young lady. Something you wouldn't know, but that you and all your gentle-hearted kind better think about. *I've been indicted for murder in every town I ever wore a star for.* Not by the bad citizens I gunned down, nor by their friends, not so much as once, but each and every time by

47

the good citizens. The ones I'm paid to protect. The ones like you. Keep it in mind, Miss Cushman. . . ." He tailed it off with a slow etch of acid to it that cut into her like quick lime. "I don't like *your kind* any better than you like *mine!*"

She didn't move nor say a thing as he started away. Halfway down the steps he stopped and called back to her.

"Did that 'nice young Mr. Ringo' know he was getting a single room, ma'am?"

"Yes . . ." said Evvie, not thinking about her answer but about what Wyatt had just told her. And the *way* he had told it to her.

"He didn't say anything about having a friend with him?"

"No . . ." The answer was still automatic, not thought about.

"Good night, ma'am," said Wyatt quietly, and touched his hat and went away down the boardwalk into the dark of the street.

He jogged Big Red down Allen Street, watching the sidewalk crowds and looking for Ringo. He was a long ways from being happy.

He didn't like the way he and the beautiful Cushman girl had got off on the wrong foot. He didn't like Behan bracing him to take up sides. Nor the fact that that brace let him know Pima County was likely rotten clean up to and including Sheriff Shibell himself. Nor that Curly Bill was here ahead of him, in Tombstone, lined up for almost certain with Behan and his bad politics. And he damn well didn't like the idea that Johnny was showing signs of big-city-itis, and setting off like he wanted to go at Tombstone at his own gait, single harness and hacka-more-free.

First things being first, as they always were with Wyatt, his aim right off was a talk with that "nice young Mr. Ringo."

He had an inside feeling for the kid like he hadn't had for any man before him. But he was beginning to wonder, pretty hard, if he'd been wrong in thinking the kid understood and shared that feeling like he thought he did.

Well, there was one way to find that out. Locate the kid and put it to him. Let him know where he stood with you, *if he wanted to,* and what you had been keeping in mind to offer him by way of a surprise, in case he did.

Big Red was just pushing the intersection of Sixth and Allen, when Wyatt's frown caught the lovers' quarrel going on down by the darkened stage door of the Bird Cage Theatre. Ordinarily, he wouldn't have considered any back-street couples' struggle to be in the deputy sheriff's bailiwick. But right at the moment he was riled-up enough by his thoughts on other subjects to look on the stage-door disturbance as a good chance to start laying a little law down along Allen Street.

He kicked Big Red down Sixth, piled off of him on a slide stop, shoved a couple of interested citizens to one side, stepped in close and laid his .44 barrel back of the nearest ear of the gent who was roughing up the lady. The tough stiffened up, spun half around, and had the courtesy to fall out onto the sidewalk where the gas lamp up the street gave Wyatt his first good look at him.

It was Johnny Ringo.

By that time he was hearing the girl's husky, "Thanks, Mr. Earp," and looking up into the heavily painted face of Lilly Belloit.

"Tombstone always this busy of an evening, Miss Belloit?" he inquired, straight-faced.

The dance-hall girl didn't miss the friendly way he said it, nor, more amazing yet, the nice, polite way he took off his big hat when he talked to her.

"No, Mr. Earp!" She deliberately raised her voice with the forced laugh. "But there's no trouble here. Your young friend just had a shade too much and decided he'd have a go at the leading lady. It's all part of the act at the Bird Cage, Sheriff, no point in making any charge on it."

She all at once dropped the loud voice, looked quickly up Sixth, moved close to Wyatt. *"I want to talk to you. Box number ten. After my act."*

Just as quick, she stepped back away from him, using the loud voice and the laugh again, this time on the little bunch of sidewalk strays that had wandered up from nowhere. "If you want to see the rest of the act, boys, the box office is open right now and I'm on in ten minutes. Tell the boys in front that Tombstone Lilly sent you around!"

The men laughed back at her. A couple made off-color

49

remarks. All of them watched her hipswing her way through the side door. After that, they looked Wyatt over, blinking twice to make sure they weren't seeing things when they spotted the pewter star on his vest. Then, not caring for the way he was handing back their looks, they sidled off up Sixth, staring back and talking, some excited, to one another.

Wyatt watched them go, not thinking about them. But thinking plenty about Lilly Belloit and her odd invite up to box ten. After a minute he shrugged, picked Johnny up off the sidewalk and slung him across Big Red's broad rump.

The old gelding didn't even switch his tail. He'd packed in more limp ones across those agey haunches than he had good teeth left in his lower jaw. One more or less didn't change the score much. Wyatt grinned wearily at him, whacked him affectionately on the withers, eased slowly up into the saddle.

"Here we go again, Red," was all he said, and kneed him around to head up Sixth.

10 ☆

The aisle passing behind the boxes built around the walls of the Bird Cage auditorium was so narrow Wyatt had to turn his big shoulders to get them past its red-hung draperies. On top of being as close-crowded as a rodeo squeeze-chute, the hallway stunk of dead tobacco smoke, cheap toilet water, dime-store face powder and spilled beer till a man near had to vomit with the choke of it.

Wyatt held his breath while he counted his way down the curtained doorways. At what he thought was number ten he held up and listened. He heard nothing right off and after a minute pulled the curtain and started in.

The man inside was fat, bald-headed and orry-eyed drunk. The bad gaslight of the box was further sickened by the reek of smoke from his stubbed-out cigar. There was enough of that light, all the same, to make out the girl he was fumbling at. She was a big juicy redhead dressed in a handy button-front outfit of dirty ruffles and stained silk, and was laying back on an old red velour settee with the fat drunk crowding her a little more than somewhat.

Wyatt was just starting to stumble back out into the aisle when she looked up and saw him. Snarling something she never learned in Sunday School, she reached for a schooner of stale beer that was setting on the table alongside the couch. The smash and slop of it busting against the doorjam missed Wyatt by inches. She was still yelling and cussing after him when he dove into the next box and pulled the drapes shut behind him.

This one turned out to be box ten and was empty as per Lilly's arrangements. He turned down the wall lamp and sat back in the far corner to have a cheroot and wait. He had built maybe half an inch of ash when the curtains pulled back and she came in.

At first she didn't see him, with the light being low and all, and he got a good chance to look at her—the first real good one he'd had.

She appeared maybe thirty, thirty-five, and like she'd spent the last twenty years of that time caking on the makeup and working every box and backroom from Kansas City to San Francisco.

That was the first look. Then, seeing she still hadn't noticed him, he had time for a second look.

She wasn't any thirty-five, maybe not even thirty. Her drawn face, white and shadowy under its thick paste of rouge and rice powder, was still strikingly beautiful. But its profile, even softened up by the gutter of the gas lamp, was hard and lifeless as a cameo brooch. The high cheekbones, tight as parchment under the paint, showed up the hollows of the sunken cheeks and the deep eye shadows. She had a short, straight nose, though, and a nice wide mouth and a clean, high chinline. Her hair wasn't cut short like most of the girls, but hung long to her shoulders and was thick and ashy blonde as Wyatt's own. Yes, for sure you had to say her face was partly beautiful. But you could see in the same breath that the whole cut and color of that face was one of hard-broke bitterness and high hopes out the window.

Her figure—and a man sure hadn't missed that even in the short moment of her entrance—was near faultless.

She was maybe a shade too thin. The black hang of her net-and-lace stage dress curved a little too sharp over the

51

angles of her hips, fell likely a bit too loose away from her bare, frail shoulders. But those high breasts and the swing of those hips were still there. Still there, mister, and still showing plenty wicked. And showing that way, Wyatt knew, for whatever man might be waiting for her in the shadows of the Bird Cage's box ten.

"Hello, Lilly . . ."

He stood up with the quiet greeting, hat in hand and feeling a little awkward. Like he'd been spying on her in her bedroom, or something.

"I didn't see you, Mr. Earp. You're a pretty quiet one." He could tell she was startled, even though she didn't let on she was.

"Tricks of the trade," he answered. "What was it you wanted to see me about, ma'am?" For some reason he felt awkward in front of this girl. He'd seen her kind and, God knew, been with enough of them to handle them without even breaking out of a slow trot. But this one had him going.

"Not alone quiet," said Lilly Bellot, pinning him with her odd, slanty eyes, "but quick, too."

Wyatt thought he'd never seen a pair of eyes just like those. Like cat's eyes, they were. Set that slanted in her face. Clear in color, too; brilliant-clear, in fact. And that steady and spellbinding in the way they trapped and drilled into you that a man knew he had either to quit looking at them or get the hell out of that box in one tall hurry.

Wyatt quit looking at them.

"What was it you wanted, Miss Lilly?"

She ignored the question again. "You're not like the others," she said, and dropped her eyes. "A woman can tell by the way a man looks at her. You're decent, Mr. Earp. A woman can tell."

Somehow it didn't unsettle him. He knew what she meant and he didn't play coy about it. "I like you, too, Miss Lilly. I like you and your kind. Not many could handle that shot-up boy the way you did back yonder in that coach tonight. I don't cotton to prissy females."

"Meaning Miss Cushman?" said Lilly quietly.

He hadn't expected that. Hadn't expected her to be so sharp about it. But it was what he had been thinking, and he admitted it.

"Her and her kind," he said.

"Her kind, maybe," nodded Lilly Belloit. "Not her."

Again he knew what she meant, and again he knew she had hit it, dead center. But this time it nettled him. "You didn't call me up here to talk about Miss Evvie. And I for sure didn't come up here to talk about her. What is it you want, girl?"

"To be on your side." She was using those eyes again. "And to warn you."

"All right." He was short about it. "Warn away."

"It's your young friend. He's mixing with the wrong crowd, talking too much. He'll bear watching. I know his kind."

"So," said Wyatt slowly, "what's his kind?" He wasn't idling about it. It was a straight question.

"Wild," she said. "Bad-wild. Drinks bad, talks bad, acts bad."

"He's just a kid, remember."

"Nobody's a kid that wears two guns, tied down, and sheds six shots of bourbon in thirty minutes."

"So?"

"So watch him. That's all."

"He's being watched," said Wyatt soberly. "What else?"

"Johnny Behan."

"Me and Mr. Behan have already had our little talk."

"It's what I mean. He told me all about it."

"I doubt *that*," grinned Wyatt. "But go on." He lost the grin as quick as he'd found it. "What's Behan to you?"

Lilly Belloit blushed. A man could see it even through the thick paint. And had to wonder that a woman in her business could still be embarrassed.

"A girl has got to get on," she murmured. "He's big in this town and doesn't bother me too much."

"Meaning you're his woman?" said Wyatt bluntly.

"He thinks so."

"How about you?"

"I never had a man, *any* man," she answered, the color still thick and dark under her rouge, "the way a decent girl wants one."

She looked at the massive, sure form of him standing there in the box shadows, the gaslight cutting bold around his thick-maned head and the whole lion's grace and strength of him. Not like I want you! she felt like crying

53

out. Not like I've dreamed to have one of your kind want me! Not like I've wanted to know and hold and have a man like you. A clean, real man. A man who would look at a girl like she was his woman for life, not his tramp for tonight.

But to Wyatt she said nothing. Only stood looking at him, letting him guess it from her eyes.

He was a better than fair guesser—with a man or with a woman. In his game, you had to be. He knew what he was going to say to the girl and felt touched by the inside kindness and gentleness that was always his way with the unlucky ones to say it to her.

"Sometimes, Miss Lilly, providing we want a thing bad enough, we get it."

She took it for what it was worth. Likely no more than a pat on the head for a lonely stray. Not reading into it any more than that. But all the same she felt the pound it put in her heart and heard the tremble it left in her low voice.

"I'm beholden to you, Mr. Earp."

"And me to you, Miss Lilly," he said quietly. "I'll watch myself. And Behan and Ringo, too." He started for the curtains. "Goodnight, ma'am."

"Wait." She was beside him, her small hand instinctively conscious of the thickness of the hard-oak forearm under the black coatsleeve. "If there's anything I can do for you. Anything at all . . ."

Wyatt laughed. He said it just to let off a little pressure, to ease her up and to sort of smooth his own way out of it.

"There's something you *can* do right now, girl. Recommend me a place to stay the night. I've already checked the Grand and the Cosmopolitan. They're full up."

"What about the Miner's Rest?" she said, and he felt the challenge in it.

"Miss Evvie Cushman is a proper lady," he replied softly. "She doesn't take in hired killers."

Lilly nodded, the brightness of her first smile for him touching Wyatt with a strange unrest.

"You see, Mr. Earp, sometimes it pays a man to know improper ladies. You're welcome to stay the night, or any night, at my place." With that, she held out to him a little padlock key on a crumpled velvet ribbon. "It's the

54

old shack on the vacant lot back of the theatre. You can't miss it. Not so bad as it looks, either. Got a real inside bathtub, and all!"

He didn't take the key.

"I better not, ma'am." He wasn't thinking about morals or any of that trash, only about Behan and the girl.

"It'll be perfectly all right." Her voice was back on its old, hard level. "I was moving out tomorrow, anyway. Back three months on the rent and no chance to make it up. It's a pretty nice shack, you might even want to rent it yourself. Try it and see how you like it, Mr. Earp."

"You got another place to stay the night?"

"Sure. With Pearl and Frankie. Friends of mine in the chorus. It's all fixed. You take the key and go on. I'll be by after my clothes in a bit. That'll be all there is to it."

He took the key now. "This makes me really beholden, Miss Lilly." He fumbled around for something more to say. "If right now you're in a little press for pin money"— he finished lame, and getting lamer—"I got a few dollars we can . . ."

It was her laugh that interrupted him. But he saw back of it to the quick tears in her eyes and caught the choke of it in her voice.

"Money, Mr. Earp? There isn't money enough in the world . . ." She stepped quickly to the curtains, pulled them to one side, turned back to him and said it and was gone on down the aisle before he could move. "You're the first man in six years to take his hat off to me!"

11 ☆

That shack was all right. Like Lilly said, it sat all by its lonesome on the vacant lot back of the Bird Cage. Also, like she said, it had a real bathtub.

Wyatt didn't know when anything had felt so good as that tarred-wood tub. After a long spell of soaking and thinking, he got out, dried himself and started to ease into the old iron bedstead. He got a second thought, put on a clean white shirt from his warbag, lit up a cheroot and looked around for something to read. The choice was limited.

He found a handpress-printed brochure of something

called *H.M.S. Pinafore,* by a couple of chaps named Gilbert and Sullivan, currently being offered at Schieffelin Hall by the Tombstone Methodist Ladies Dramatic, Choral and Home Arts Society. That, and a string-bound bunch of old *Epitaph* newspapers, and a nice new book titled *A Fool's Errand,* by a bird, or maybe it was a lady, named Tourgee, or some such.

He took ahold of the latter, figuring from its title that it might have something in common with his own shaky business in Tombstone. It didn't, and ten minutes later his cheroot had gone out in his hand, and he was sound asleep.

He was still in the old rocker, sawing away, when something set off his jumpy nerves, and he was up and out of the chair, pressed up against the wall back of the door, waiting.

He watched the latch lift, then the door swing in with barely a sound from its strap-leather hinges. The next second he kicked it shut, grabbed blind, and wound up with his arms full of Lilly Belloit.

He let go of her like a hot stovelid.

"You gave me a turn, girl," he growled. "You don't ever want to sneak up on a man that way."

"We're even," said Lilly, gulping. "You scared hell out of me too, mister!"

"I'm sorry," mumbled Wyatt. "After so many years an old cat gets whippy." The sleep was getting out of his eyes about then. He looked at the girl, his big jaw coming out. "What happened to *you?*" he growled angrily.

She was a sight. Her blouse was torn, her hair badmussed, her face considerable marked up. She was shaking like an aspen leaf in a high country wind, too, and not from being scared by Wyatt's grab.

"Lover's quarrel," she grinned, tight-lipped. "I'll get my things."

Wyatt's eyes stopped her. "Behan?" he asked.

She saw his wide lips flatten and knew she shouldn't tell him. But she was tired, and hurt, and she was a woman. She nodded. "It's all right, Mr. Earp. There's a first time for everything." She tried hard for the little smile and just made it.

"A first time," said Wyatt ugly-like, "and a last!" He didn't match her try at the smile. His eyes were burning like a loafer wolf's just outside the throw of the campfire.

"Don't make anything of it," she asked him earnestly. "He just found out from one of the housemen about me seeing you in the box. He had a right to be mad, I guess, the way he saw it."

"No man," said Wyatt slowly, "has got a right to hit a woman. Not *any* woman," he added. And he knew she caught what he meant.

"Now, please, Mr. Earp . . ." she began again. But Wyatt cut her off.

"You'll need a hot tub and some fresh clothes. I'll heat the water. Get your things off."

"No, no. I'm all right. Really I am. You . . ."

"Get your things off, girl," he repeated gently, and turned and went out to get the wood and the water.

When he came back, she had drawn the ragged curtain across the corner where the tub was and he saw the flimsy camisole and the long sheer of the black net stockings hanging across its rusty draw-wire. There was a basin and a water pitcher in there, along with the tub. He heard her already splashing away and allowed she was cleaning up her face. He didn't say anything and they didn't talk much while he was getting the water hot.

When it was ready, he handed it in to her through the curtain.

He heard her pouring it and getting into it. Presently, he reckoned he was listening a little too hard and that she might be thinking the same thing and be getting a little embarrassed by all the stillness. He managed to cough a little and to scrape his feet around like he was right busy with his own doings and not thinking about what was going on back of that patched old drape. But that wasn't any good, for she nailed him on it, right off.

"Why don't you give up and bed down, Mr. Earp?" she called. "I'm going to soak a spell and I can let myself out. Now just quit stomping and snorting around out there and get to bed."

He felt the blood go up into his face and wondered if a "hired killer" could blush. He noticed, too, that a lot of the tiredness seemed gone out of her voice. He felt the goodness of that warming him. Then felt at the same time his own weariness getting to him. "All right, girl!"

57

He actually laughed. Quiet, maybe, and some soft about it, but he did laugh. "You caught me. I'll go ahead and turn in. You want the lamp left up?"

"No, turn it down. I've got candlelight enough in here. Good night . . ."

"Good night, Miss Lilly."

He got in between the worn cotton sheets, feeling the welcome of their coolness hit his skin. And not missing the drowsy-clean perfume of *her* that was on them, either.

"See you tomorrow, girl . . ."

His eyes were closed almost before the springs quit sagging under his six-foot bulk. He didn't hear her delayed, soft-laughed reply.

"Tomorrow's a mighty long time, mister!"

When he awoke, the candlelight was spilling out from back of the curtain and she was sitting on the bed beside him. It seemed hours had gone, but he knew it could only be minutes.

His face was in a shadow from the part-closed curtain, so that she didn't see him open his eyes. He shut them back down, quick, watching her through barely open lids, his heart pounding loud enough, he was afraid, to jar her off the bed.

She was in a loose wrapper, like nothing he had ever seen. A filmy thing of net mesh and little pink silk roses and a tiny blue satin ribbon looped into the eyelet lace that came up high and tight at her throat, and short and puffed-out at the shoulders, above the slender bareness of her arms. Soft as was that light from beyond the curtain, it filtered through the sheer of that wrapper in a way to put the blood so thick in a man's throat he scarce could swallow. Wyatt saw the willowy grace of her body, and he saw all of it, as bold and clear as though there was nothing between it and him but the candlelight.

She moved a little to brush back a stray wisp of hair, and his eyes pulled to her face.

His breath came in so sharp he near gave himself away.

She had her long hair piled high atop her head, held there by a fresh silk ribbon, and all duck-curly with the little damp ringlets where she'd pulled it up and away from her neck in the back. The paint and the rouge and the rice powder were gone, while in their place he saw a rose-petal flush of high natural color that would have broken the heart of a schoolgirl. That was the thing that took his breath away—that whole, radiant, child-young look of her, there in the candlelight!

Seeing her like that, a man knew she could not be far past twenty. He knew, too, that he had never seen such natural, wild-soft, uneasy beauty in a woman's face before.

She had been looking down on him when he first opened his eyes, and now she did again. For a long, quiet time. Just staring at him. More of gentleness and worship and pure wonder in it than most men ever get to see on any woman's face. Then, he saw her bend forward and start her hand toward him and he closed his eyes tight, so's she wouldn't discover him. He felt her touch his forehead, easing back the hair that was tousled there. And he could feel the nearness of her leaning close above him, just before the warm, light flick of her mouth touched his.

He opened his eyes then, looking full up at her.

She started back a little, their eyes tying up and holding, hard. There was a strange, wonderful spell of silence while they looked at each other. Then she said it, unsure and scared and halting as a child about it. "Is it all right —Wyatt?"

"It's all right, Lilly," he muttered hoarsely.

As she came to him beneath the faded coverlet, soft crying her hunger and her love and her loneliness for him, he took the frightened, trembling fragrance of her slim body to his, holding her fierce and close and telling her again and again that it was all right now. That she was safe, and forever would be safe. Here by his side and in his arms. For always . . .

When he next came awake, the dance and sparkle of the winter sun was glary-bright against the window, and Lilly Belloit was gone.

He got dressed and walked over to Fourth Street, then slowly up it to Frémont and the jail. A half inch of powder snow had fallen during the night. The high, thin air got down, sharp and clean, into a man's lungs, making him feel like it would be a pretty good day to open up shop in Tombstone, after all.

59

He found Johnny Ringo still rolled up in the blankets of his cell bunk, where he'd wrapped him up and left him the night before. Seeing the kid was still out, he stirred up a fire in the front office stove. But when he was done with that, he rousted him out, none too gentle, and got down to cases.

"Pardner," he rapped it to him, not wasting any sentiments over the lump he'd put back of the boy's ear, "you and me are going to come to an understanding. Right about now. You hear me?"

"I take it, it was you that laid me out last night." Johnny said it sullen and ugly, not looking at Wyatt and not wanting to.

"For the second time, kid."

"There'll be no third!" He was still ugly about it. "Goddamn you and your lousy sneaking up behind a man!"

"That's whiskey talk," said Wyatt, a little too soft, "but don't try any more of it."

"Kiss my foot!" snapped the kid. "I don't fear you, *nor* your big reputation."

"Your mouth was always bigger than your belly, boy. Come on, let's go get a cup of coffee. I've got a proposition to offer you and I don't want any sourmash decisions on it."

"Not interested. Gimme back my guns."

Wyatt looked hard at him and saw it was no use, just then. He got the guns out of the desk drawer and handed them over to him. "You've got all day to think it over. Sundown, tonight's, the deadline."

"I don't know what you're talking about, and I don't give a good damn. Get outa the way."

Wyatt said nothing, just stood clear of him and the door. Then he nodded.

"You're off on the wrong foot, Johnny. Pull back and check to my raise."

The kid was not so hung over that he didn't catch the earnest, quiet way Wyatt asked it of him. But his belly was giving him three kinds of hell and his head was twice too big for his hat size. He was a whiskey-sick boy and in no mood for listening to lectures from the law.

"I'll travel my gait, you go along at your own."

"Travel it, then," said Wyatt. "Yonder's the door."

The kid brushed past him, buckling on his guns. Wyatt

followed him out into the street. "Think it over, Johnny," he called quietly after him, "you've still got till sundown."

Ringo went on walking. He didn't answer him, nor he didn't look back.

The kid went into the Can Can Chop House, had his coffee, but couldn't face the three eggs he'd ordered. Instead he went back down the street to the Palace and put away three bourbons. That saved his life.

He was feeling better and beginning to think about how he was going to make up to Wyatt again when Behan walked in. He had Frank Stilwell and Pete Spence with him. Two more morning jolts were in order and Johnny took both of his without complaining any, only too glad to do it and to have somebody that understood him to talk to.

But it was Behan did most of the talking.

"Understand your big friend stretched you last night. How come?"

"I was making a damn fool out of myself, that's all. Likely had it coming. Started pawing at Miss Lilly, I guess."

"So I hear. I still don't see Earp had any particular call to lay you out. You were drunk, boy."

"He don't cotton to drunk," nodded Johnny. "Nor to lady friends of his getting pawed."

"Lady friends of *his*?" Behan scowled it.

"Sure. He's hotter after that flossy gal of yours than a two-dollar Mexican popgun. As who ain't?" he suggested with a pale grin.

"Meaning you, my young friend?"

"Him," interrupted Stilwell, with a mile-wide wink, "and me and Pete and any other son of a bitch with enough blood in his veins to keep his pressure up. Hell, John, you'd ought to know that gal by now. God knows you bin at her long enough yourself. And," he grinned it friendly-like at Johnny, "as Ringo says, who the hell ain't?"

Behan let it pass. It was for sure not what he had in mind swinging the talk to, anyways. "Well, if Ringo enjoys getting his skull massaged in the middle of Sixth Street, I reckon it's his business. I understand it's a better act than any they got at the Bird Cage."

61

"What the hell you mean by that?" growled Johnny, belligerent right now.

"Oh, nothing, kid," shrugged Behan. "Just that they're laughing about it all over town. They say a man ought to go on the stage and get paid for it, providing he's got real natural talent like you."

"Awful damn funny, ain't it?" snarled Johnny, starting to push his chair back.

"Simmer off, kid." Stilwell put a big hand on his arm. "John don't mean to ride you. It ain't rightly his fault if Earp made a damn fool of you in front of the gal and all them sidewalk bums."

"Sure, kid, forget it. We're all friends," grunted Behan. "How about another one, all around?"

The other one was ordered and just about to be had, when young Billy Claiborne broke in at the street doors, making for their table like he had something considerable on his mind. Which he did. Also something in his hand.

He threw the paper down in front of Behan.

"That new sheriff's a busy little pistol," he nodded. "There's one of these tacked up in front of Hafford's, the Oriental, Campbell and Hatch's and the livery stable. I tore this one off'n the wall, out front of the Palace, here. How you like them potatoes, John?"

Behan didn't.

He threw the paper across to Stilwell. Frank picked it up and Pete and Johnny leaned in to help him look at it.

It was hand-scrawled in pencil on the back of a wanted flyer for some penny-ante rustler from over in Maricopa County. It wasn't any literary masterpiece but it said what it meant to say and said it straight.

> CITIZENS AND OTHERS WILL
> NOT WEAR GUNS WITHIN THE CITY
> LIMITS UNLESS AUTHORIZED.
> EFFECTIVE 6 P.M. THIS DATE.
> *W. Earp*

Stilwell laughed. So did Claiborne and Spence. After a second, Johnny Ringo, feeling the morning's whiskey getting into him and wanting to be counted one of the boys, reckoned it was pretty funny, too, and joined in on the guffaw. Only Behan kept quiet. He didn't even crack a grin. In fact, he was looking a little sick. But then he was the only one facing the street doors and seeing who had just drifted in through them to stand tall and quiet behind the happy ones.

"Well," said Frank Stilwell, wadding up Wyatt's notice and chucking it over his shoulder, "so much for Mr. Wyatt Earp and his early morning billy-doos. Down the hatch, boys. Here's to a damn fool and a dead sheriff . . . !"

He had started his shot glass up, the others starting theirs with him, when they all noticed Behan not touching his and just sitting and looking past them like he'd been hit in the belly and hadn't got his wind back yet.

Stilwell put his glass down slow and careful. Spence and Claiborne played theirs the same way. Johnny still had his in mid-air.

"Get up," said Wyatt. "Back off and turn around slow. You stay where you are, Mr. Behan."

He knew the Pima politician was not a gun. He carried one and that was all. The other three were professionals. You could smell that a mile off. And there was no need guessing about Johnny Ringo. Him you knew, and never quit watching.

Stilwell was the first up, the first around, and took it the best. "Morning, Sheriff. We was just hoisting one to your memory."

"So I heard," said Wyatt. *Who tore it down?*

By now, they had all gotten up and around and had seen the wadded-up notice where it lay in the sawdust between Wyatt's spread feet. They had also had time to look up and to see the stagged-off Parker double cradled in the hollow of his right arm.

Billy Claiborne looked at his companions. None of them bothered looking back at him. He flushed, took a step forward. "Me!" he snarled defiantly. "Who wants to know?"

"Pick it up."

"The hell you say!"

Wyatt hooked a big thumb over the double's hammers. The twin clicks bit into the stillness.

"Pick it up."

Claiborne got white. He knotted his hands till the knuckles showed blue.

Wyatt dropped the shotgun's butt to his hip.

Claiborne figured the distance from its muzzles to his belt buckle. Five feet. Maybe four and a half. He bent over and picked up the paper.

Wyatt nodded. He put his left hand in his coat pocket, tossed a little dime-store hammer and a nickel bag of roofing nails onto the table. "March," he said.

Young Billy Claiborne was tough. He was honest-to-God tough, no two ways about it. But the greatest softener ever invented was the sawed-off shotgun. He picked up the hammer and nails and marched.

"After you, gentlemen," said Wyatt to the rest of them. "You stay put, Mr. Behan," he repeated. "We won't need you."

They started off after Billy Claiborne, awkward and sulky as so many sheepdogs caught in a strange cowtown.

To Behan, Wyatt only nodded, *"Don't ever touch the girl again,"* before turning and stalking off after them.

12

It's the little things that add up. Mayor Clum was among the handful of early risers that morning, who stepped back as Wyatt herded Ringo and his playmates out onto the boardwalk in front of the Palace. Naturally, this was news. It was all over town inside of two hours—or just as fast as Clum could leg it over to the *Epitaph* and run off a special edition. The account wasn't a classic, likely, but it was close.

". . . Entertainment in the town is definitely picking up these days. Possibly the finest act to be presented hereabouts since Mr. Eddie Foy appeared at the Bird Cage was put on in front of the Crystal Palace this A.M. by a group of gay young players under the skilled direction of our new sheriff. All of the troupe were adequate in their roles but the hit of the day was undoubtedly the Tack Hammer Number in Act Two, performed to perfection by our very own Billy Claiborne. Assisting Mr. Claiborne in his difficult interpretation were the Messrs. Stilwell and Spence, of this city, ably supported by a most promising newcomer from the

Texas circuit, Mr. John Ringo. We understand Act Three is scheduled for 6 P.M. tonight, and needless to say we are all looking forward to a grand curtain number. Admission is free but you are urged to be early as "standing room only" promises to be the order of the evening along Allen Street. . . ."

Also, needless to say, the critical appreciation of Johnny Behan's young troupe was somewhat less jovial than that of Mayor Clum and the *Epitaph*.

After making Billy Claiborne tack the six-gun notice back up in front of the Palace, Wyatt turned him and Spence and Stilwell loose with the warning that next time it wouldn't be played for laughs. Then, quietly reminding them of the sunset deadline, he moved off down Allen Street shoving the unhappy Johnny Ringo ahead of him.

Once back at the jail, he kept it crisp.

"Look, boy," he nodded to the sullen Ringo, "I'm sorry you got caught in that squeeze. But you were in it, and fair in it. So this is the last talk you'll get from me. I allow you'd better listen."

"Save your wind," grunted Ringo. "You've made a damn fool out of me twice in twelve hours, and you've done it a'purpose. We got nothing to talk about."

"I think we have," said Wyatt. "Johnny, things are going to happen fast around here, now. I've tied into a bad bunch. I'll need help. Gun help. From what a man can see, all the professionals are on the other side. That leaves you and me."

"It leaves you," scowled Ringo, dark and ugly.

"You're nettled, boy," shrugged Wyatt. "I'm asking you to forget it. It's only natural for a kid to be sore about getting handled in front of strangers. I like you, son, and I want you to stay with me, you hear?"

"You're shouting into a snowstorm, Wyatt." He let up just a bit. "This town is lousy with loose money and I mean to scoop up my share of it."

"You quoting Behan?" asked Wyatt quietly.

"You figure it out, you're the big new sheriff!" He was nasty again, just as quick as he'd eased off the minute before. "Now, lookit here, Wyatt. I know that the way you figure it, you pulled me out of a bad hole back yonder in

65

San Angelo. But that don't make me beholden to you for life. Why don't you get off my back and stay off of it, goddamnit?"

"What you mean, the way I figure it, Johnny?"

Ringo shrugged. "I reckon I'd have got those two house toughs in the Hairy Dog without your butting in. You seen me gun that dealer and you seen me handle my Colts, since. You unravel it from there."

"A little travel certainly broadens a young man's viewpoint," observed Wyatt caustically.

"I'm good!" boasted Ringo defiantly. "Natural-good. You said it yourself!"

"I thought I knew you, Johnny." He gave him the old, sober headshake. "Thought you could take a little pat on the back without it shook your brains loose. Go on, boy . . ."

Ringo shifted his feet around, awkward-like. "I reckon I've said it. I just don't aim to be your nigger no more. I allow I can make it without your wetnursing, from here in. Leastways, I mean to give it two hellish big tries!" With the loud-voiced claim, he proudly slapped at the leathers of his old-pattern .44's.

"You set your main store by those guns, don't you, kid?" asked Wyatt pleasantly and sort of off-track-like. Ringo saw him tugging at his mustache and knew for sure that question wasn't as simple nor as easy as it sounded. He said his piece, regardless, and still bad-proud about it.

"They're the difference, and *you* know it! The way I see it, the best man in these parts is the first and fastest with his guns."

"You reckon that nominates you, eh, boy?"

"You said it, mister!" bragged Ringo rashly.

"Well, there's just one way you can keep wearing those guns in this town, Johnny. *My way . . .*"

Wyatt opened the desk drawer. He took out an old, green-tarnished deputy's star. Still quiet and easy about it, he tossed it onto the desktop, toward Ringo.

The kid looked at it, knowing what it meant to Wyatt. And what Wyatt meant by shoving it at him without any details. He could take it or leave it, and that was all.

Ringo hesitated. He didn't know all there was to know about the famous Dodge lawman. Nor near all he was going to know about him before he was through with him.

66

But there was one thing he should have known about him already, and for sure. That was that "line fence of the law" business him and Wyatt had talked over long ago.

Wyatt could be a lot of fun and could take a good salty view of almost any trouble that washed his way. But about that one thing he was dead-set. For him, it was where all friendship shut up shop and the hen-hockey froze solid to the roosting pole.

You couldn't laugh with Wyatt about the law.

But the kid was a lot closer to where Lilly Belloit had pegged him than to where Wyatt had. He showed that now, and he showed it in the worst possible way he could have thought up.

He laughed.

He laughed at Wyatt and at the pewter star on the desk.

He laughed at the star, flashed his wonderful draw and shot that star off the desk and spinning with a crazy whine through the air over Wyatt's head and ricocheting off the wall behind him.

Then, he blew the smoke out of his gun barrel in that high-school way a green gunhand always does, and flipped the big Colt back into his right-hand holster with a fancy spin. "No thanks, Sheriff!" The damn-fool grin was still working. "I'll wear 'em in my own way." He hitched at the heavy gunbelt, arrogant and cocksure. "Should you want to know where they'll be, come sunset, you're looking at the place right now!"

Wyatt didn't say a word.

He leaned over in his chair and picked the bent star up off the floor.

He held it up in front of him with his right hand, studying it thoughtfully, while his left hand went back to twisting at his mustache.

The kid's offhand, hip shot had centered the badge, ripping a jagged hole right through the middle of it. After a minute, Wyatt put it flat down on the desk, reached in his coat pocket and got out the little tack hammer he'd taken back from Billy Claiborne. Slow and careful, he pounded down the sharp edges of the metal around the tear. Then he held it up and looked at it again. Finally, he nodded like he was satisfied, and stuck it in his vest pocket.

"I'll save it, Johnny," was all he said. "Someday I'll pin it on you."

"Over my dead body!" laughed Ringo, still taken with the off-trail idea the whole thing was some humorous.

"You guessed it," said Wyatt plenty soft, and got up and stepped out and away from behind the desk.

He let the cold of the words and the easy slouch of his big body take hold of Ringo and settle into him. He watched the wild grin halter down into a sick-cat smile. Then he put the rest of it to him just as soft and careful.

"Now get out, kid, and don't ever look back. For you won't like to see what's standing behind you. . . ."

13

Nowadays you hear a lot of fancy reasons why kids go bad. Mostly, they're all tied up with poor twisted little minds, no rightful opportunities to make good, no proper schooling and suchlike trash. They even got brain doctors to dig into the kid and tell the judge that the reason he stuck up the corner grocery store and shot the poor old Widow Brown in the belly was on account his mother wouldn't let him keep his pet turtle in the bathtub when he was a boy and he cut down the other old lady just to get even for that. It isn't ever that he's just plain no damn good to begin with. Or that his reason was already mighty old-fashioned when Ringo was in kneepants. Or that it hasn't changed any, since, nor is likely to.

Money, mister. That's your reason. Fast money and money that's got without a kid has to work a week of regular hours to get his hands on it. And big money. As big, say, as can be got hold of in five minutes of light exercise setting a fast horse in front of a halted stage along a dark and lonely road, and that would take six years of ranchwork at forty a month and found for an ambitious boy to set by, providing he went at it legal-like.

It may hit you as the long way around, setting down all this preaching to get at the itch that was scratching Johnny Ringo when he swung his roan off Third and up Allen Street right after Wyatt had offered him that star. But it isn't.

Sure, he was mad at Wyatt. Sure, in his mind he was thinking he'd some day get square with him for pushing a man around like he wasn't old enough to wipe his own nose; and for doing it first in front of that cat-bodied Lilly Belloit and then in front of Johnny Behan and those other good eggs at the Palace. But the main sweat that was lathering him was that he'd drunk up the last of the money Wyatt had given him and was on the seat of his jeans in a strange town, without the price of a nickel cup of coffee to his name.

When he'd got that far with his worries, it came natural for him to think of where he'd seen plenty of the long green, which same was on and around Johnny Behan. And to think, too, that the night before, Behan had offered him good-paid hire as a gunhand, with no limit on the amount of overtime work to be had.

Riding along up Allen Street that fine morning Ringo was thinking it was about time he looked up Mr. Behan and had his talk with him. But history pulled the switch and shunted him over onto a side track.

As the roan came abreast of the O.K. Stable, Frank Stilwell along with Pete Spence and Billy Claiborne came riding out of it, heading up Allen and out of town to the north. That put them to moving straight into him. He pulled up and so did they. Stilwell started the talk off, apparently in some hurry about it.

"You want to see Behan?"

"I reckon."

"Made up your mind?"

"Yeah. Where can I find him?"

"You can't. But you're just in time. We're heading out on a little job, now."

"Fair enough, I'll just ride along." He started to rein the roan around but Stilwell checked him.

"You might as well start getting smart, right now. You work with this outfit, you don't advertise it in the middle of Allen Street. Ride on out of town, south, then cut around and hit back into the Burnell's Springs road. We're heading for Tom and Frank McLowry's spread over at Sulphur Springs. Got to see Curly Bill on a little business. We'll hold up for you."

Ringo got a little edgy. "Where's Behan? I was aiming to see him."

"In this business," replied the squat outlaw, "birds of a feather don't bunch up in the same bush. Behan don't go out'n his way to ride the main stem with the boys in broad daylight. Besides," the burly rider eyed him, "he's gone to Tucson on a little urgent business. Small matter to do with Charley Shibell getting a mite careless who he passes out Pima County stars to." He grinned knowingly. "I got a rough-curried hunch says your big pal's tin badge ain't gonna be worth the tomato can it was cut out of, time John gits back from Tucson. Meantime, I was told if I saw you I was to take you along with us. That is, if you was of a mind to go."

"I'm of a mind," said Ringo. "What's up?"

"The new sheriff's number," grinned Billy Claiborne, busting into it.

"Yeah," grunted Stilwell. "We got orders to rewrite that there six-gun billy-doo of his, come six P.M. tonight."

"It figures," agreed Ringo, breaking out that wild grin of his. "But why wait for sundown?"

Pete Spence edged his pony nervously toward Stilwell's. "Goddamnit, Frank, we're holding up traffic. Let's git a move on."

Stilwell swung his horse, throwing a quick eye at the boardwalk in front of the livery stable, and to the people beginning to slow down along it. "Git riding, Ringo," he nodded shortly. "Don't hurry it none. We'll wait for you."

Johnny returned Stilwell's nod, pulled out to let him and the others pass. They went on down the street with their horses at no more than a shuffle walk. They didn't look back and neither did he, as he put the roan on up Allen and out of town the other way.

The last spade was out of the slot. That bad faro hand, begun in San Angelo and held up by Wyatt's three-week try at settling the kid down, was all done. The dealer's box was empty, the case-ace played and called.

Johnny Ringo was on his way.

In his first, fast-moving, fifteen minutes at the Sulphur Springs Ranch, Johnny found out plenty.

The ranch, main headquarters for the San Pedro Valley desperadoes, was the property of the McLowry brothers, Frank and Tom. Along with them, most of the other main-springs of the local wild bunch were in or around the bunkhouse when the men rode in from Tombstone about one o'clock in the afternoon. The names that went with the hard-eyed handshakes rolled out like a badman's Who's Who of Pima County and points southwest.

There was first of all, after the McLowrys, the Clanton boys, Ike, Phin and young Bill. Then came Zwing Hunt, Billy Grounds, Harry Head, Jim Crane, a slit-eyed Mexican breed named Cruz but, for reasons clear enough in his Apache face, called "Indian Charlie," and four or five others that came so fast he couldn't hang onto their handles.

But the one that stood out was Curly Bill Brocius.

He was a five-foot, ten-inch man, thick-bodied and a shade older than most the others. His face was dark-skinned and handsome, his big head topped with thick black hair that ringed up near as tight as a carnival gypsy's. He had a quick, good laugh that he used plenty and that wasn't put on in any way and he was as good-natured a cutthroat as they came. He just didn't have anything against life that he couldn't overlook, and he aimed to make every minute count on the side of roughhouse fun. As long as Ringo knew him, he never remembered him to cry over a bad turn in the trail nor to duck his fair share of dirty work as it might come along.

Among the others, he took an offhand, natural liking only to young Billy, the baby of the Clanton Clan. As to the rest of them, he spotted Ike for a blowhard, Phin for a grouch, and both McLowrys for mean-quiet ones you had to watch, particularly Frank, the older one.

The gang operated in two sections, one for rustling, one for road work. The Clantons and McLowrys handled the rustling; Stilwell, Spence and the others, the stage hoists. Ordinarily Curly handled the road-agent crew, but Old Man Clanton, the father of the boys and the regular head of the rustler bunch, had just got himself bushwhacked by a swarm of mad Mexicans trailing some stolen cattle up from the border. Accordingly, the whole deal had passed to Curly and he'd had to take over the rustling and sort of let up on the road-agent work for a spell. He didn't admit that Wyatt's downing of two of his boys had had anything to do with that let up, but he did say he was looking for a good new hand to take over the stage jobs while he looked to the rustling. Ringo knew he was hint-

71

ing at him, but he didn't grab the bait right off and only kept his mouth shut and listened for a change.

Naturally, before he had got around to introducing Ringo to the boys, Stilwell had told Curly about Wyatt's six-gun order of that same morning and about Behan heading for Tucson the minute Wyatt had walked out of the Crystal Palace. What Curly thought of the order was first to snort, then to bust out his big laugh and go to naming off which hands he wanted to ride along with him back into town to call Wyatt's bluff on that business of nobody wearing guns inside the city limits past sundown that day.

"Let's see, Frank"—he was talking to Stilwell—"you boys just come from town, so you'd maybe best lay over here at the ranch and leave some of the others of us handle this job. Ike, you and Billy come along." He turned to the McLowrys. "And Tom, you and Frank. That's five, but I like lucky numbers so we'll make it seven. "Pony," he pointed to Pony Deal, a shaggy-headed youngster of about Ringo's age, "you ain't bin in town nor in trouble lately. Git your hoss." He looked around.

One of the waiting men grinned at him. "Well, there's you six. With me, it's seven, and we're all set."

"All right, Pat, you're in." It was Frank Patterson but Curly always called him Pat to cut him out from the other Franks in the crowd. "Climb your pony and let's ramble."

"Hold on," waved Ringo, flashing his bad grin and cheeking up to Curly bold as brass and like he'd known him all his life. "I'm the one that's bin put off on the most by Earp. Seems I'd ought to get to tag along and watch the fun."

Curly looked at him.

He saw a tall kid, over six-two. Slender, he was, and with a fast grin and a hard laugh near as quick, if not so good, as Curly's own. He was a little narrow and wild in the eye but he had a way about him, what with his wind-deep tan and his short red hair, that got to a man right off. That and the fact his guns hung on him like he knew where to find them providing he wanted to get to them in better than a normal hurry.

"All right, kid, cut yourself a fresh hoss out'n the corral. Eight's always bin a bad number for me but maybe you can change my luck."

"Let's git the hell gone, Curly," snapped Frank Mc-

Lowry. "You talk worse'n a damn woman, once you're wound up."

"It's like the feller says, Frank," smiled the outlaw leader, stepping easy up onto his saddled pony. "The female of the speeshies, she's the little son-of-a-bitch you got to watch."

Seeing the little freeze that hit Curly's grin when he said it, Johnny Ringo nodded to himself, shook out his rope, headed into the work-stock corral. Curly Bill Brocius, no matter that he was sudden to grin and quick to laugh, was for sure one you had to watch.

14 ☆

During the rest of that day, after his early morning brush with Ringo and his pals in the Crystal Palace, Wyatt was fair to middling busy. First, there was the coroner's inquest over the dead boys from the stage holdup the night before. This took no more than ten minutes, with Dr. George Goodfellow giving the bodies a short look and advising the six good members and true of the Citizen's Safety Committee, who'd been lined up by Mayor Clum as a coroner's jury, that a verdict of mighty justifiable homicide was indicated.

The suggestion was followed right fast. So fast, in fact, the town didn't even know there'd been an inquest till they read about it down below the article on Wyatt's six-gun notice, in the special noon edition of the *Epitaph*.

After that, there was the business of trying to find a few deputies to swear in for the fun that was bound to hit town around six o'clock, providing Curly Bill and his bunch took up Wyatt's challenge. But none of the sober citizens of Goose Flats had lost any gun-toughs. Word had got around by now that Stilwell and his bunch had left town by the Burnell's Springs road. Nobody needed to be reminded that Sulphur Springs Ranch lay over across the Dragoons in that direction. Nor to be reminded who ruled the bunkhouse full of bad lots who hung out there.

His name might be William Brocius in Dodge City but it was just plain Curly Bill in Pima County and nobody in his right mind wanted to argue about the way you spelled it; which was with two Cavalry Colts in capital letters, with the eyes dotted right square in the middle by a one-ounce slug of .44 caliber lead.

Result was, the winter sun got down back of the Whetstones and six o'clock rolled around while Wyatt was still whistling into the wind for his deputies. He was good and damn mad about it you can bet, when, just before six, the door to the jail office eased open and Ferd Wagner walked in.

"Ferd . . . !" It wasn't often Wyatt showed any start. "Where in God's name did you drop in from?"

"Over to Fairbank," grinned the other, taking Wyatt's hand easy and natural, like it wasn't the second or third time he'd done it. "I was on the day-run down from Benson. Meant to lay over in Fairbank but heard you was looking for a deputy or two and not having any luck."

"Thanks, old salt." Wyatt left it at that. "You still working undercover for the Company?"

Wagner was a secret agent for Wells Fargo. One of that little-known crew of brave men who worked as spies for the express companies, getting less pay than a top stagedriver and often as not drawing their final check from the Winchester First National Bank over the signature of some road agent who had caught them working after office hours and out of bounds.

"Sure. You can't teach an old dog to roll over. I see you're still doing business at the same old stand, too."

"Yeah, you know how it is."

Wagner nodded. "Company sure is pleased with the way you stretched them two kids of Curly Bill's. Old Monk Wilson has got it spread clear to Phoenix and back, the neat way you done it. Office up to Tucson wired down that if you ever needed a job, you knew where you'd be welcomer than paper money in a passed plate."

"I'll remember it," said Wyatt.

He got a badge out of the drawer, came around the desk and hung it on Wagner's vest.

"You're sworn," he said. Then he grinned. "I'll thank you to notice that isn't just any old deputy badge, mister. That's the one the town marshal turned in when I took over. As of now, you're the new town marshal of Tombstone, Ferd!" His voice sobered, the dry good nature gone out of it. "Now, mind you, be careful. Don't make any

74

play unless you have to. You're just to back me and see I don't take one between the shoulder blades. I'll do the talking and what forcing needs to be done. Understand?"

"Sure, there'll be no trouble with you handling it."

"Likely not. Let's go."

They went out the door and off down Frémont. It was already dark, with a driving wind and a sleety snow bucketing down off the Dragoons, across Goose Flats. For a night where there wasn't going to be any trouble, it looked uncommon black and ugly.

It was just a little after six when Wyatt and Ferd Wagner eased up Allen toward the Palace. They kept on the north side of the streets, staying close in to the buildings, where the shadows were solid ink. At the O.K. Stable, Wyatt told Ferd to wait up a minute while he went inside to check what horses might be in there with lather between their legs. He was back out in no time.

"Salty bunch," he nodded to Ferd.

"How salty?" asked the stand-in town marshal.

"My boy Ringo, along with two each of the Clantons and McLowrys. Then Pony Deal, Frank Patterson and the old he-coon, himself."

"Curly Bill," groaned Ferd unhappily.

"As ever was," grunted Wyatt. "Come on, I got something I want to get over at my shack. Got a hunch this'll be a night for barrel-bending."

At the shack, Ferd held the lamp and watched him rummage in his warbag. Ferd grinned nervously at what he dug out and held up to the light.

"Remember this?" said Wyatt, returning the grin without the nerves.

Ferd hesitated. He remembered it all right. Once a man had seen the Buntline Special, he didn't forget it. There'd been only five of them ever made, all to old Ned Buntline's personal order. One had gone to Wyatt, the other four to some brother star-wearers, just as famous in their own ways as the big man himself: Bill Tilghman, Neal Brown, Charlie Bassett, Bat Masterson.

The Special was a regular heavy-frame Colt with an outsize twelve-inch barrel. It was a weapon made not only to Buntline's order but to Wyatt's. No better beltgun was ever figured out for the risky art of buffaloing.

75

"Well, hell I reckon!" Ferd broke the pause and dropped the grin. "You allow it's going to be real close work, likely."

"Likely. The sweeper up to the livery said they'd been in town since five. That's an hour of whiskey any way you cut it. Always like to work inside a man's reach when he's liquored up."

"They bin talking, I guess."

"Enough. They none of them checked their guns at Campbell and Hatch's. They all still got them on and are allowing out loud they mean to keep them there." He moved for the sagging door. "Douse the light, Ferd. Let's go."

Outside the darkened shack, both men held up suddenly, listening intently. From the direction of Allen Street a well-oiled bass was announcing to the winter night that the lad behind the loud mouth was a kinky wolf from the Chiricahuas, was uncurried below the hocks, and didn't mean to have any burrs pulled out of his tail nor shooting irons lifted off his hip.

"Sounds like the first one of our coyotes tuning up over yonder," muttered Wyatt. "We'll just sneak up and skin him out before the pack starts gathering."

"How'll we work him, Wyatt?"

"He's about in front of the Bird Cage, judging from his yammer. We'll go around the block, you north, me south. Move in easy along the buildings and let me have the first whack at him."

Minutes later, they were closing in on their weaving challenger. Wagner, in his nervousness, had walked too fast and had gotten around the block first. He had already gotten that close in on the pistol-waving drunk, he didn't dare back away from him to wait for Wyatt. Then, at the same time he saw the latter, now moving up fast on the far side of their man, he got his first good look at the bird they had boxed.

It was Curly Bill himself.

Nobody ever found out why Ferd Wagner did what he did then. Likely, it was just that he was stampeded by seeing it was Curly. Or maybe just made foolish by thinking the outlaw was too boiled to know what he was doing. At any rate, he took a drop on him and ordered him to hand over his Colt.

Curly surprised him by laughing, good-natured-like, and holding the gun out butt-first.

Ferd grabbed at it and, quick as he did, Curly spun it around on his trigger finger so that Ferd caught at the barrel rather than the butt. Ferd gave it a yank and Curly's finger bit into the trigger. The slug took Ferd through the right lung, about four ribs down, dropping him for the night and then some.

But when that happened, Curly didn't laugh any more. He only stood there dumb for a minute, as though he didn't understand what he'd done. He always claimed he never meant for Ferd to shoot himself like that, and a good many perfectly honest folks held with him on that claim all their lives. But not long after that, no matter it was maybe an accident, that tricky way of giving up a gun got to be called the "Curly Bill spin," and wasn't looked on as the sort of parlor stunt calculated to make a man popular with peace officers.

Nevertheless, Ferd's going down like that gave Wyatt three seconds of time. Of which same, he used only two. One to leap in behind Curly, and one to wrap the Buntline barrel around the back of his hat.

By now, several of the solid citizens were nosing up for a look at the shambles. Wyatt deputized one bunch of them to lug Ferd over to his shack and fetch Dr. Goodfellow. Then he tossed the jail keys over to another bunch and told them to drag Curly over and lock him up. The whole outfit of them were still standing around with their mouths open, when he rammed the Buntline Special back in his belt and took off across Allen, toward the Palace.

He got a good break there, for both McLowrys were just coming out and didn't see him sliding along the front wall of the building next door. He stepped into the shadow back of a big pile of packing boxes, letting them come right on past him.

Not being out to make a hero of himself, he played the house percentages for all they were worth, no different than he always did. He eased out behind them, fed the barrel to Frank, first, rightly figuring him for the most trouble. He could tell by the way the steel went home into his head that Frank was out of it. He put his knee into brother Tom's kidneys before he got the Buntline well away from Frank's skull. Tom snapped straight up and

77

spun around helpless with the pain. Wyatt just reached out and slashed the barrel alongside his jaw, slanchwise, near cracking the bone and laying the meat open clean down to it.

He leaned back against the packing boxes and waited for a few of the bolder Tombstone boys to filter on across Allen and come up to him.

"Put these birds in the hoosegow with Curly," he told them, low-voiced. "Keep the noise down and get them out of here quick and quiet. I don't want to flush up the others if I can help it."

He looked up as a man ran across from the Bird Cage. "We got Ferd fixed up," he panted. "Doc Goodfellow says he's real bad off, though." He paused, gulping for breath and saying the rest of it slower. "Sheriff, me and the boys wants to back you. If you'll hold up for five minutes, we'll have our bunch rounded up."

"Thanks," said Wyatt. "I reckon I won't need to wait, friend. You go along with these boys, over to the jail. Hang around there and take charge till I bring the rest of them in."

"The rest of them! Good God A'mighty, Mr. Earp, there's six, eight more of them in the Palace, there!"

"Five," corrected Wyatt drily. "And two of those are boys. Get going like I say, and hold the noise down. Hop it, now!"

He was away and around the pile of boxes and moving for the glass doors of the Palace before there could be any more argument.

They watched him hit the doors and shove them right open to walk in like he was there to collect the rent or play in the band or something. Then the man from across the street got his breath back, started feeling a little special from being patted on the shoulder by the new sheriff, and began throwing orders around, the same as if he'd been a policeman his whole life.

His good friends and neighbors had just taken hold of Frank McLowry to throw him into a handy buckboard at the curb, when everybody held up to drop their mouths open at what was coming back out of the Crystal Palace.

You can get an argument on most any angle of what actually went on in Tombstone while Wyatt was there.

But everybody that ever remembered it from being there and seeing it happen, agreed on one thing: nobody went into the Palace with Wyatt that night; several somebodies came out of it with him.

He did it so quick and simple it was all over before it got started.

The only stop he made was just inside the doors to adjust his eyes to the bright light and to locate his customers.

He spotted them at the bar, was satisfied to see they hadn't spotted him yet. He moved straight across the room through the push of the table crowd, not slow nor stalky nor any of that, but just unrushed and sure and stepping long.

The first they saw of him was in the back-bar mirror. Naturally, that was way too late.

He took the two nearest him, which just happened to be Ike and Billy Clanton. Ike went down the first clip he hit him. But Billy had enough spunk left, after taking his barrel-cut across the back of the head, to stagger around and fumble for his guns. Wyatt slashed him twice more, full across the face, and the kid went down clawing at the blood in his eyes and cursing in a slip-lip whimper that sounded nastier than a trapped lobo trying to chew his front foot off.

Ringo and the other two didn't move; Ringo, because he knew better than to try to draw out on Wyatt when you were turned, back-to, away from him; and the others because they wouldn't have had the guts to brace the Dodge City gunman by their lonesomes with less than five feet of solid rock, a dark night and a pair of .44-.40 Winchesters between them and him.

"All right, boys." It was short, even for Wyatt. "Let's take a little pasear over to the jailhouse."

And to the jailhouse they went, Ringo leading the way among the staring tables. Pony Deal and Frank Patterson followed him. Ike Clanton came last and guided the staggering, blood-blinded Billy.

The whole action had taken something like sixty seconds. And two minutes could not have passed from the time Wyatt entered the Crystal Palace till he was back out of it. Which is mainly how come the boys over by the packing boxes next door were so flabbergasted they dropped Frank McLowry into the gutter and damn near let him get drowned in the horse-water from the Palace hitch rack while they were standing there staring.

And which is entirely how come Wyatt Earp to pistol-whip five big gunmen in ten minutes, and to put Curly Bill Brocius and all seven of his Sulphur Springs bad boys to bed in the Frémont Street jail without their suppers.

And likewise without their six-guns.

15

Wyatt had said things were going to move fast.

They did.

For forty-eight hours he held Curly Bill and his bunch in the Tombstone hoosegow under a charge of carrying unconcealed weapons. *"For the time being,"* he'd added, in a scum-ice way they didn't like a little bit. And with good reason. That "time being" had to do with Ferd Wagner.

The Fargo agent was still alive.

He hung on all day Saturday, the second day; then gave up and went down with the sun that night. He did it like the gentleman he was, too, sending for Wyatt and two witnesses and making a statement that the shooting had been an accident and his own fault. He had Mayor Clum write it out and he signed it, Wyatt holding him up so's he could make it.

After he was gone, Wyatt went back over to the jail. He stalked through the front office and into the cell block. Curly and a couple of the others were playing Three-toed Pete with the jail deck and a stack of burnt matches for money. Their heads were not aching so bad as the day before and the lot of them had chippered up somewhat since noon, when the flunky who brought their grub over from the Can Can Chop House had told them Ferd was feeling better and like to get well, after all.

But when Wyatt walked in, Curly didn't need more than one look at the set of his mouth, to know the card game was over and his luck had changed.

"Ferd just died, Curly," Wyatt nodded. "He said it was an accident. I'm asking the court to call it murder. How about a laugh on that?"

It hit the big outlaw hard, a blind man could see that. "I'm right sorry to hear Ferd's gone, Wyatt," he said. He held his head down, along with his words. "Likely you know I ain't funning when I say it."

"I'll tell that to his wife and those three kids of his up to Benson," replied Wyatt. "Maybe they can pay the bills and live fat off the fact you're sorry."

Curly didn't answer. He knew about those little kids of Ferd's. He just turned away and walked over to the far wall and sat down on the bunk, looking sick.

"I'm holding all of you," Wyatt told them slowly. "Judge Cartright is sitting a circuit session up to Benson next week. Monday morning we'll just hop the stage and run up there for a little batch of arraignments. Tomorrow being Sunday, you got some time to think about what you're going to say to Ferd's widow. You'll see her in court."

He turned his back on them, twisting his mouth to get rid of the bad taste talking to them put in it.

"You can't hold the rest of us, legal!" Ike Clanton snarled after him. "You'd best damn well git Sid Skidmore over here and let us talk to him, or you're apt to be answering some charges your ownself, by Christ!"

Wyatt eyed him. He knew all about Mr. Sidney Skidmore. He was the leading dim light of "Rotten Row," Tombstone's name for the nest of lawsharps hanging out their shingles along Fourth and Toughnut Street, around the corner from the new courthouse.

"Mr. Skidmore's already been here," he said quietly to Ike. "We had a nice long talk about the law. He agreed with you."

With that, he went on out, kicking the door shut behind him. They yelled and cussed around a bit, then quieted down. The quiet held for maybe ten minutes, before Ringo cracked.

"Wyatt, lemme out! I got to talk to you. I got to tell you something. You hear me in there, Wyatt?"

There wasn't any answer for a long time. Then the door opened and Wyatt came in. He let Ringo out, followed him back into the front office.

"All right, kid, say it short. It's a little late for a long wind."

Ringo glanced nervously toward the cellblock, dropped his voice to a mutter.

"Wyatt, this ain't my mess and you know it. I didn't rightly have nothing to do with your deputy getting hisself killed. I don't see you've any call to tie me into it, at all."

"You come out to ask for special treatment, boy?"

"No, Wyatt, that ain't it. I want to talk about you and me."

"What about you and me?"

"I bin an idiot. It's the first time I bin sober enough to hit a balloon with a ballbat, since I hit town. So, I reckon you know it's me talking now, and not the whiskey."

"I'm listening."

"All right . . ." It was hard for him to get it out, and he hung up on it for a minute, looking to Wyatt as though he expected some help with the rest of it.

He didn't get it.

Then he bent over the desk, breathing hard, and it came out of him all in a rush and a tumble.

"Wyatt, I'm sorry I turned on you and I swear I won't do it again and I want that there star you offered me the other day!"

He might as well have been talking to the wall. Wyatt didn't move and he didn't look up. After a bad minute of waiting, Ringo backed away from the desk and tailed off with a wobbly, "I guess that's what I had to say. . . ."

The minutes ticked off long and slow. He thought Wyatt never would leave off tugging at his mustache and staring at the floor in that empty-eyed, far-off way of his. But at last he began to talk.

"A man fools me once," he said slowly, "shame on him. He fools me twice, shame on me. It's an old saying they got, up in the border country, kid. It's one I never forgot. I've been thinking about that saying a lot these past few days, and about you along with it, Johnny. You've fooled me once, boy. I'm afraid the rest of it comes out pretty simple."

Ringo cleared his throat. So far, Wyatt hadn't looked up from the floor, and he still didn't.

"Uh, how's that, Wyatt . . . ?" he got out, at last.

"Nobody fools me twice."

Wyatt said it soft and unhappy-like and he still didn't look up from the floor. But Ringo felt the bitter end that was in it and hadn't been said. He knew his last question

82

was only asking chapter and verse. But he had to say it.

"Where's that leave us, then?" he muttered.

Now it was that Wyatt's pale eyes looked up. They held on Ringo, deep and still as winter-cold water in a desert tank when the day wind has died at sundown.

"It leaves *you*," he said softly, "facing a hanging charge as accessory to the murder of Ferd Wagner."

At six P.M., Sunday night, the day stage from Benson and Tucson rolled up in front of the O.K. Stable. At 6:01, Mr. Johnny Behan got down out of it and headed up Allen for the *Epitaph* office, where editor Clum's light was still burning in the front window. At 6:05, Clum was looking at the legal paper Behan shoved across his desk, and at 6:10 he was into his overcoat hunching unhappily down Allen Street at Behan's side. At 6:15 P.M., they were in the front office of the Frémont Street jail, with Wyatt studying the paper Behan handed him, not hearing editor Clum's unpublished remarks about the shame and the pity and the pure hell of it.

A man looked at that paper, he read Charles E. Shibell scribbled in ink across the bottom of it, and he knew where he was.

And where he was, was looking for a job.

As of tomorrow morning, Tombstone had herself a new sheriff by the name of John C. Behan.

Bright and early, Monday, Behan turned up at the jail with lawyer Skidmore and a copy of Ferd Wagner's signed statement clearing Curly Bill. The Sulphur Springs outlaws were turned loose, stopped at the Can Can Chop House for breakfast, and rode out of Tombstone an hour later, unhurried and free as the Arizona breeze.

Wyatt took the bone of all this into his teeth and slunk over to his shack back of the Bird Cage to chew on it all day. After eight hours of pacing and mustache-pulling and growling to himself, he spit the splinters out and started packing his warbag.

Like any frontier peace officer, he'd had to put up with his share of shady politics and well-hidden higher-ups. Them, and the gutless, sheep-stupid tax-paying citizens who stood still for them. But enough was too much. For the past year he'd had in mind going out to the West Coast

83

and setting up some sort of business that didn't need to be done back of a star. This was as good a time as any to get to it. He was all done with Tombstone. There was just one thing the town might still hold for him, and he would get that answered right now.

It was something that had been in his mind since the minute he'd rolled up to the Benson stage-stop, riding shotgun. And not only in his mind, but in his body. Something that wouldn't let a man rest and that he had to get shut of. To be absolutely sure about. No matter his head kept telling him his heart was dead wrong about it. There was always that last chance. Maybe, now that he'd decided to give up his guns and stars, she might see it somehow different.

One way or the other, a man had to find out.

Had to go and see Evvie Cushman.

And to ask her about him and her, flat out.

She answered the door herself, standing trim and tall in its lamplit frame. She saw him there, waiting with his big hat in his hand, but she said nothing and made him speak out first.

"Miss Evvie, I'd like to talk to you if I may."

"Yes? What was it about, Mr. Earp?"

"I'm leaving Tombstone," he said simply. "But before I did there was something I had to say to you, ma'am."

"Really, Mr. Earp, there can't be anything for you to say—not to me!"

"Yes there is, Miss Evvie. May I come in? It won't take long and I'll make it just as straight as I know how."

It wasn't coming easy for him, she was female enough to see that. She was decent enough, too, to remember her manners at the last minute. Especially, when the thought crossed her mind that he'd most likely come by to apologize for being rough and short with her before. "Why, of course. Please excuse me, Mr. Earp. I'm afraid you and I just got started rubbing one another the wrong way. It's not that I mean to be rude, sir." The smile was small and tight around the edges. But the moon was in Wyatt's eyes and he wouldn't see it that way.

"Thank you, ma'am. You sure do have a nice place here."

She stood aside for him, waving her slender arm toward the sitting room. "There's no one in the front parlor, Mr. Earp. Do go right in."

He moved past her to turn and stand uneasily in the center of the little room, waiting for her. She followed him in, all at once uneasy herself.

He looked huge in the warm, close fall of the lamplight, dwarfing the spindly furniture, pulling the rose-papered walls in toward them, seeming to fill the whole room. He stared at her, saying nothing. Suddenly the fear of him, and the frightening feel of the man in him, rose up in Evvie Cushman and she knew why he was there.

"Now please do sit down, Mr. Earp. You make me downright uncomfortable, standing there like that." She tried to keep the uneasiness out of her voice, glossing it over with another of the neat little smiles. Wyatt caught the bluff this time but put it down for that natural sort of embarrassment you'd find in any young girl with a new gentleman caller in the front room and nobody to home in the back part of the house. "Well, thanks, I'll just stand, ma'am," he smiled back. "Kind of figure it makes us even. I'm a mite uncomfortable myself."

She only nodded, not saying anything nor offering to set down herself, but just sort of moving back away from him and waiting there for him to go on.

"You see it's like I said, Miss Evvie. I'm leaving Tombstone. I'm going into business for myself out in California and . . ."

"Mr. Earp," she broke in on him quick and sharp, "please say what you have to say." She tilted her chin at him defiantly. "You know I don't like you and you know I don't like the business you're in. Now please get on with it."

She wasn't smiling any more and neither was Wyatt. It was a miserable bad way to go about telling a woman that you thought you were in love with her, but he didn't have all winter to waste and was anyways, and always, a man to go ahead and toss his steer once he'd grabbed him by the horns.

"I mean to, Miss Evvie," he said quietly, "and was just trying to. What I wanted you to know is that I'm quitting the law business. I'm all done with the sort of thing that

85

has made you think I'm a hired killer and that has so set you against me. I thought knowing that might make things some different between us. At least, I hoped it might."

He broke off to take a half-step toward her, his big hands reaching out stiff and clumsy.

"Miss Evvie, I know I haven't any rightful call to ask you a question like this, but I just couldn't bring myself to leave Tombstone without I did. And without I got your certain-final answer." He hesitated, then let the rest of it come out in that blunt, straight way of his. "You're woman enough, and plenty woman enough, to know what I'm talking about, Miss Evvie. And to guess how I feel about you. Question is, girl, is there any last chance you could someday come to feel the same way about me?"

She didn't move, nor say a thing. Just stood there looking half away from him and biting that beautiful bottom lip of hers. He knew he hadn't really said all of it yet. Hadn't got down to that one last word on the subject which a man always had to come around to, one way or another, before any woman in the world would let him off the hook.

But love can be an awful tough word to get out, especially when a man is forced into pushing it at a high-proud girl he's talked to only once or twice before, and who has already told him she can't stomach his kind in general, and him in particular.

Wyatt waved his hands again, in that helpless way a man will when he thinks they can talk better than he can. He moved a little more toward her, swallowed hard and almost got it said—but never did.

The minute he moved, she did too.

He hadn't a thought in mind actually to put his hands on her. He was just using them the way any worked-up man would, to try and show her how much more he wanted to say than he could put into words. But no sooner did he motion them toward her than she jumped back away from him like he'd cut at her with a whip. And the gasp came out of her in a frightened, little-child way that put a shiver into Wyatt, colder than anything he'd ever known.

"Don't touch me! Oh, please, Mr. Earp, don't touch me . . . !"

He dropped his hands. Stepped back. Felt all the tightness and the desire and the want of her go out of him.

Felt, in its empty place, his own man-strength rushing back into him. He looked at the misery and the fear of her trembling there against the wall, and knew that for him Evvy Cushman's beauty must become a destroyed and lifeless thing. And that she, herself, was only to be pitied and turned away from with all the kindness and gentleness a man could show.

There were women like that, he knew. Ones who went almost crazy if a man crowded them, pouring all they had of love and sympathy onto all men, so's they'd never need to answer to any one man. Evvie was that kind. You had to admit it even though it near tore your heart out doing it. You had to admit, too, that you'd never get the picture of that cameo-clear face out of your mind, nor the memory of that faultless, beautiful body of hers out of your thoughts. No, you could turn your back on her and mean never to look back again. You could maybe even, in enough years of trying, look back and be glad you had sense and guts enough to know when you'd been beat and to walk away with your head still high and your pride in one chunk. But one thing you'd never do with Evvie Cushman. *You'd never forget her.*

Before he turned away from her, Wyatt touched his hat and told her in that slow, kind way of his, "I'm right sorry I frightened you, Miss Evvie, ma'am." Then soft and gentle, and like a man would say it to his kid sister or to his own little girl, "Poor little thing . . ."

That was all.

He left her still huddled against the parlor wall. He didn't look at her as he went out past her, and didn't see the starting glitter of her tears nor hear the quick-choked sob with which she fought them back.

He swung up on Big Red, turned the old gelding away from the neat white pickets, let him take his own way down the street.

16

Somehow, he wasn't surprised to find Lilly there when he returned to the shack for his warbag. What he hadn't expected was the unsettling, warm glow it gave him.

"Hello, Lilly." He didn't realize he was using that soft smile of his on her. But she did, you can bet, and felt it clear down to her size-three slippers. "Where you been keeping yourself?"

"Around, Sheriff." She gave the smile back to him at something better than six percent interest. "Looks like maybe you're figuring to run out on us." She held up, studying him with those slant eyes of hers. "It's not like you, Wyatt. Don't you do it."

"I got to. There's nothing here for me now. You heard what happened last night."

"Sure. What I'm waiting to hear is what happened tonight."

He knew what she meant. He didn't back around it. "Nothing," he said. "I reckon she just isn't my kind."

"She isn't any man's kind, boy. I could have told you that. Any woman could."

"It wouldn't have done any good. I'm the sort has got to find things out for himself. Thick skulls run in the family."

"And thin hides?" she asked quietly.

"What you mean?" It nettled him a little. "You know what a man's up against here. Behan's hooked to Shibell in some way, and Shibell to somebody in Prescott, and him to somebody else, clear on up. You can fight what's in front of you, but you can't draw a gun on somebody behind your back in Tucson or Prescott. I know what it is. I'm sick of it."

She just looked at him a minute, then nodded. "You want to hear something else that'll make you a site sicker?"

"I've heard it all. The hell with it."

"If you've heard this and mean to take it laying on your back and waving your feet in the air, you've sure fooled me."

"I've fooled a lot of people in my time," he growled. "What you talking about, Lilly?"

She gave it to him, uncut. "Behan is spreading it around that in your fast four days as sheriff, nobody's stuck up any stages. That's the first time more than forty-eight hours have gone by but what some outfit hasn't tried to make a hoist somewhere along the line."

"Maybe I'd ought to thank him for the compliment before I leave. That what you mean?"

"What I mean is that I don't think you're leaving, Wyatt."

"Better think again, girl."

"You better," she said abruptly. "He's saying it's pretty hard to stick up stages and be sheriff all at the same time."

Wyatt laughed. A man had heard some silly things in his time, but the idea that he'd been in any personal way mixed in with knocking over the local payrolls and mine shipments was pretty far out on the edge of the herd. "That kind of talk doesn't even call for an answer," he grunted. "Nobody would listen to it. I wasn't even near this town up to this week."

"Can you prove it?" she asked quickly.

"Sure. Ringo was with me. We came over from Texas, three weeks on the way."

It was her turn to laugh and, nettled as he was, he couldn't help feeling what a good, clean sound it was. "Ringo!" she said. "Now, there's a wonderful boy for an alibi! Why, he was all this morning drinking and blowing off right along with Behan. Telling it big that Tombstone wasn't wide enough to hold both him and you. Wake up, Wyatt! Ringo's no good to you, nor to anybody else."

"Likely you're right about Ringo," he granted her. "But neither Clum nor his Citizen's Committee, nor any other man of good sense hereabouts, is going to question where I was two, three weeks ago."

She nodded. "And how about two, three hours ago?"

The way she said it, coming up off the bed where she'd been sitting, holding him hard with that anxious, bright-eyed look of hers, told him she was dead serious; that they were getting square down to what had brought her to the shack.

"All right," he said slowly. "Let's have it."

"You've already had it." She answered him just as slow. "Where were you two, three hours ago?"

"Here in the shack, for God's sake! I've been here all day."

"Fine." There was frost on it and he felt it. "Now, all you got to do is prove it. Can you?"

His jaw trapped shut, his pale eyes, narrowing.

"No, by God, I can't. There's been nobody near the shack. I've not seen nor talked to a soul other than you and Miss Evvie."

89

"It's what I mean. You're in trouble, Wyatt. Real trouble."

"Go on, girl . . ."

"Your horse outside?"

"Sure."

"He's warm? Lathered some?"

"I told you I just rode out to Miss Evvie's and back. Likely, I was a mite nervous. No doubt I gingered Red some, coming and going. He's lathered."

"All right, there you are. No stage jobs since you hit town. Then you turn in your star and disappear all day. Come nightfall, you're back here with a hot horse and packing your bags in a big hurry. All we need now is for the posse to ride up outside and feel under your saddle."

"Goddamnit, girl, say what you mean!"

It was the first time she'd heard him use rough language and knew from that how deep he was taking it. She laid the rest of it on, harsh as raw salt in an open cut. "The Benson stage was stuck up at Boquilla Springs three hours ago. Monk Wilson was shot and killed, and the Company lost the Lucky Cuss payroll. Upwards of $14,000 in greenback cash."

He didn't say anything for a minute. Then he made it soft and ugly and deep in the belly. *"The bastards! The dirty, murdering bastards . . . !"*

With that, he was moving.

He slid past Lilly, grabbed the lamp off the table, blew it out. Next, he took his warbag and threw it under the bed. "Got to travel light," was all he said before running to the front window and looking out.

When he came back to her, he was grinning. But not in a way to make anybody comfortable.

"My luck!" he said. "It's coming on to snow. They'll be able to see Red's tracks going away. You'll have to cover for me. Say I was here, got my things and took out on a high lope. Say you hadn't heard anything about the stage holdup and wondered why I was in such a hell of a hurry. Tell them I told you earlier in the day that I was leaving and that you could have the shack back. You got all that now, Lilly girl?"

As he'd gone along, her face had taken on a hard set. Not so much hard, either, as sad maybe, and let down. "Sure," she whispered. "But never mind that 'Lilly girl' stuff, Wyatt. Just go on and run. I owe you a couple. Least I can do is give you cover."

It was his second laugh, and it puzzled her. It sounded almost like he meant it, and was happy about something. He stepped close to her, putting an arm behind her and pulling her in close. He held her like that only a second, then reached down and kissed her tender and gentle on the cheek.

"You remember me, Lilly," he told her. "For I'll promise not to forget you."

Then he was easing the door open, taking a last quick look around, and slipping through it. She was at his stirrup before he could get Big Red reined around. "Wyatt, don't go! Stay with me! Don't quit like this . . . !"

The third laugh was crisper yet, ringing clean and sharp in the night air. "I'm not quitting, ma'am, I was fired!"

"Wyatt . . . !"

"Back in the shack before you freeze, girl. Hard work, that's what makes the world go round, Lilly. So, don't you worry your pretty little head about old Wyatt, now. Your boy is mainly off to see a man about a job!"

The noon stage for Tombstone left Benson on time the following Wednesday—with the Contention payroll in its usual place between the shotgun rider's feet. There wasn't a blessed thing to mark its departure from that of the previous Wednesday's run, unless a man happened to be looking for little things.

Like the fact that it had a new driver in place of Old Monk Wilson, and a new shotgun rider in place of the one that had suddenly felt called on to go home and visit his poor sick mother—subsequent, of course, to having Old Monk shot off of the seat alongside him on the Monday run.

And like the fact that only one passenger got on at the depot stop.

The run was even an hour late getting out of Fairbank, just like the one Wyatt had ridden into Tombstone the week before.

It hit Boquilla Springs about twilight, the same as the other one, and twenty minutes later was easing into the rocky cut north of Watervale, with full dark coming on and the coyotes beginning to tune up.

91

Even the shadowy horsemen that melted out of the rocks to yell up at the new driver looked about the same. There were seven or eight of them and their leader, though it wasn't the same one as before, appeared to be enjoying his job and being real pleasant about the way he laughed and suggested that the new rider throw down his shotgun and kick the cashbox overboard.

At this point there was one slight turn from the other pattern, for the new rider was no Wyatt Earp. He let go of his .12 gauge as requested, butt-foremost. By the time it hit the dirt alongside of the coach, things were smack back on schedule.

A double-barreled Parker blasted the night and two bandit saddles were standing empty, exactly as before.

But from then on, all similarity ceased.

The outlaw leader and his surviving partners had only time to realize the belch of the Parker's tubes had rolled out the near-side, coach door window, when the door itself slammed open and the solitary, black-coated passenger was hitting the dirt, heels first, bucking a cavalry model .44 Colt into the packed mass of their horses.

It was a tribute to his speed that he had emptied the first gun and border-shifted the second one from his left to his right hand and into full action, before the first of the outlaws got going with the Winchesters they already had out and aimed when the passenger opened up with the Parker.

Even then, it was no contest.

They ripped a couple of carbine slugs through the coach, with maybe six, eight others into the empty air around it. But the passenger's right-hand gun had emptied a third saddle by that time and the first shot from his left-hand gun, following the invisibly fast border shift, had winged their leader.

At the moment, none of them knew that it was just a scratch; that the .44 slug had hit the breech of the leader's Winchester, ricocheted off of it, knocking it out of his hand and numbing that hand and its whole forearm with the shock of a grazing wallop from half an ounce of lead traveling 840 feet a second. They only heard him yell and saw the Winchester go spinning away from him. They didn't wait to hear nor see any more. Three down and one drilled inside of ten seconds was too fast and fancy. It wasn't the kind of arithmetic that added up to easy money in any man's mind.

They got out far and fast, and their lately laughing, wing-hit leader wasn't the last one to leave the scene, by several.

For the next minute or so things got back onto previous pattern, for it sounded like much the same easy voice that now called up to the driver and his shotgun rider as had talked to the bandits the week before. "You can get down now, boys," it drawled. "Show's all over for tonight."

During the brief, wordless rest of it, it was largely the same as last Wednesday. With one little exception.

This time there was no need to help any lung-shot road agents into the tonneau where they could stretch out and die comfortable. The three boys sprawled in the dirt along the offsides of the nervous wheelers, were down for keeps. There wasn't any one of them feeling any pain when the quiet-voiced passenger and the hard-swallowing stage crew dumped the last of them into the empty coach.

Five minutes after that, Red Rock Cut was as quiet as a country cemetery at midnight and the old Concord was long gone up the Goose Flat Grade.

It was just 7:15 P.M. when the Benson stage pulled up to the O.K. Stable stop, and Tombstone got her first word that Wells Fargo had hired on a new express messenger.

He was a big, quiet, pale-eyed man, who the boys along the boardwalk in front of the livery barn were certain they'd seen somewhere before. And some recent, as well.

Unless the lamplight was bad, or a man's memory going back on him, that was Mr. Wyatt Earp crawling out of that Concord and stalking off up Allen Street with the Contention payroll box under one arm and a sawed-off Parker double under the other.

17 ☆

Bad news never was a slow traveler. Word that Wyatt was riding for Wells Fargo got to the right places in plenty of time. By now there were three mine payrolls a week coming down from Benson: the Lucky Cuss on Monday, the Contention on Wednesday, the Tough Nut on Friday.

For the first full week on record, the road agents looked the other way. Not a try was made at any of the runs.

Wells Fargo was delighted, the stage crews took a new lease on life, the insurance companies were ready to talk about reducing premiums.

Only Wyatt was unhappy.

He had not come to Tombstone to ride seventy-five-dollar-a-week shotgun for Wells Fargo. It was one thing to hire on for a short spell to clear up any bad air about who was lifting the payroll boxes or dust shipments. It was two others to look forward to a career of setting a stage-driver's box six days a week for sowbelly and beans money.

There was no Sunday run from Benson, so he had laid over in Tombstone Saturday night, not tickled any undue amount with the prospect of climbing back on the box Monday, either. He hadn't seen Ringo or any of the Sulphur Springs boys since he'd left nine days ago. On purpose, he'd avoided Lilly Belloit. He'd heard she was back in the shack but he'd not wanted to see her for reasons he wouldn't admit to himself. He *had seen* Evvie Cushman, for he'd had the rough luck to bump into her on the street the day after the Boquilla Springs brush. She'd evidently had time to get over her scare of him and to get back on her high horse. She had stood her ground, looked him square in the eye and smiled that pat little smile of hers, and he'd had to take off his hat and give her the sidewalk. He hadn't said anything but she had, murmuring some chin-high dig about "hearing he hadn't gone to California after all, but was still doing business as usual in Tombstone," as she brushed past him and swept on down the street in that grand lady way of hers. Adding it all up and not liking the total, he came out with one little bit; he'd taken a regular room at the Cosmopolitan and slunk into it in a high grouch.

Pacing that musty room late Saturday night, his mind was in that rankling state of flux and flow where a man knows he's got to do something and do it quick, but where he can't quite decide what the hell it is he's got to do.

After maybe another ten minutes of walking back and forth from the street window to the hall door, he grabbed his hat and drifted.

At the Crystal Palace the first customer he spotted was Johnny Ringo.

The kid was sitting in at the front poker table. Wyatt held up, not thinking anything in particular about it but just to watch him a minute through the frost of the plate glass.

He was about to move on when he thought he noticed something a little odd about the way he was handling his cards and chips. He checked a few seconds more, then his eyes got real still and went to narrowing in that cold way of his. The kid was shoving his stack around and fumbling his pasteboards *all with his left hand*. His right was on the table a good part of the time but the stiff way he kept it, half-open and with the fingers not moving, a man could guess he'd turned his wrist or hurt it in some other way, so that it wasn't too much use to him for the time being.

That bad look was still in Wyatt's eyes when he shouldered in through the rock-crystal doors. But by the time he got up to the kid's table you'd have thought from his expression that he hadn't seen Ringo in a ganted-up coon's age, and was some happy just to run across him again.

Knowing him at least a little, Ringo wasn't about to buy that faraway grin at face value. He shoved back away from the table and got onto his feet. Still, Wyatt kept it easy, moving straight on into him, smile and all. "Why, hello, kid. Where you been keeping yourself?" Before Ringo could talk, or even think to talk, he reached out and grabbed that hurt right hand of his in a grinning shake. "Mighy good to see you out and around again, boy." With the idle words, he shut down on that hand like a bulldog bench-vise.

Ringo, who had only winced a little at the first grab, turned white with the pain of the second. "Goddamn you, Wyatt, leggo my hand!" He ripped it away, crouching back as though he was going to draw. Then, at the last minute, he seemed to remember he was bucking the original, two-handed tiger, and himself with only his left hand fit to back the play.

"Sorry, kid," said Wyatt evenly. "Didn't notice you had a bad hand. Looks pretty puffy at that, doesn't it? What'd you do, get it caught in a saloon door?"

"None of your goddamn business what I did!" snarled Ringo. "I don't see no tin star on your chest no more, big man, so lay off the questions. You'd best back off and

95

haul your freight before me and the boys fixes your wagon for good."

Wyatt had already had his look at "the boys." They were Pony Deal, Ike Clanton and a couple others of like shortweight measure.

"Always admired your mouth, Johnny. You got more wind in your belly than a blue Texas norther."

With the hard iron of the statement, he gave Ringo his second look at something he hadn't seen since the Hairy Dog Saloon back in San Angelo. The cavalry .44 didn't maybe "appear by magic" the way the story-writers put it. Likely it was just that Ringo and his pals were watching Wyatt and not his gun. Anyways, there it was just back in San Angelo, laying there idle and easy in his right hand, not threatening anybody in particular and only sort of wandering around aimless and pleasant-like.

Along about then, though, things got off the aimless and pleasant track.

"Unhook your belt and drop it," said Wyatt. The way he said it was every bit as good as if he'd had more stars on his vest than Uncle Sam himself.

Ringo unhooked and dropped. But even as the big Colts hit the Palace floor, he had his mouth going again. "Try that again when I got two hands!" he got it out halfway between a strangle and a snarl, but the ugliness of it only brought one of those calculating head-chucks from Wyatt.

"Kick them away from you," he ordered.

Ringo looked at the gentle wave of the wandering .44 and wasted no more time. He kicked. The heavy gunbelt slid through the sawdust, brought up against a nearby table leg. "All right, big man, now what?" he rasped.

"Now," said Wyatt slowly, "I'm going to give a wet-nose kid a licking he should have gotten a long time ago."

"You picked the right time to do it!" grated Ringo. "When I got one bum hand!"

"That 'bum hand' is exactly the reason you're going to get whipped." Wyatt wasn't loud about it, just plenty clear. "I know how it got hurt and you know I know how it got hurt. In case you got any lingering doubts about it, you drop around to my room at the Cosmopolitan after you wake up, and have yourself a good look at an octa-gon-barrel .44-.40 Winchester that got left behind at that Boquilla Springs stage stick-up last Wednesday night."

He paused, eyeing the motionless group at the kid's table. "Now, just for the record and so your referees can rule it was a fair go-round"—he held up his right hand—"I'll guarantee not to lay this one on you, and we'll start dead even otherwise."

By this time, every drunk and dance-hall girl in the place had moved up. You could have heard a duck feather drop into that Palace sawdust. Nobody had any trouble catching the thud of Wyatt's gunbelt hitting the floor planks. Nor the scraping slide of it, as he kicked it away from under his feet.

"Give it your best try, boy," he said quietly to Ringo. "Nobody's coming up behind you with a Buntline, this time."

He was through talking. So, for a change, was Johnny Ringo. He growled something bad-deep and without words in his throat, and went for Wyatt.

Next morning around Tombstone, you could get a hundred and forty versions of that one-arm fight, or one for every customer that was crowded into the Palace when it got started. Three things about it, all the same, are still in the *Epitaph* and *Nugget* files, and nobody arguing about them even fifty years after.

Number one was the damage bill of $487 turned in to the city council by the Crystal Palace owners next day, under the natural assumption that the Citizen's Safety Committee had hired Wyatt to wipe up the place. The bill was itemized down to the last hand-carved back-door mirror, busted bottle of eight-dollar hooch, and imported-from-San Francisco, felt-top poker table.

Number two was the fact that Johnny Ringo was the man left laying in the sawdust when it was all over, beaten into a pulp in five minutes of one of the bloodiest barroom free-for-alls in frontier memory.

Number three was the point-short speech Wyatt delivered to the boys at Ringo's table, before picking up his guns and going back to the Cosmopolitan to clean up.

"When he comes around," he said softly to the Sulphur Springs gamblers, "give him a message for me. Tell him the next time I catch him with a busted hand, following a stage stick-up, he's as all through in Tombstone, Arizona, as Jesse James in Clay County, Missouri."

So Ringo was the first thing Wyatt bumped into when he began to drift through Tombstone that long ago Saturday night. The next and last thing was a ragged, big-eyed Mexican kid that shagged telegrams from the Western Union office over on Toughnut Street. All the kid had to offer Wyatt was that Jake Shagrew, the night operator, had a confidential message for him down at the station. And would he, *"por favor, señor,"* come down right away and get it?

The little chili-picker was pleased as spiked punch when Wyatt thanked him in his rough Spanish, and was somewhat more than just plain puffed up when the big *gringo* flipped him a whole silver dollar and smiled him a sober, *"vaya con Diós, amigo!"* Maybe it isn't the kind of a thing a man ought to detour to tell about, but it's not every night in the week a hired killer gets to be a hero for the price of a plate of ham and eggs.

The wire was from the United States Marshal for Arizona, Crawley P. Dake at Phoenix. It didn't say much, just GOOD WORK BENSON STAGE LAST WEEK. URGENT SEE YOU AT ONCE, but Wyatt was old enough at the game to guess what it didn't say. And to feel the short hairs on the back of his neck go to lifting with the guess.

Unless he didn't know Crawley Dake and the long, slow way of the federal law, the north side of Allen Street was in for the biggest shock of its short life.

He was tugging at the left side of his mustache and looking far away, when he gave Jake Shagrew his one-word answer, COMING, and had him sign it WYATT.

An hour later he had checked out of the Cosmopolitan, shoved his written-out resignation under the door crack of the Wells Fargo office, and pointed Big Red's roman nose into the night and the northwest, due for the Salt River Valley and Maricopa County.

18

Wyatt was gone the better part of two weeks. What he did with all his time when he was away is anybody's guess. What he did with his time when he got back is a matter of remembered fact.

It was a Saturday night, at about the same hour of evening he'd pulled out the fortnight before, when Frank Stilwell and Pete Spence, coming out of the Palace, spotted him riding up to the O.K. Stable with another horseman. At about the same time, he spotted them and flagged a wave at them to hold up.

His companion waited where he was, holding their horses in front of the livery stable, while Wyatt swung down and walked over to them.

"Boys," he greeted them civilly, "I'm back to make a little deal with you all. We've had our ups and downs, it's so. But it hasn't been my fault that we none of us knew from one day to the next where I stood. Things are going to be some different from now on, I can guarantee you."

The two outlaws didn't know just how to take his approach. Was it a covered-up threat? Or a legitimate offer to throw in with the gang? A man couldn't rightly say, offhand. But, damn it, he had said "make a deal." That didn't sound like any rough stuff. Likely, it would do to listen to him.

"What's your proposition?" asked Stilwell, directly.

Wyatt grinned. "Well now, Frank, if you and a few of the boys will get together in the back room, yonder"— he thumbed the Palace doors—"say in about an hour, I think I can give you all the details you'll need to know. What do you say?"

"We'll spread it around," shrugged Stilwell. "Can't say how the boys will take it. Can't guarantee you no audience. I reckon some of 'em will show, though."

"The more the merrier," said Wyatt. "I've brought a friend with me that wants to be cut in on the play, too. He's new in these parts but he knows his business. See you later."

He left Stilwell and Spence staring after him, as he went down the sidewalk and followed the other man into the stable with their horses. They watched the livery door for a couple of minutes but Wyatt and his friend didn't come back out right away, so they cut and drifted uptown to round up the bunch.

They could have waited a couple of hours and still not seen Wyatt and his companion come out onto Allen Street. For the simple reason they didn't come out onto it. They handed their horses over to the buck-toothed stableboy, walked right on through the barn and out into the alley behind it. Inside the next half-hour they had gotten Mayor Clum out of bed, had him rustle up a rump session of the Citizen's Safety Committee, and brought the midnight meeting to order behind the drawn blinds of the *Epitaph's* pressroom.

Wyatt's subject was "Politics and Peace Officers," and he must have spoken right well on it, for inside of ten minutes the Committee, which was ninety percent composed of city council members and was sitting as such the minute they heard Wyatt's proposition, had passed a resolution supporting his program and welcoming his guest to Tombstone, all in the same and mighty eager breath.

The pressroom was dark again a quarter of an hour after they'd filed into it, and Wyatt was walking down Allen toward the Palace with his so-far silent friend.

The two stalked through the front-room poker tables to disappear through the back-room door without so much as a look or a word for anyone. For their parts the customers dropped their chips, choked on their drinks, shook their heads and asked themselves if they were seeing double. They weren't, and Wyatt was presently making that fact clear to the little bunch behind the back-room door.

When he closed that door to peer through the cigar smoke and sourmash fumes of that back room, he counted a pretty good house. There were Frank and Pete, naturally. Then Ike and Phin, of the Clantons; Pony Deal, Frank Patterson, Billy Claiborne and four, five others new to him. Behan wasn't there, of course, nor were Curly Bill or the McLowrys. Ringo was missing, which, assuming the boys had given him Wyatt's message, was more or less to be expected.

Wyatt made it unmercifully direct. Before he'd talked thirty seconds all doubts as to what kind of a deal he had come to offer went up to the ceiling, along with the smoke from the forgotten cigars.

"Gentlemen," he said elaborately, "allow me to present my friend." He hesitated, giving them a chance to get the tobacco fog out of their eyes and squint at a tall, muscular cuss of about six-one, who looked enough like the ex-sheriff to be his brother. Which same, natural

100

enough, he was. "I'd like you to meet my brother, Virgil," concluded Wyatt pleasantly.

Nobody said a word, so he got on with it.

"As I told Mr. Stilwell earlier in the evening, there's going to be a new deal in Tombstone from here on. I wanted to tell you about it to your faces so's there would be no further misunderstandings such as have marred our relationships in times recently past.

"I have just come from a meeting of the city council. As you will recall, I left office here without having time to get a town marshal apointed to replace Ferd Wagner. I am authorized by tonight's special meeting to introduce to you the man who will look after the local law and order from now on. He and I have drawn up a little set of six rules which the council has passed favorably on, and which you might do well to listen to right about here. They'll be read through once, slow and careful. After that, it's every man for himself. Virg."

He broke off and stepped back, giving the floor to his brother.

Virgil Earp pulled out a wad of penciled notes from his vest, waved them around, and took up where Wyatt had left off, his voice as soft and slow as his famous brother's. "They're all put down here in legal language, boys, and you can read them that way in tomorrow's papers. I'll just give you the guts of them, to save your valuable time."

He ticked them off, using his big fingers to count them for the scowling outlaws. They sounded simple enough, but as usual in a game where you were playing table stakes and couldn't buy in for less than a stack of blues, there was a wild joker in the deck.

Number one said there'd be no more riding horses on the board sidewalks; number two, that said animals would no longer be permitted inside saloons with the owner topside; number three, that popping off firearms in the city limits, saving on Christmas, New Year's and the Fourth of July, was out the well-known window; number four, that six-guns would *not* be worn low on the hips this season inside the corporate confines of Tombstone, excepting by gentlemen who could furnish acceptable proof they were strictly passing through the town with no idea of

101

spending the winter; number five, that gun racks would be set up in designated saloons, hotels, stores and corrals, for the purpose of allowing the locals to check their hardware on arrival and reclaim it on departure.

Number six was the joker.

It just said that unmanageable drunks would be subject to a free night in the city jail. It might as well have said what it meant, for it was clear enough to each and all of the listening outlaws. From now on the town marshal could put the clamp on anybody that was in his way and had liquor on his breath. Which would be to say any male American in Tombstone, old enough and strong enough to hold a bottle.

When Virgil had done with it, there was a scuffling of boot heels, a puffing away at cold cigars, a scraping of chairs and suchlike general signs of nobody knowing what to say, but wanting mighty bad to say it. Ike Clanton, the self-elected loud-mouth of the bunch, got his feet under him first.

"Well, talk don't grade no higher here than it does in hell!" he challenged the Earps. "I reckon now you bastards have made your point you might as well bow out. Yonder's the door."

"So I see," acknowledged Wyatt. "But my point is yet to be made. It's one I wouldn't dare make in public, for legal reasons, but I'm going to give it to you boys for what it's worth." He paused, sweeping them with his empty stare. "From the minute I leave this room, I mean to hunt down and kill any man that resists arrest—no matter what charge he's wanted on."

Ike was no smarter than he looked. It didn't sink into him worth a cotton cinch, and his bluster showed it. "I said it once!" he sneered at Wyatt. "Yonder's the door. Use it!"

Tighter mouths and better minds than Ike Clanton's were present. Frank Stilwell moved forward. "Wait a minute," he called to Wyatt. "I smell more to this than rubbing our noses in that manure of getting your brother appointed town marshal. By itself, that don't cut enough grease to clean the skillet. Johnny Behan is still sheriff. No city policeman is going to put much of a dent in his badge. I got a question comes natural to mind. Where's your kicker in all this, Wyatt?"

Wyatt had already started for the door, the silent Virgil dogging after him. He held up at Stilwell's request for information. He snapped his fingers and shook his head in a mile-wide, put-on way, as though to say, "Doggone me, I plumb near forgot to tell you what it was brought me here in the first place!"

What he did say was, "Sorry, Frank. Meant to make that point without being asked. Right proud to oblige."

He stepped back toward them, stopping only when he was well in under the glare of the green-shaded gas lamp. He fished in his pocket, careless as though he was digging for a quarter to pay for his beer. His big fist came out closed around something small and shiny. But it wasn't any quarter. At least if it was, it was the first two-bit piece ever minted with a snap-pin on the back and six sharp points around the edge.

He snagged it onto his vest, still easy and careless about it, not seeming to mind that it hung a little slanchwise and that Stilwell had to twist his neck a mite to see what was engraved across the face of it.

"Read it," Wyatt nodded to the peering outlaw, "but don't weep yet." The easiness and the carelessness evaporated frostily. "Save your tears for the funeral, boys. It might be your own."

He and Virgil were gone then. The door was closed behind them and Frank Stilwell was straightening out his neck. Straightening it out and feeling around it, maybe, the raspy touch and dead-hay smell of the hemp.

Frank was a fugitive from the fifth grade. He could just about lip-read the labels on the tomato cans at Parson's Grocery Store. But he had read that block-letter engraving on Wyatt's new star without any trouble at all.

It was simple enough for anybody.

It said DEPUTY UNITED STATES MARSHAL—ARIZONA TERRITORY, even when you read it slanchwise with your eyes full of stale cigar smoke and your uneasy insides telling you that local stars had just dropped to a dime a dozen.

The federal law had come to Tombstone.

the tightest, quietest time. Wyatt stood for law and
let Behan do the politicking. The bad accessory of that
fact was that Wyatt's law was the federal law, and Behan's
bad law was cussed, which in most cases meant the

19 ☆

Now began the tightest, quietest time, law-wise, in the
town's two-year memory. For six months Johnny Behan
and Wyatt Earp fought it out. In the end, federal star
or no federal star, it was not Wyatt but Shibell's deputy
who stood ahead in the game.

The Pima County machine was too much for the short
limits the U.S. put on its badge-toters. Time and again
Wyatt would make his arrests. Time and again Behan
would hold them a few hours to make it look good, then
turn them loose for "lack of evidence." Even when that
evidence was to be had, pat and cold, there was no beating
Behan and Charley Shibell and their Prescott crowd. Inside
those first six months no less than five men, brought in by
Wyatt on charges either of murder or manslaughter, or
accessory to same, "broke jail" and made it away. In each
case Behan had some smooth story to make it read
reasonable in the *Epitaph* and *Nugget* reports next day.
It appeared to make small difference that in each report,
somewhere along the line, the same string of words—"an
accomplice with a saddled horse was waiting in the alley
behind the jail"—kept cropping up.

In this sort of dirty war Wyatt was no match for the
Tombstone sheriff. Behan knew people and how to use
them. Wyatt didn't. He knew his law and his guns and his
gunmen. Behan knew the man that ran the hardware store,
the one that clerked in the Cosmopolitan, the cowboy from
the San Pedro, the miner from the Dragoons, the Mexican
that swept out the Bird Cage and the stablehand that
swamped manure in the O.K. Corral. He knew Tombstone
and what made it tick. Before long he had it ticking pretty
loud against Wyatt Earp.

It's a fact—tolerable hard to understand but a fact just
the same—that there are still honest old codgers in Tombstone who'll tell you Johnny Behan was the best sheriff the
town ever had. There are just as many who'll put their X
to an affidavit that Wyatt was nothing better than a murdering bastard that hunted down innocent boys and framed
law-abiding citizens till hell wouldn't hold half his mean-
ness.

The unfair fact was that Wyatt stuck to his law and let Behan do the politicking. The bad accessory after that fact was that Wyatt's law was the *federal* law, and unless that law was crossed, which in most cases meant that the U.S. mails or money shipments had to be messed with, he couldn't even get an indictment through his own office, let alone Behan's.

This simply meant that the cushy-fat rustling trade could carry on as usual under Behan's protection or, at damn thin least, under his lack of prosecution. Wyatt couldn't begin even to touch it unless the cattle came in from Mexico and could be caught crossing the border. Which meant a man had to run a patrol from Nogales to the New Mexico line right around the clock.

Along about this time another thing happened. It just about put Behan out of reach. The Prescott crowd got busy and surveyed a line right square down the middle of old Pima County, lopped off the east half of it, along with Tombstone, naturally, and slapped a new brand on it —Cochise County. Charley Shibell, for faithful services rendered, got to handpick the new county's sheriff. You guessed it. From about four months after Wyatt took over as Deputy U.S. Marshal he had to face up to the nasty fact that Johnny Behan was full Sheriff of Cochise County.

All of which isn't to say for a minute that the Earp boys were whipped.

Right off, Virgil and his six rules put a lid on Tombstone the like of which the town had never winced to. By the time two of the rough-string boys had been shot dead on Allen Street for resisting arrest, the gang knew the Earps had to go.

They got Virgil, quick enough. Behan simply had him thrown out as town marshal and a good friend of the gang's put in his place.

But Wyatt was awake. He pulled open his desk drawer, hung a U.S. deputy's badge on his brother, and kept right on cracking down with all six rules.

All this was so much see-sawing, though. Both Wyatt and Behan knew it. Both knew what the real stake was. And who held the hole-card on it.

It was Wyatt.

And the stake was the stage holdups, not the rustling jobs.

105

For six solid months he kept the road agents quiet. He did it by so simple a trick it near drove the outlaw boys to look for honest work. He just saw to it that every last mine shipment or payroll carried U.S. mail along with it. Even if, as happened more than once, he had to write his own letters.

Piling blunt insult atop sharp trick, he got Wells Fargo to put Bob Paul on, to ride shotgun for those shipments. To begin with, Bob was a sure man with a scattergun. But aside from that he was a man about as down on Johnny Behan as you could get. He'd run for Cochise County Sheriff against Behan in the first election after Shibell got the latter appointed. He beat him, too, sound and square. But Behan had rigged a crooked ballot count in the outlying county towns, and come off the dirty winner.

All in all, toward the last, it narrowed down to the one thing. Wyatt had put a boot on the bad boys that pinched plenty. With little damn difference that Behan had him beat at every other turn. The mine shipments had all along been the gang's gravy, the real easy money. When Wyatt cut them off, it meant one word—war.

It was only a question of sooner or later.

In the dictionary Curly Bill and his wild bunch thumbed through, there wasn't any such listing as "later." Behan somehow managed to stall them those first six months by arguing that pretty quick he'd see to it Wyatt got relieved of that U.S. badge.

But Marshal Crawley P. Dake was no Charley Shibell. His orders came through from Washington, D.C., not Prescott, Arizona Territory. Wyatt's star stayed pinned.

Some shortly, Curly Bill had his restless bellyful. He put out the word for the boys to "round up the strays" and drift along over to the Sulphur Springs spread. There was going to be a little bunkhouse lecture. Its subject: "The Preparation and Feeding of Pure Lead to Deputy U.S. Marshals."

20

When you set about stalking out-of-season game like deputy U.S. marshals, you don't rush it any. Not when you're after a record head like Wyatt's. You circle the long way, downwind, and you take your careful, sweet time about it, knowing it's not quite the same as any other big game in the book.

The shift that brought Wyatt his warning came from a quarter of the Tombstone compass nobody in the Sulphur Springs bunch would have thought to keep an eye on: Johnny Ringo.

It was a blustery, sand-drifting night in late September that brought Ceferino Sebastiano Jimenez Paz y Gutierrez dog-trotting through the whirlygusts of Toughnut Street and shivering up to Wyatt's office door.

He went in, after knocking timidly, and stood with his tattered sombrero barred across his skinny chest, waiting while Wyatt finished talking to Virgil. When the latter had left, he stepped forward.

"Dispense me, usted, señor Weecott." It was as close as his soft Sonora tongue could curl itself around the harsh *yanqui* name. *"Por favor . . ."*

It was not the first time, nor the fifteenth, that the little Mexican had come bearing messages through the night in the past half year. And with the exception of two, three telegrams from Marshal Crawley Dake, those messages had all come from one source; one a site more interesting than the U.S. law officer up to Phoenix.

"Hola, Chico!" No matter the little chili's mile-long name, all Mexican kids were Chico to Wyatt. *"¿Que pasa con usted, compadre?"*

"Nada," shrugged the kid, grinning shy-like. *"Justamente una otra cosa de la señorita, no mas."*

"Por supuesto!" Wyatt returned the shrug and the grin. *"¿Que otro, amigo?* She want to see me?" he wound up asking in English.

"Inmediamente, señor, ¡Haga me el favor de venir en seguida!"

"Right behind you, *paisano.*" Wyatt dug in his vest pocket, flipped him his silver dollar. "Don't forget to close *la puerta* on your way out. *Por favor, señor.*" He picked up his big hat and gave the coffee-colored sprout a polite flourish with it.

"Mil gracias, patron. Vaya con Dios." Chico bowed himself stiffly out, tugged on his own floppy straw, and bent his thin body into the whipping dust devils. He was

107

gone in less time than it took Wyatt to smile after him. But pretty quick Wyatt dropped the smile, clamped his black Stetson on, and headed up Toughnut toward the rear of the Bird Cage.

"Come in, man! You're welcome as good news from home, but that sand is pure hell on a schoolgirl's complexion!" Lilly stood aside for him, holding the rickety door while he slipped inside, got his broad back to its planks and eased it shut for her.

"It's a real roof-lifter," he grinned, hunching a shoulder to the howl of the wind outside the little hovel. "Haven't seen it to blow like this since Kansas. Makes the old shack feel right cozy, I allow."

"I allow it always feels that way when you're in it," said Lilly, soft-voiced.

"It takes two to get comfortable," replied Wyatt, not missing what she meant. He put his heavy arm around her thin shoulders. "I reckon you know that by now, girl."

She didn't answer, only snuggled closer and held onto the little moment of nearness. Wyatt was a strange one. She had known him all these months, worshipped him outright and he knew it. Yet in all that time he hadn't laid a hand on her more than half a dozen times. And not once, since that first night, in the way she hungered to have him do.

Quick enough he moved away from her now. For his part he didn't know how he felt about Lilly. Except he was certain he didn't love her. Not like a man imagined it would always be when he finally trailed onto the one woman there was supposed to be somewhere in the world for everybody; not, for sure, like he had felt about Evvie Cushman. Still, there was that about the Bird Cage girl which bothered him some when he was away from her and bothered him plenty more than some when he was hand-close to her.

He put his backside to the glow of the old potbelly stove, spread his long legs and cocked his shaggy head to let on like he was all business.

"Chico was a mite stirred up," he grunted. "Like as if there might be something blowing around Tombstone besides the wind."

"I'd say there is, Wyatt. Something you'd best listen close to."

"Such as?" he said.

"Johnny Ringo. He was here earlier tonight."

"By God, you've not been seeing him!" It was a flat statement, not a question. There was a deepness and ugliness to it that put a wonderful shiver to racing Lilly's slender body.

"You wouldn't be jealous now, would you, boy?" she whispered huskily. "You tell me you are, you'll see the happiest woman west of Fort Worth."

"I'm telling you nothing," denied Wyatt. "You're telling me, and I'm waiting to hear you tell it."

"Wyatt, boy," she murmured, moving in on him, "there's one man in this world for me. You know his name isn't Ringo."

He stepped away from the stove, and from her. He shook his head, talking mean. "I only know Ringo, and all his studhorse kind. There isn't a mortal reason would bring him to nosing around you, save one thing. I know that no-good bastard, Lilly. Don't put off on me!"

"I never thought I'd see you pawing corral dirt and tossing yard hay over your shoulder on my account," she smiled. "It's a rare wonderful sight. But you're dead wrong about me and Ringo. And about what brought him here tonight."

"How wrong?" glared Wyatt, not letting up on the reins a bit.

"He wasn't here two minutes. He never even took his hat off. Just left his message, got back on his horse and drifted."

"Message?"

"For you," she said slowly.

"Go on," he ordered, his eyes narrowing. He was all at once over his mad. That built-in alarm system of raw animal wariness, that no working gunman lives long without, was prodding him plenty now. He was suddenly thinking all about Ringo, none about Lilly Belloit.

"He said to tell you the boys just had a meeting over to Sulphur Springs and you drew the black straw. It's not Behan this time, but Curly Bill. He's put the word out to get you, any way, any time, any place. Just so it's clean and sure, with no cat-mess left that Behan can't dig a good enough hole to cover over."

Wyatt let his breath go, eased off the clamp of his jaw. "That all?" he asked quietly.

"Saving this. He said to tell you he reckoned you and him were even for San Angelo. Whatever that means."

"It means what it says," nodded Wyatt. "He owed me one from back in Texas. It's his quirky-wild way of paying it off, that's all."

"Quirky-wild, or not," said Lilly Belloit emotionally, "he's payed it off. Likely I've had him wrong, all along."

"You haven't," said Wyatt slowly.

He was at the window now, staring out into the howl of the night. He shook his big head, his voice, of a sudden, no longer harsh nor bitter.

"When I was a boy," he began softly, "I had a dog. . . ."

He held up so long she thought he had forgot to go on. But a man's mind travels the back years painful slow, and the hurt in them always takes the same time to go around. Pretty soon, he took up again.

"My father brought Shep home one winter night, half-starved and so pitiful scared he wouldn't come up to any-body. He wasn't more than six, seven months old, maybe not that much. My father had got him in town. He'd pulled him away from a pack of grown dogs that had jumped him and weren't meaning to let him up.

"There was four of us boys. My father called us all into the kitchen and showed us Shep, shivering and growling, back in under the stove. He told us to go ahead and call him out, providing we could.

"Naturally, we all whistled and stamped at him, clap-ping our hands and carrying on like boys will with a new pup. Shep only growled the more, and hunched on back in under the stove. Pretty quick, my father said to let up on him, that he'd just wanted to show us something—that you couldn't crowd even a dog into being your friend. Then, he told us to go on out of the room, one at a time. 'He'll likely take to one of you,' he said, 'and follow along after that one. That will be the one he trusts, and that he wants to be his friend.'

"Morg, he went first. Then Virg and Warny. Shep never moved, only to follow them with his eyes and to hair-up

110

at each of them in his turn. When I started out, he quit growling, gave a sort of wait-up yelp, and came halfway out from under the stove. I stopped and he snuck on over to me and began pawing my overalls. I patted him and right off he went to thumping his tail on the floor and to licking my hand like I'd raised him off his mother.

"My father just bobbed his head and said, 'You've got a dog, boy. See you look after him.' "

Wyatt broke off his story, still looking out the window and far away. Lilly didn't say anything, knowing that wasn't the whole of it.

"I loved that pup," he said at last. "He picked me out to side up with. A boy doesn't ask much more than that. Nor," he added thoughtfully, "does a man."

Now, as he held up again, Lilly asked him quietly, "What happened to Shep, Wyatt?" knowing from the way he had talked, all along, it was something still hurtful to him, clear down the years.

"He took to killing sheep, before he was a year old. My father caught him at it. He put a rope on him and brought him home to me. He gave me the end of the rope, then fetched the old Sharps' bullgun from the corner back of the woodbox where it was always kept. He looked to see that it was capped and primed, nodded to me and handed it over. All he said was, 'He's your dog, boy. Look after him.'

"It was the hardest thing I ever did, Lilly."

He turned from the window, now, his pale-blue eyes dark with the memory of it.

"But I did it.

"I did it, and I swore, then, I would never let another living thing think he was my friend, or tag along with me. I would travel alone as far as the trail might lead, not asking any man to share my load, nor letting him touch any part of it. I meant and kept that promise for twenty years."

"Then?" said Lilly, seeing it was coming hard and wanting to ease it for him.

Wyatt said it slow and bitter. Not bitter with the other one; not blaming him for it, nor hating him for it; but bitter with himself. And putting the hate and the blame where he thought it belonged.

111

"Then, I found Johnny Ringo under the stove. I called him out and I let him follow me off. I patted him on the head and held still for him to lick my hand."

Lilly was afraid of him, then. Suddenly and deep inside. She knew, before she said it to him, what his answer would be. She knew it, even as she put her small hand to his arm. Even as she looked up to him and pleaded, husky-voiced.

"Let him go, Wyatt! There's no rope in your hand, now. There's no gun in the corner, here. Let him go, boy, let him go!"

"He's my dog," said Wyatt dully. *"I got to look after him."*

The way he said it put a chill through Lilly Belloit. It was the utter hardness of him. The final, terrible strength. Back of it you might see those rare, soft spots of the real kindness that was hidden in him. But before them, and always before them, you saw that terrible, fierce sense of the right and the wrong. It was what set him apart from other men, what made them hate and fear him and seek forever to destroy him.

And in the final, bitter end, it was what made him hate and fear himself; and what would bring him to destroy himself.

It was not a pretty thing. Not in Wyatt Earp, or any man. It came too brutal close to setting yourself above other men; to treading on range that was fenced off to any man, where the signs didn't just say, "no trespassing," but spelled it out in full, "forgive us our trespasses as we forgive those who trespass against us." You could love him like Lilly did, and worship every inch of God's ground he'd ever stood on. But, in the end, it was God's ground, and not his.

You knew that, and you had to tell him you knew it.

"It's not yours to say that, Wyatt. Not yours, nor any man's. You're wrong and your father was wrong before you. Men aren't sheep. Nor they aren't dogs. You can't just lead Johnny Ringo over the hill and shoot him. That's not within your law!"

Wyatt had dropped his head while she talked. She still had her hand on his arm and was begging him with her eyes, when he looked back up.

"And whose law was it within," he asked slowly, "when

he shot up the Benson stage six months back? He could have killed any or all of us."

"You know what I mean, Wyatt. If he does a murder, he's got to pay for it. But he's not owing for it, to you. It's yours to catch him, not to kill him, for what he's done. He's bad, Wyatt, we know that. But any man deserves his full chance before a judge and jury. Bring him in, Wyatt, but for God's sake not like you brought those other poor boys in on the Benson stage."

He looked at her a long time.

"You're all alike," he said at last. "You, no less than Evvie Cushman, or any of the others.

"You tell a man that he's the law. You pin a star on him to prove it. You say to him, it's your job to keep the peace. To keep the bad ones from running over the good ones.

"You hire him because he's got a record for being able to sort out the bad ones from the good ones, and to salt them safe down.

"Then, when he comes up against one of those bad ones, you want to grab his gunhand and tell him to hold off; to wait up and let that bad one shoot first. So's everybody can be good and sure he is bad. So's anybody who isn't sure he is, can look into the lawman's coffin and tell himself, 'Well all right, I guess you can go ahead and try him for murder. The marshal looks pretty dead, at that.

"Let me tell you a little something about bad ones, Lilly. Maybe, it'll let you see them the way I do. Maybe it'll let you see that I don't necessarily figure I'm horning in on the Lord's territory, nor taking any play away from the legal law when the times comes that I have to handle one of them without waiting for the courts to help me.

"There's something every police officer that honors himself and believes in the right that's been given him to protect the decent, law-abiding folks, comes to know in time. That something is bad ones; bad ones, and how to recognize them when he runs across them; how to know without God Almighty, or anybody else, has to tell him so, that those bad ones are born that way." He paused, to narrow down and fasten those light eyes on her, harder still.

"What poisons them is in their blood. You'll always

113

hear different, but any man in my job knows better. About Ringo, you can hear it told that he's from a fine family of God-fearing folks, that he's got a good education and the best of upbringing, that he only gambles and drinks and raises the hell he does because he's trying to forget the way he's let his folks down. He puts that line out himself, lets people think it's true, maybe even gets to believing it for his own part. They've all got some sort of a story and the way they see it they aren't ever to blame.

"The fact about Ringo is that he comes by the bad that's in him, by blood and breeding. He's kissing kin to the Youngers and Daltons up in Missouri and Kansas. He's even got an eighth or sixteenth James blood in him. Like gets like. No man can tell me different. You breed a vicious stud to a crazy mare, you're not going to get any sugar-tit suckers for your colts. Ringo's bred that way. You never handle his kind with an apple and a hackamore."

It was the most words she'd ever heard him string together. The force and the thought that was in them held her quiet. When she saw he was through and not going to say any more, she asked him carefully.

"So, what are you going to do about him, Wyatt?"

"I told you," he said harshly, the thoughtfulness and the quiet gone out of his voice. "If I ever come up to him with fresh blood on him, I'm going to kill him."

Contrary to what he'd told Lilly, his first thought after leaving her place wasn't for killing Johnny Ringo but for keeping Wyatt Earp alive.

He was never the one to horse himself any about the romance or other nonsense connected with being a famous peace officer. It was a hard, dirty job. It took hard, dirty work to hold it. When you'd put the years into learning it, that he had, you didn't worry about using back alleys or brass knuckles when the game got that far down into the deck.

Wyatt was using a back alley now. The one that ran along behind the Allen Street store buildings on the south side. He was using it to get down to Fifth and over to Toughnut and the telegraph office without he was bush-whacked on the way.

What he did when he got there was to hunch in out of the wind and ask Jake Shagrew about his Missus and the new baby boy. Then he waited for a late cowboy customer from Galeyville to finish scrawling his inquiry to old C. H. Hyer up to Olathe, Kansas, as to what the hell had happened to those sixteen-inch red-top boots with the four-row stitching he'd ordered custom-made three months ago. After that, he held the door for the irate waddy on his way out, turned to Jake and put in a terse, ten-word telegraph order of his own—for a pair of brass knuckles from Dodge City.

The way Jake got the order, was this:

>J. H. HOLLIDAY
>C/O GEN. DEL.
>DODGE CITY, KANS.
>
>DOC. COULD USE TWO GOOD DEPUTIES.
>BRING MORG. NO HURRY.
>
> WYATT

Jake read it back to him, put it on the key without wasting any comment. When it was gone, he shoved his eyeshade up, shot a stream of Brown's Mule into the open door of the office stove, squinted at Wyatt, and unburdened himself.

"Trouble, Marshal?"

"It hangs to some like stink to a sick dog." Wyatt's answer came back of his hard-eyed nod.

"I can smell it now," said Jake Shagrew, hitching his shoulders like to a draft only he was feeling.

"Keep your nose open and your mouth shut, then," advised Wyatt. "Otherwise it might leave you ailing somewhat, you understand?"

"It's your money, Marshal," he muttered uneasily. "Once she goes through that key, I'm shut of her. Can't recall a word I sent for you, not for the life of me. You looking for an answer, Marshal?"

"Yeah," said Wyatt. "Along about sundown Thursday at the Benson Railway Depot. Allowing Number Nine's no more than four hours late."

"Number Nine, Thursday! Thought you said there wasn't no hurry!"

"Thought you said you didn't remember what I said."

There was a frost on it that would have turned a pumpkin in July. Jake curled up, went limp around the edges.

"You sure thought right, too, Marshal! Uh—ah—good night. . . ."

"Good night," said Wyatt Earp, and went out into the whip and cut of the wind and the sand.

21 ☆

Jake Shagrew didn't let it out, that's for sure as water's scarce in Chihuahua. But when you've got guns the caliber of Curly Bill, Frank McLowry, Phin Clanton and Billy Claiborne hunting for you, you don't sashay out of town for forty-eight hours, without you're missed. Not when you're a deputy U.S. marshal, you don't.

The Sulphur Springs bunch got wind of Wyatt's disappearance the day after he left. Right off, they set out their lookouts, north and south of town, watching for him to come back by either stage or saddle. They knew from the O.K. stableboy that he'd ridden out on Big Red, but old hands watch all trails, and sleep mighty light.

Accordingly, the arrival of the regular Friday stage run from Benson was covered blanket-close. The give-away was that rawboned sorrel gelding trotting behind the boot of the coach. It was what put a man to watching the driver's box and seeing up there only the regular driver and his shotgun rider, then what put him to jumping behind the baled hay south of the stable entrance and pinning his look on the coach door and what was about to come out of it.

First, it was three run-of-the-line passengers who didn't count one way or the other. But the last three were anything but ordinary stagefare. If you were totting them up by gunman's arithmetic, you'd likely do well to start multiplying the last three by about ten.

Wyatt, you knew. You let him ease out and down, not needing to figure his ten's worth. The second man out made you blink your eyes and look again to make

116

sure the first one had been Wyatt. Then, if you'd thought Virgil looked like his brother, you stood to refigure right now in favor of this new one. Nobody had to tell you who *he* was. In any light less than full day and from more than twenty feet off, he was the spit-image twin of Wyatt. If you'd seen the latter and could describe him to the last eyelash, you had only to subtract a couple of years of age to save your wind in telling anybody what the new brother looked like. Or what his name was.

This one had to be Morgan Earp, and a gunhand as clearly worth ten ordinary men as was ever brother Wyatt.

Right there, though, the guessing game let up.

The third man out stopped you cold. You knew you'd never seen him and didn't know him from the eighth jack down in a twelve-mule hitch. But you sure didn't need to know *who* he was to spot *what* he was.

He was frock-coated and prosperous dressed, like the Earps. He wore the gambler's wide black hat, shoestring tie and pinstripe, pegtop pants, the same as his friends. After that, the resemblance cut sharp off.

He was winter-thin as an orphan mustang colt in late March, pale as a new-washed bed sheet, hollow-eyed and sick-looking as a wet dog with distemper. But he swept his strange, fish-blue eyes across the little crowd, bold and snake-flat as any Earp, and he shouldered through it and off after Wyatt and Morgan with the same contempt and cat-crouch to his walk that they had.

You would never guess to look at him that he was a gentleman-born, to one of the finest of the old Confederate families, from clear down in Valdosta, Georgia; or that he was a graduate of one of the Old South's best-known colleges; or that he honorably held one of those Bachelor of Science degrees in dental surgery, and had long been licensed to practice that profession.

What you would guess, and be right about it as spring rain, was that he had put in more time with the fifty-two pasteboards than with the forceps; more labor over the bourbon jug than the antiseptic bottle; more practice with the two Colts he wore cross-belted beneath his frock coat than with the jawbone drills and chisels he carried in the little doctor's satchel in his hand.

You might also guess, from the sunk cheeks and rattley,

117

heavy way he breathed that he was better than halfway gone with the lung fever.

Then, if your eyes were good, you could leave off guessing. For he was walking by your stack of hay bales and you were seeing the flecked-off stamping of the gold-leaf letters on the old satchel, J. H. Holliday, D.D.S.

With that, you swallowed hard, slid back around the bales, hightailed it up the alley for the back door of the Crystal Palace. There wasn't any doubt you'd found your third ten in your little game of gun multiplication, nor that you'd best turn in the total sum to Curly and the boys, right now.

That last one off the Benson stage was Doc Holliday.

One Earp had been a bad enough batch of slum to begin with. When Virg showed up to make it two, the stew got thicker. When Morg climbed down out of the Benson coach, making it three, the mulligan stuck to the bottom of the pot. By the time Doc Holliday swung off the stage, it was beginning to smell burnt.

For a solid week the Sulphur Springs chefs stood back from the fire and fought the smoke out of their eyes.

Now, it wasn't any longer a simple question of just picking Wyatt off by his lonesome some dark night. He never left his office without at least one of his new deputies, and most times two of them, tagging him hand-close. Any damn fool, or combination of same, that would deliberate a' purpose tie into a couple of Earps and a Doc Holliday, dark or daylight, would only be ordering his own bed sheet and six feet of boothill dirt to dump it in.

All that was left was that there had to be a way to draw Wyatt out of Tombstone. The hell of that was, there was a way. Just one way. The one they'd steered spooky clear off, all along. But they had to come to it now or admit they were licked.

It was mess with the U.S. mail, or do nothing.

Curly Bill hadn't got where he was, as a do-nothing boy. He ordered in Ringo and six of the "ranchhands" and laid it on the line.

The stage that went back up to Benson Wednesday nights took along the Contention's bullion in place of the payroll cash that came down on the morning runs. Curly had it on inside authority that that Wednesday's shipment of bar silver would go better than $50,000. No point in wasting a strike. Might as well lift a load of bullion while grabbing the mail sack to pull Wyatt out.

The job orders were for no rough stuff. Killings always made it hard on Behan when it came to covering up. Just get the silver and Uncle Sam's sack and clear the hell out. He handpicked Ringo to run the show because the kid had the best reason for getting back at Wyatt; also because he'd been pulling at the bit to make up for the botch he'd made of the job where Wyatt had stretched three of his bunch and near busted his own right hand into the bargain.

This time there was no leak.

Ringo had settled his past dues with Wyatt by that first warning he'd left with Lilly. He was grinning that crazy grin of his when the frost-clear moonlight saw him heading his six helpers up across Dragoon Summit and down the far slope toward the channel of the San Pedro and Six Mile Grade. Likely, now, providing things went his way, him and Wyatt Earp could finally shoot it out at something better than condensed milk cans thrown into the air, or empty Arbuckle's coffee bags pinned on the chaparral.

But every damn thing went wrong.

When they jumped the stage just short of the top of Six Mile Grade, with the teams pulling slow enough to make it look easy for one amateur, let alone seven professionals, Ringo thought he had it made.

He'd left four of his boys in an old adobe shack back off the road a piece, waiting there with the packhorse they'd brought along to carry the bullion. Him and the other two had gone on to the road.

Now, with their Winchesters shouldered and covering Bud Philpot, the driver, and Wyatt's friend, Bob Paul, the shotgun rider, it looked like there'd be nothing to it but backing off with the bullion and the mail sack.

But Wyatt had picked a man in Bob Paul.

"Throw down that mail sack!" yelled Ringo.

"She's throwed," said Bob Paul.

Ringo caught it, hooking its lock-chain around his saddlehorn. "Where's the bullion?" he barked. Then, as

Philpot eased off on the nervous leaders a mite, "Hold up there! Pull in them goddamn hosses!"

"We don't hold up for anybody!" Paul yelled back at him. "Lay the leather to 'em, Bud!"

You don't need to imagine he was thinking to bluff it out with just that mail sack and the yell. Wyatt had told him, above all, to see that the outlaws got the mail sack whenever they might jump his run, whether they asked for it or not. Past that, he'd said to use his own judgment. Bob Paul was using that judgment now. Along with his shotgun. The old double was up and blasting right along with his yell to Philpot. As it did, somebody else was yelling.

One of the bandits was hit, for sure. But Ringo and the other one were letting drive with their saddleguns. The kid's first snap drilled Philpot, heart-center. In the middle of laying his whip to the wheelers, Bud spun up off the box, fell headfirst, down in between the wheel team, his body hanging up across the trace chains.

It was a full runaway.

Bob Paul managed to grab up the lines as Philpot let go of them, but with the latter's body banging around between the wheelers and with the night-dark full of gun blasts and bandit yells, there was no heading nor holding the stage horses.

Ringo and his two pals got their mounts free of the lunge of the coach in time to watch it rattle by, top the grade, go lurching out of sight down the far side. And in time, too, to throw a scatter of wild shots after it. It was only a little added fact that two of those shots smashed into the belly of a boot passenger named Peter Roerig, killing him deader than last year's elections. It was only another two-bit addition that in the boot with Roerig rode $80,000 in ready-sacked bullion.

The main thing was that there had been a U.S. mail sack between Bob Paul's boots, and that somebody had had the bad sense at last to try to interfere with its legal delivery. Moreover, Bob Paul had had a clear look and listen to that somebody in good Arizona moonlight.

The high fence of the federal law had been crawled over and Johnny Ringo had snagged the seat of his Levis. His troubles were only getting started. When he got down to the ground on the far side of that fence, he had some-

thing a little tougher than his torn pants to take a look at.
Wyatt Earp.

The fact men had been killed, knocked hell out of
the original idea of dry-gulching Wyatt when he came
out to follow the getaway trail. It meant that Johnny
Behan would have to go along with the regular sheriff's
posse, the same including deputies of the cut of Billy
Breakenridge that wouldn't buckle to any bribe or bury
any evidence.

Ringo knew that much without any bunkhouse lectures
from Curly Bill. So did his two pals. From here, it was
every man for himself and the hell with the four poor
bastards that had been left holding the pack-horse.

They put their ponies on down the Benson road right
behind the stage, where the heavy prints of the coach
teams would clutter their own hoof sign. Five miles
along the line, they split up and left the road, cutting
across country on bare, rocky ground. The wounded boy
headed for the Sulphur Springs hideout, not being so shot-
up he couldn't make it by himself. Ringo and the other
one were back in Tombstone well ahead of midnight, buying drinks in the Palace and the Oriental for all hands
around, free and cocky as though they'd been there the
whole night, with nobody the wiser.

It didn't go so slick for the others.

Joe Ruiz, an old Mex sheepherder, long known around
the mining camps down the San Pedro, had come up to
the shack looking to get some water from its well. The
four *bandidos* had built a coffee fire, bold as brass. When
the old herder got up close enough to make out who was
siding that fire, he just turned back into the brush and
faded for his flock. When he saw Wyatt and his little
posse milling around the holdup site next morning, he
slipped over, pointed out the old adobe, and read off its
last night's guest list. His tally came out Bill Leonard,
Jim Crane, Harry Head and Luther King. All four were
short-caliber Clanton men, known rustlers and wild bunch
boys.

Wyatt was off on their tracks before Behan and his
main posse got out of bed and had breakfast.

After five days of trailing they nailed Luther King
coming out of an abandoned line camp on the old Red-

field spread. After his gentle way with such kind, Wyatt got the boy to talking. He named Ringo as head of the bunch but said he didn't know the two that were with Ringo on the stage end of the job. He also agreed the Mex herder had called his own three pals on the button, but claimed they had all lit out for Sonora the night before.

As Wyatt held up, wanting to go on after them but saddled with King and knowing that in him he had a witness too valuable to mess around with losing, Johnny Behan and the main Tombstone posse rode over a near hill and pulled up for a parley. The Cochise sheriff demanded they turn King over to him and Wyatt, seeing he had his top deputy, Billy Breakenridge, along, decided to risk doing it. Breakenridge was a four-square lawman and could reasonably be trusted to see no monkey business went on about the prisoner.

Him and his own little bunch, Virg, Morg and Marsh Williams, a Fargo special agent from Benson, rode on south after Head, Crane and Leonard.

They might as well have been chasing shot-at coyotes. They squandered another week at it, gave it up, and rode back into Tombstone with nothing but pinched bellies and wind-broke horses, late the night of October 23rd.

They had a nice jolt waiting for them.

Their wind of it didn't come by way of *The Nugget's* printed report, but if it had they could have read it this way.

> ". . . Luther King, the man arrested at the Redfield's ranch, charged with being implicated in the Bud Philpot murder, escaped from the sheriff's office by quickly stepping out the back door while a bill of sale for the disposal of his horse was being drawn up by Deputy Sheriff Wood. He had been absent for a few minutes before he was missed. A confederate on the outside had a horse in readiness for him . . ."

No matter which way you read it, nor how you cursed and clamped your jaw, if you were Wyatt Earp it all came out one acid way.

Your case against Johnny Ringo was as highblown as a dead cow's belly six days in the sun.

22 ★

Wyatt was a gambling man. Nobody, in his time, made a good living off of just being a peace officer, and Wyatt was a man that liked a good living.

He had dealt for the house in every big layout from Fort Hays through Abilene and right on up to Dodge City. Fact was, he was near as famous for a working cardsharp as for a hardcase lawman. All he'd ever learned about burying an ace or palming a ten-spot he'd got from the best teacher to be had—Doc Holliday.

There's been a whole deck of lies dealt out about Doc, good as well as bad. But one thing nobody's ever argued. He could hold his own in any man's game. He'd throw you four pat queens, with an ace kicker; then call you down to your last blue and draw out on you with three cards to the middle of a six-high straight.

Remarking on this talent, along about here, isn't steering as far around the well to get water as it might sound. An hour after Doc and Wyatt had checked back into their rooms at the Cosmopolitan, Marsh Williams was pounding on the latter's door.

"It's open," called Wyatt. "No need to knock the decent customers out of bed proving it."

Marsh came along in and gave it to him without trimmings. "Located him for you," he nodded, tense-like. "Been on a high lonesome ever since the stick-up. Told him you wanted to see him. He only laughed that loco way of his. Said, if you wanted to see him, you could come a'looking. He'd be right where I left him."

"Where was that?"

"The Oriental. He's on a streak. Been a big game running since early yesterday. He ain't been out of his chair the past eight hours. They tell me he's better than $3,000 up and still winning."

"Been drinking much?" Wyatt's eye corners drew in.

"Barman said he'd had his quart for breakfast, with half-pint chasers on every pot since."

"Doc!" There was a rare excitement in it.

"It's what they call me." The thin gunman loafed in

123

through the connecting door that opened off Wyatt's room into his. "What's the ante?"

"Ringo's in a big game over at the Oriental. He's riding a high streak, and dead drunk."

"Well, it can't last," shrugged the other. "What that greenbelly doesn't know about poker, Hoyle could be lynched for. What you getting at?"

"We've got him!" rasped Wyatt. The excitement was still there, but held under by a hard hand now. "Maybe it's only a Comanche's chance in Texas but by God we'll give it the long play and find out!"

"Well," grinned Doc, the pull of his gray lips under the sockets of his dead-fish eyes putting you in mind of a skull that had just thought of something funny, "you never can tell about the luck of a lousy calf. Fill me in, pardner."

"I've played with the kid and watched him play with others. They busted the mold for bad losers after they'd poured Johnny Ringo," snapped Wyatt.

"So?"

"So, listen. And listen good. Given anything better than the house break, we'll have the little bastard under lock and charge before he's another hour older." He went on, tight and short, laying it out in four-letter words. When he had done with it, Doc only grinned that slack, skull grin and reached for his hat.

"How deep you want him cut, pardner?"

"To the bone," said Wyatt.

Ringo cursed foul and ugly as only a man that's slobbered drunk can.

It was the seventh pot he'd dropped since Holliday had bought into the game an hour and twenty minutes before. And the last three of those pots he'd lost with two fulls—aces-over-tens and queens-over-jacks and a king-high diamond straight, dealt pat. The gall-bitter part of it was that every last one of those seven losing hands had come on Holliday's turn to deal. And every one of them had been lost to a high flush or double brace of natural fours, shucked to himself by that lousy skull-faced shadow of Wyatt's.

Doc's "phenomenal" luck had been too much for the other players. The last two of them folded as the deal now came to the ex-Dodge City dentist for the eighth go-round. With only Ringo left, and him with no more than a couple of hundred in scrambled red and blues still on the table in front of him, Doc said it quietly.

"Want to call it a night, boy? You still got enough to buy your stagefare back to Texas."

"You son-of-a-bitch!" shouted Ringo wildly. "You deal 'em! And, by Christ, you deal 'em off the top and god-damn slow!"

Doc shrugged, deliberate in the way he ignored words that had led to dead men in many another case. "You got to learn to lose, youngster. Any tinhorn can win and grin. How'll you have it, now, plain or fancy?"

Ringo was drunk, and mad drunk. The rage and the whiskey were so thick in him his voice had to fight to break through the crust of them. He shoved his stack to the middle of the table, pushed his chair back free and clear of it. "Straight poker!" he choked. "Face up and one at a time!"

"Showdown it is," nodded Doc easily, and slid him the deck for the cut.

He broke it into five little piles, mixed them back in, cut them again, and yet a third time. Watching him, Doc just shook his head and lifted his lip a little bit over his yellowed teeth.

He took the deck back, careful not to riffle so much as the top card of it. He didn't look at the pack, nor the chips, nor the table. Only watched Johnny Ringo and his hands.

The first card was the ace of spades.

Ringo watched it fall in front of him, eyes stary, hands grabbing the table edge.

To himself, Doc dealt a small heart.

Ringo's next was the ten of clubs. Then the diamond ace. Doc dropped himself two more small hearts, now had the deuce, tray and six going for the low flush. Ringo's fourth was the spade ten-spot. He was paired-up, and sitting on a possible full.

The crowd pulled in now, packing in close behind Ringo. There was no sound in the place, save for here and there a nervous chinking of glasses or scrape of chairs, as latecomers left their tables to drift up and watch the last ones fall.

Doc's fourth card slapped the felt, skidded and settled into line. It was the five of hearts.

Ringo licked his lips. The oily sweat stood off his forehead and temples like spring water on a wax lily. Doc slid him his fifth card across the table. It wavered on edge, fell, face-up. It was the club ace.

Aces-over-tens, full!

And there was nothing against it but four little hearts to a flush that figured, by more odds than a man had hairs in his beard, to go bust on the fifth card.

It was only then, while they waited for Doc to drop himself his last one, that Ringo and the crowd noticed the way Wyatt's watchdog had dealt his first four in place—the deuce and the tray paired on one side, the five and the six on the other—with an open hole left between them for his payoff pasteboard.

Doc now dealt the pasteboard into that hole.

The crowd got pale-still.

It was the fifth heart—and it was the *four*.

Dr. Holliday had filled his flush the hard way. Inside and straight. The highest hand in poker, barring a royal. And the deadliest to deal yourself in a tablestakes game.

Ringo played the hand out just the wild way Wyatt had gambled he would. He scattered his full house onto the floor and bet into Doc's flush with a pair of wooden-handled sixes.

The ancient Confederate-issue Colts flashed up and out.

"Goddamn you!" he snarled at Doc. "I'm cleaning the table. Every mother-frigging dollar on it!"

Doc didn't move.

"Houseman!" he called pleasantly to the bank. "Cash these chips for the boy. He wins with twelve lead aces."

As the houseman started for the cash box, Doc nodded to the crowd. "Ease off now, folks. Don't start any stampede. The boy's bad with a gun and he means business. Please give him plenty of room."

Nobody said anything, and nobody moved.

The houseman came back, counted in the chips, handed Ringo a sheaf of the long green, thick as a mail-order catalogue. The kid holstered his left-hand gun, grabbed the money, backed for the door. "All right," he croaked hoarsely. "I got mine. Anybody tries follering me, gits his!"

"It's your pot," Doc told him flatly. "Go along home with it."

Ringo glared at him, but didn't answer. He backed on out through the Oriental's double-hung doors.

He was still backing, two uncertain steps later, when he felt something familiar bite into the small of his loin, square between the kidneys. It was about the size of two buffalo nickels welded side-by-each and any fool, drunk or sober, could call its gauge for twelve.

"Drop it," said Wyatt softly. "And turn around slow."

Ringo dropped his Colt and turned.

The Parker's muzzle bores followed on around his ribs, wound up in his belly.

"You're under arrest," said Wyatt. "Hand over the money."

There's nothing for getting over a ten-day drunk in a hurry, like a dose of shotgun salts. Ringo was sobering fast but he had two snarls left in him.

"On what charge, by God!" he demanded with the first one.

"Highway robbery," replied Wyatt, straight-faced.

"The hell you say! Just who's making that charge?" he snapped with the second.

"I am," said Doc Holliday, easing out through the doors behind him.

And, "Get going!" was all that Wyatt Earp added.

23

It was just short of midnight, the 23rd, that Wyatt got John Clum out of bed for the second time since taking over as Deputy U.S. Marshal in Tombstone.

After he'd suggested that the mayor had best get into his riding pants, and while the latter was doing same, he layed it to him.

"John," they'd come to first names that past six months, "I've got Ringo in jail, along with a pretty fair hunch where Harry Head and the rest of the holdup gang are hid out. I want to go get them and I'll need you and every

127

Safety Committee-man we can scare up, to back me on it."

"Now, hold up, Wyatt." His Honor was still sleepy and having trouble with his boots. "I took it you'd lost track of those rascals when I heard you'd come in earlier tonight without them. Behan told us you'd started off running trail on them down into Sonora. What's this hunch business? Kind of sudden, isn't it?"

"Sudden, or otherwise," said Wyatt, "I never slap an easy saddle on my hunches. I ride them, sore-backed."

"You'll kill your horse some day," grumbled the testy little mayor. "Get on with it." He had just got his left boot home solid, and it was giving his pet corn hell.

"There never was any trail, no matter what Behan said," Wyatt went on. "Just King's claim the others had headed for the border. We didn't cut a clean set of prints the whole five days. Riding back gave me a little time to turn hunchy. I'm now convinced they never even set out south, but hit east into the Dragoons and turned north to hightail it for home. I'll lay you odds on the devil, and give you God for your banker, they're over at the Sulphur Springs ranch right now—not forty miles away—and having a free laugh with Luther King while they lay out the next job."

He paused and Clum, having long ago learned about that little trick he had of tugging at his mustache, let him tug and waited up for him to go on.

"John, we've got a federal case on them this time. It changes everything. If I can get King back, or even grab any of the four others, I'll have me a man that'll turn state's evidence. Bucking the federal pen is a tiger none of these county hoodlums cares to get into. It'll mean we can put Ringo, and any of the others we snag, back of bars long enough to raise a kid and put him through college."

"But, man," complained Clum, "what good will it do? They're all small fry. The big ones will get away like they always do. It's Curly Bill and the Clantons and Mc-Lowrys we've got to get!"

Wyatt nodded and said it quick. "John, it's them I mean to get."

"How in the devil do you figure that? There's no charges outstanding on any of them." The same time he was arguing it, Clum was shouldering into his old

128

sheepskin coat. Fall nights turn sharp at 4,000 feet and the mayor had argued law with Wyatt before.

"You got to know one thing about the way these outlaws bunches operate, John. They can't stand convictions and arrests don't mean a damn thing to them. But if you can put so much as one of them *actually* away, they know it's no step at all to the next one, or two, or three. And only a hop and a skip from there to where the whole outfit is strung up and salted down for the winter."

"All right, even so," protested Clum, buttoning his sheepskin. "It will take months, maybe years, that way. Where's your tonight's excitement in that? They'll have the town bled dead by that time."

"That's right," agreed Wyatt. "Unless the town bleeds them first."

"How's that, man?" He held up on the last button.

"They'll fight. We go out there and lift some of their boys right out of the bunkhouse in the middle of the night, they've got to fight. They've no choice. I know Curly. He won't take it. He can't afford to."

"Neither can we, damn it, man!" Clum put some heat in it and Wyatt scowled a little.

"Come again, Mayor?"

"I mean we can't afford to ride out there and blunder into a showdown fight at Sulphur Springs. Good men would be killed, and for what? To bring in a couple of hangdog stage robbers that Johnny Behan would have out of the city jail before you could get to the telegraph office to wire Crawley Dake for instructions! I won't do it, Wyatt, and I won't ask my friends to do it. Now, you know better than that!"

Wyatt grinned. At least it was supposed to be a grin. His lips curled up, anyways. "There'll be no fight at Sulphur Springs. It'll be at Tombstone. You and the posse won't be within a mile of it. You trailing me any better now, John?"

"No, sir, by the Lord I'm not!"

"Well, trail this, then. Like you say, it would maybe take years to round them up by ones and threes. Then, maybe we get convictions, maybe we don't. The way I now got it in mind, we've a good chance to grab all their topdogs in one swipe. Providing we can, I'll guarantee you *some* convictions."

"Say what you mean, Wyatt," declared Clum irritably. "Don't circle it like it was four days old."

"All right, it goes like this. Inside of twenty-four hours after we make our strike on Sulphur Springs, they'll make theirs on Tombstone. When they do, I'll have my court ready to sit on their case. There'll be no legal delays and no hung juries. They'll get heard under two judges and twelve jurymen that haven't failed to pass a death sentence in thirteen years."

As he said it, it looked to Clum like he just sort of shrugged his shoulders a mite. But there they were, laying easily in his big hands. He held them out, with a little, palms-up lift, toward his companion. "Now you read my sign, Your Honor?"

The mayor brought his eyes up from the ivory-handled Cavalry Colts. He looked at Wyatt a long three breaths, and said it quietly.

"It's murder. Neither I nor any responsible man in Tombstone will be a party to it. You know I will not go outside the law, Wyatt."

"All right," said Wyatt thoughtfully, "you're a lawyer." He paused, eyeing him. "Answer me this. Are we within the law to make up a posse and ride out to Sulphur Springs to arrest suspects, implicated by a confederate's confession, in the Six Mile Grade mail robbery and murders?"

"Certainly, sir! What are you getting at?"

"And you're willing to form up that posse to make those arrests?"

"Of course, of course," nodded Clum impatiently.

"Well, then," said Wyatt, setting his teeth, "get your hat. That's all I'm asking you to do."

He started to turn for the door, but Clum cut him off. "Just one minute, now. What about the rest of it? Do I have your word you'll keep it within the law, Wyatt?"

"Sure, Mayor . . ." He put those pale eyes on him, with the suspended agreement. "There'll be nothing done that the law won't back me one-hundred percent. And I can give you my personal word on that."

He broke it off to stand aside for Clum. Then he followed him out of the house and closed the door quickly behind them. He held up on the stoop for a minute, letting the other get out of earshot, then announced it, flat and quiet. Into the October darkness. So that only the whistling wind heard it. And picked it up and carried it away into the night. Soft and ugly and full of the meaning of legal murder.

"I *am* the law," said Wyatt Earp.

Like most things about Johnny Behan, it's pretty hard to prove he let Ringo go, deliberate a'purpose.

You just have to look at the facts and make up your own mind.

About one o'clock in the morning, word came to him at the Palace that Wyatt and Clum were readying a hell of a big posse. There was already some thirty horses under saddle in front of the U. S. Marshal's office, with more Safety Committee-men shadowing up through the dark by the minute.

You don't get thirty or forty honest citizens out of bed and mounted up in ten minutes. Nor you don't do it without what, somewhere along the line, some one of those honest citizens doesn't bark his shins on the beanpot and spill the *frijoles* while stumbling around in the rush to get ready.

By 1:30 Behan had a better than fair idea where the law-and-order boys were bound.

At a quarter of two, Mr. Sidney Skidmore was getting shook out of his blankets over on Rotten Row. By two, sharp, he was over at the city jail showing Sheriff Behan the fastest, shysterest writ of *habeas corpus* ever handed out in Tombstone.

Right on the dot of 2:15 Johnny Ringo was stepping up on his rat-tailed roan in the alley back of the jail. Five minutes later, he was riding with the gaslights of Goose Flats to his back, hell-for-sweaty leather, up and over Dragoon Summit on the Burnell Springs road.

Wyatt's men closed in on the outlaw ranch from four sides, so close-mounted in the last few yards before the bunkhouse a packrat couldn't have got past them without he was squashed by a shod hoof. The trouble was, there wasn't even a packrat left in the Sulphur Springs bunkhouse.

Only a mighty scared, half-Apache rat.

When Wyatt hailed them to show a light and come

out with their hands elevated, the sole response he got was Indian Charlie Cruz coming whining out into the gray of the five o'clock daylight, in his long-handled drawers, and shivering with more than the chill of the late fall morning.

Virg and Morg got down and shoved the breed around a little, while Wyatt sat by on Big Red and listened. He didn't hear a damn thing. Not that the Indian didn't talk. He just didn't say anything.

He'd gone to bed with the rest of the boys about ten o'clock, he claimed. That was to say, with Curly Bill, Phin and Ike Clanton, both McLowrys, Pony Deal and three, four others. How was that? Could those three, four others have been Luther King? Jim Crane? Harry Head? Bill Leonard? Yeah, could be. Seems like he'd guess maybe they was. But no, Frank Stilwell and Pete Spence hadn't been there. They was over to Galeyville selling some cattle.

"Mex cattle?" cut in Wyatt quietly.

"Dunno," grunted the breed sullenly. "Didn't get no chanct to try my Spanish on 'em."

Virg slashed him across the collarbone with the barrel of his Colt, knocking him back against the bunkhouse logs, down onto his knees. "Don't get smart when a white man asks you a civil question," he told him.

"Get up and keep talking," advised young Morg.

"Dunno no more," muttered Cruz. "Like I said, I bunked in with the others but didn't ask no questions when they left."

"When they left?" said Virg, running his fingers along his Colt barrel by way of encouragement.

"Somebody come busting up on a horse in a tall hurry from over Tombstone way. There was some fast talk and they all cleared out."

"How long ago was that?" asked Wyatt.

"I dunno, I ain't got no watch."

"It was getting light, maybe? You could see some little?" It was Morg again, now.

"Maybe."

"Enough, likely, to tell us who it was come out from town in such a lather?" Still Morg.

"No. I never got out'n my bunk."

132

Virg hit him cat-fast. But not with the gun. With his balled fist. Big and hard as a chunk of quartz ore. Square in the groin. He was into the dirt again. Twisting and thrashing like a stomped-on snake.

Morg helped him up, waving Virg away from him. He pinned him up against the bunkhouse logs, not roughing him any that he didn't have to. "All right, *compadre,* we'll start once more. Take her from the jump-off and don't fight the bit this time." His voice was softer than Virg's, not having the same bite and whip in it.

"Yeah," said the latter, making sure the breed understood Morg was talking for himself, "take your time. We got all night. Which is to say," he rasped, moving in on him, "all of about two minutes!"

But two minutes, or ten, or twenty, you could see it made no difference to Cruz. He'd said as much as he meant to, or could. When Virg started for him again, Morg stepped between them, told him to slack up on the rough stuff. Wyatt kicked Big Red forward, made it official.

"Yeah, hold up, Virg. We're licked. Somebody's beat us to our birds. We all got a pretty good idea who it was, I reckon, but there's no use killing this cripple when the main covey's long flushed. Let's go."

"Wait a minute!" Virg jammed his Colt into Cruz with the challenge. "You're not meaning to leave this bastard here to get back into the brush, are you, Wyatt?"

"You heard me." It was flat, no argument or explanation meant to be in it. "I said let's go."

Virg looked up at him a minute, then shrugged. He knew Wyatt and he knew that dust-soft way he went to talking when he'd had it, and when he didn't want to have any more of it. "It's your posse," he said, and went for his waiting pony.

Morg followed him, knowing Wyatt as well as Virg did, and maybe a little better. He swung up on his own horse, put him alongside Virg's, and followed Wyatt and the Tombstone posse out of the ranchyard.

They stayed paired up and hanging back behind the others.

Virg let the silence hold for a spell, watching Morg. The kid was a lot like Wyatt, he thought. Only not

133

near so tough. Not that he was afraid of any man alive, but only that he didn't have Wyatt's bone-hard, dead-set way of seeing things.

For Wyatt, as for himself, too, thought Virg, there wasn't any such thing as a gray cat. They were all either black or white. It made them easier to see and to keep track of. A man was either on your side or on the other side. There wasn't any place in between for him to stand, the way Virg and Wyatt saw it. If he insisted on standing out in the middle, he got shot at, that was all.

But Morg, now—well, the kid, he saw it some different.

You didn't need to be his friend, or his enemy. Morg didn't give a good damn whose side you were on, providing you left him alone on his. He had no bothersome ideas about the law, either, such as had always plagued him and Wyatt. In fact, both Virg and Wyatt knew, and had talked of it as far back as Abilene, that Morg was a lawman for only one reason—Wyatt.

The kid thought Wyatt weighed twenty-four ounces to the pound.

Watching him now, as the posse pulled away from the deserted ranch, Virg knew something was worrying Morg, and that it was more than likely something to do with Wyatt.

"All right, boy," he nodded at last. "What's eating you? You don't like the way your big brothers play with Indians?"

"No," said Morg, slowly. "It's not the breed. Though you needn't to have hit him that second time. It's Wyatt, Virg. He's not the same as he was back in Kansas."

"What the hell you mean, Morg? He doesn't strike me any different. Looks the same. Acts the same. Still doesn't drink hard liquor or cuss much. Has got the flossiest girl in town following him around. Can still out-deal anybody but Doc across a poker table. Dresses as good as ever. Got the same damn old red horse. Still smokes fifteen-cent seegars and never gets a haircut. Where's your big change in all that, boy?"

"I didn't say anything about a big change. That's just it. It isn't anything big. Just little things. Like the way he doesn't laugh as quick as he used to. And the way he quits grinning too fast, even when something does strike him funny. And he's jumpy, too. He never used to be goosey like that. So quick to crawl a man the minute he does the least little thing wrong. That's not like Wyatt. You know that. You reckon it's the girl that's got him going, Virg?"

"Hell no. I don't reckon it's anything got him going. Just your imagination, maybe. He always was a moody cuss, Morg. Good-natured enough, long as things were rolling his way, which is to say the way he reckoned was the right way. But fair mean, the minute they wasn't. He's like me, in that. Can't stand to have any man sass him or size up to him or to make it look for even five seconds that there was any real question of who was in the right and who was in the wrong. My God, boy, you're sure to remember that about him!"

"By God, I do, Virg, and that's *it!*" said young Morg instantly. "Somebody's been making him look wrong. I mean, making him look wrong to himself. You've hit it square on. Somebody's not only sassed him and sized up to him, they've got away with it. They've beat him out on something big, and made him like it into the bargain. Only it wasn't any man did it. It was that damn girl. There's a site more to her than flashy looks and catsy ways. It's my notion she's got him going."

Morg was talking about Lilly Belloit, for neither him nor Virg nor anybody else in Tombstone, saving Lilly herself, ever knew about Wyatt and Evvie Cushman. Morg's hunchy guess was as close as anybody ever got to the real truth of Wyatt's inside trouble. The kid had hit the right idea, but the wrong woman.

Virg finally shook his head, breaking the little spell of silence. "No, it ain't the girl. No woman's ever got Wyatt going, you know that."

"There's a first time for everything." insisted Morg. "Something's got him itching where he can't reach to scratch. I'll bet a pair of trays into three tens showing, that it's a woman. Leastways, I aim to have a talk with him on it soon's we get back."

"You go right ahead, youngster," advised Virg. "You wait and have your talk like you say. Me, I'm not going to wait to have mine. I don't buy your deal about him and no woman, but I've got my own little piece of beef to chaw with him on another matter. I reckon I'll ride up and chaw it with him right now. You'd best come along

135

with me, too, for if ever a pair of Earps have bought into a bad pot with their middle brother, it's you and me."

Morg didn't say anything to that, just put his pony to loping after Virg's and kept his thoughts to himself. When they had caught up to Wyatt and sided their horses in alongside Big Red, he still kept quiet, only listening while Virg got shut of what had been sticking in his craw.

"What the hell was the idea of letting up on that breed like you done back there, Wyatt?" he growled. "You getting soft-headed in your old age?"

"Maybe," said the third of the Earps thoughtfully, "maybe not. Like the old saying goes. You got birds of the same brood, they'll sooner or later covey back up again."

"Meaning what?" Virg was still huffy about it.

"Meaning I got a better than four-bit hunch that Cruz will live just about long enough to lead us to the main hatch. You understand?"

Virg thought it over. "Yeah," he grudged. "I reckon it makes sense, all right."

"Morg, what do you think?" Wyatt put it quietly to the youngster. And just touched it with that little smile of his. For him, this boy could do no wrong. He saw in Morg more than just the baby of the family. He saw in him all of his own strength and sureness, without any of that strength's harshness, or that sureness's arrogance. He saw, still bright and alive in Morg, what he had seen in himself as a boy. And what he had somehow lost, or let die, as a man.

The youngster was a long time in answering. When he did, it wasn't so much what he said as it was the way he said it.

"I guess I don't understand but one thing about you any more, Wyatt. And that is, if your hunch is up to average, somebody won't live too long."

"That," grinned Virg, hard-eyed, and missing the boy's point a country mile, "is for sure as a skunk smells worse on a wet night."

Wyatt said nothing. Only put the spurs to Big Red and sent him along.

He hadn't missed Morg's point.

24 ☆

Wyatt was a man of more than several talents. In addition to being handy with a gun, sharp at cards, and hell on highwaymen, he was quite a prophet. It was just twenty-four hours after he hit the Sulphur Springs ranch that the wild bunch rode into Tombstone in retaliation.

Wyatt and his posse got back about noon of the 24th. Things were quiet all the rest of that day, but right at noon of the 25th Curly Bill and Ringo rode into town along Fifth Street from the east, likely meaning they'd come over from Galeyville. Back of them they had just about every boy that had ridden the ridges in Cochise County the past three years.

There never was an accurate count run on those boys because right off they split up and spread around in the various saloons and dance halls and because, saving for Curly and the kid, they weren't any of them what you would call known outlaws.

That may sound funny but it isn't. The big bulk of the men that backed Bill Brocius and the Clanton-McLowry rustler outfit passed themselves off as honest "cowboys." The simple fact, after that, was that better than half the decent folks in Tombstone never caught on they were anything otherwise. You can still get an argument down in Cochise County that lots of those boys were innocent, hard-working cowhands, only in town to let off a little steam and having no better sense than to hang with Curly Bill's bunch while opening their valves.

Choose your partners and take your sides. Wyatt always said that in his day down there you didn't spell cowboy any different than you did outlaw.

Taken that way, it wasn't so funny that when he heard Curly and Ringo had hit town with a dozen Galeyville "cowboys," Wyatt got the old Parker down off its wall pegs and went to checking the hang and feel of his .44's.

Satisfied with that much of it, he got on with the "legal" end of it.

When he'd promised Clum he'd stay within the law, he hadn't just been letting his tongue ramble.

137

One side of him that has never come down through the years like it should, was what went on inside that lion-sized head of his. And it's important. Anybody that wants to take a square look at the record has got to see that Wyatt was smart. Not that he was ever coyote-tricky like Johnny Behan, because he wasn't. But smartness comes in all sizes. And every brain has its blind side. Wyatt always weighed out short on political savvy and on the ways to butter-up people and make friends and defenders of them with one hand while robbing them blind with the other. At the same time he had the kind of a mind that all slickers hate, and that they can't understand nor handle.

He always thought in a dead-straight line.

You couldn't bribe him, you couldn't make him lie, you couldn't turn him aside.

He saw across your head to what he wanted on the far side of you, always warned you to get out of his way, then made his move. Once he started, you were either bright enough to take to the sidewalks or you got run over. Right now, he saw across the swaggering heads of Curly Bill and his Galeyville crowd to Mayor Clum and his Citizen's Safety Committee.

Some weeks before, the Committee had put Virgil back to work for the city. They'd made him chief of police at Wyatt's suggestion, Wyatt selling them on the idea it would let him and Morg operate in certain emergencies where they couldn't legally horn in as deputy U.S. marshals.

Meantime, there hadn't been any emergencies to turn up that would fit this bill. But where one didn't fit, Wyatt wasted no time in manufacturing one that did—right out of the whole cloth. It had been his full idea back of the Sulphur Springs raid, naturally, and Curly and his bunch had bought the entire bolt of it right down to the bare spindle.

He waited only long enough for them to get all-day drunk and for night to come on to cover his own moves. Then he called Clum and the Safety Committee to order.

"Gentlemen," he put it to them. "As you may just possibly have heard, Curly Bill Brocius and John Ringo are in town. They are drunk and disorderly, armed in defiance of our civic statutes, and are announcing to anybody

138

who will listen that their purpose here is to wipe out certain duly appointed peace officers and open up Tombstone wider than a gored bull's belly.

"Mr. Clum has expressed certain reservations about the legality of my intentions to see that these boys are served up what they came after.

"It will be legal. Virgil, here, has deputized Morgan and myself. We propose to move uptown right now. Local law is being broken and we are properly sworn in as local lawmen. If there are any questions let them come about here. We're set to go."

He got his first surprise when Clum backed him all the way, and his second when the Committee backed Clum. He thanked them politely but said he would not move uptown one step unless him and his brothers were allowed to go it alone. Giving second thought to their loving wives and cozy homes, and to the reputations of some of the celebrators, namely Curly and Ringo, the would-be deputies sat down a mite quicker than they'd stood up. Twenty minutes after the meeting was called, Wyatt and his brothers were moving up Allen Street—alone. It was ten P.M., October 25th. As good a night and time as any for killing a couple of "cowboys."

The only trouble was that the Earps were sixteen hours ahead of history. And ten minutes behind some blabbermouth on the Committee.

Somehow, word had got out about the meeting.

Wyatt never felt that anybody in Clum's bunch did it deliberate. It was just that where you've got a couple dozen mouths walking out of a back room, tight closed, one of them is bound to flap open the minute it hits outside air. One way or another it's certain that Ringo and Curly Bill caught the smell of sudden trouble coming up Allen Street some short minutes ahead of Virgil Earp and his two "new deputies."

The kid later claimed that him and Brocius would never have backed down except that the Clantons and McLowrys, who were supposed to come along up from down south in Charleston, had failed to show on schedule and Curly didn't want to tackle the Earps without them.

It was a legitimate excuse and some still believe it.

Wyatt never was one of those.

When he moved in on the Oriental where he'd been told they were holed up and waiting, only to find them gone, he called it a night. "All right," he said to Virg and Morg, "let's go. They're gone and they won't be back. You'll not catch the likes of those two being heroes by their lonesomes."

"What about these other heroes?" Morg threw his dry grin toward the five Galeyville cowboys, still lined up at the bar but not enjoying their drinks near as much as they had been when the Earp boys entered.

Wyatt just nodded. "Boys," he said quietly to the lot of them. "You go get your ponies. Round up your friends and get scarce. We're not looking for you and we're not looking for any trouble from you. Nor do we mean to rush you. The night's young. You're invited to help yourselves to the rest of it."

He broke off, giving them a little time to shift their boots around or make any speeches they had in mind. Nobody seemed inclined to take the stump in behalf of civil liberties so he put the rest of it to them. "Come daylight, however, you'll be setting another horse. As from sunup, any man of you that rode in with Ringo and Curly Bill had best be well on his way up the Burnell Springs road. Any of you that might meantime meet up with either of those two gentlemen can tell him the same saddle fits them—only hair-cinched and double-rigged. Any questions?"

During the following five long seconds the bottom fell out of the curiosity market with a thump of silence that could be heard clear out in Allen Street.

Wyatt gave them another long pause to make sure nobody felt cheated of his free-born American rights, then eased around and started for the door. Virg and Morg flanked him right and left. None of the three looked back. Or felt he had any need to.

It was a rare man who wasn't willing to take an Earp's word for the surest thing ahead of taxes.

The next morning Tombstone was as free of outlaws as a dipped sheep of vermin. Not a rustler roamed the wide open spaces of Allen Street. Many a marshal in his boots would have been saying, "Peace, brother, it's wonderful," but not Wyatt.

The bait he'd ridden eighty miles to put out had sprung the trap of its own weight and the "big ones" had got away again. He shut himself in his office and carried on like a lion in a cage.

When Clum called around to get a report for the Committee on last night's results, he wouldn't see him. He wouldn't even talk to Doc Holliday who came by about noon to cheer him up. Doc, never the one to overlook a qualified excuse for killing a quart, got mad and huffed off to Hafford's Saloon to drink his breakfast alone. Even Virg and Morg let him be, after coming in to report the town was holding millpond-quiet.

But if the carefullest-laid plans of Safety Committee mice and special deputy lawmen had gone astray, so had those of the Sulphur Springs rat pack.

It's never been quite clear how come Curly Bill Brocius and Johnny Ringo got their wires crossed with the Clanton and McLowry boys. Some say they didn't. And that what followed was pure, innocent coincidence. Some— even some real straight ones like Mayor Clum—bought Ringo's yarn that him and Curly just missed connections with the others, accidental-like. A few others, a very damn few, such as namely Wyatt and his two brothers, always held that Curly and the kid had run out on their pals, leaving them to walk into the trap without warning.

One thing alone is mighty certain.

They walked into it—or rather rode.

It was just past noon of the 26th that Virgil Earp, coming out of Hafford's Saloon where he'd gone to try and slow Doc down, saw Ike Clanton and Tom McLowry riding up Allen Street from the south. He jumped back inside the doors for they hadn't seen him and it gave him thirty seconds to think.

He knew, from the cut of the crew they'd had with them, that Ringo and Curly Bill had come over from Galeyville to the east. Now, Ike and Tom were coming in from the south, which likely spelled Charleston. They would need to have left there pretty early to get up to Tombstone by noon. It had been close to midnight when Ringo and Curly had pulled out the night before. That would have given them time enough to get down to Charleston and warn off Ike and Tom had they been of that mind. Right now, a man had to figure they hadn't, and that Ike and Tom were riding in cold. Either that, or it was a damn trick of some kind, with these two being used for bait. Knowing Ike, you had to throw that out right off. He hadn't the kind of guts to be riding point for any peace officer ambush.

Along about this far in his thinking, the two outlaw horsemen were jogging past Hafford's, heading for the O.K. Stable down the street, and Virg was seeing something which gave him an idea. What he saw was to forecast the first shot fired in a street war that's still talked about wherever old westerners get together with five minutes to spare for thinking back to the smoky days. But it's mighty safe to say that Virg had no such thoughts of making history when he drifted back through Hafford's and down the alley to the rear of the O.K. Stable.

All he saw was that Ike was wearing two Colts and riding with his Winchester across the horn of his saddle.

And all he thought was that he didn't cotton to his and Wyatt's local rules and regulations being fractured right out in the open like that.

Ike and Tom rode their horses on into the stable, being old hands enough not to bother climbing down out front to lead them in. It was cool and dark inside the livery barn. Both of them were still blinking to get the bright noon sun out of their eyes when Ike, just legging down off his buckskin, heard Virg's pleasant greeting hit him in the small of the back like a bucket of tossed ice water.

"Morning, boys. I'll just take the artillery, Ike. Easy does it, now. All the way around, careful."

Ike should have recognized the family drawl but apparently he didn't for he came all the way around and anything but careful about the way he did it. Which was with his saddlegun still in his hands.

Virg never gave Ike's kind the breaks that Wyatt was in the habit of giving them. When Virg called a man from behind like that, he did it with his Peacemaker already out and in hand. Accordingly, during the time Ike squandered on his turn-around, all he had to do was reach out and tap him.

He didn't aim to drop him, just to straighten him up. Which same is what happened.

Ike stiffened as though somebody had slapped a hot

mustard plaster on his bare backside. He dropped his Winchester into the mulch of the stable manure and stood there with his head buzzing worse than a swatted beehive.

"Behave yourself, Tom." Virg ignored Ike while he warned his companion. McLowry wasn't armed and there wasn't anything else he could do about him just yet. "Me and Ike are going to have a little talk with Judge Barrett. Meanwhile, I'd suggest you give both his horse and yours a shot of hot bran. You'll be wanting to ride them again real soon."

Ira Henry Barrett, the local magistrate, was something of a Behan man. He fined Ike twenty-five dollars and set him scot-free. But Virg had Ike's guns and didn't linger to argue the verdict any. Fact was, he was walking into Wyatt's office down the street before Ike ever got out from in front of the bench.

He hadn't any more than given Wyatt the first of the good news when brother Morgan was stalking in from over on Allen Street with the rest of it. "You think you've got something with Ike and Tom, Virg?" He put the quick family grin back of it. "Come on, quit hoeing the little ones, boy! I just turned up three big potatoes in my patch!"

"How big?" snapped Wyatt, not being in the market for any family fun just then.

"Medium," drawled Morg. "Frank McLowry and Billy Clanton, along with another bad spud I thought was put down in the root cellar for the winter."

Wyatt eyed him, feeling the slow rise of the excitement beginning to come up in him now.

Virg's word that Ike and Tom had blundered into town had hit him good and deep, like a shot of sourmash on an empty belly. Then, Morg's report that Frank McLowry and Billy Clanton had tailed them in came like a second jolt, welcome and warm and strong, right on top of the first. But he knew his easy-going younger brother. And he knew that faraway trademark grin that was so like his own.

He called for the third shot, full aware it was going to be some fingers stiffer than the first two.

"The suspense is killing me, pardner . . ."

He said it dry and flat but it didn't fool Morg. He was used to looking back of those pale eyes. He could see the grin there now. No matter the droop of the haystack mustache didn't lift a straw to it.

"It's apt to, brother." Morg said it just as dry. "They've got Billy Claiborne out. He's along with them."

Wyatt took it quiet.

It was some potato, all right.

Young Claiborne had been doing a thirty-day stretch in the Charleston jail for disturbing the peace by gut-shooting one Jim Hickey. Hickey's big mistake had been insisting, more than twice, that Claiborne let him buy him a drink. When he wouldn't take no for a civil answer and came at the boy with his third offer to set them up, Billy just turned around and shot him in the belly.

This little set of facts was adding up in Wyatt's mind right now.

He was interested only for a minute in the point that under the kind of law that was handed out in Behan's Cochise County bailiwick a man could get thirty days for crippling a friendly drunk for life. He was mainly concerned with the fact that that man had got himself out on bail before his month was up, was running loose on Allen Street right now, and was, barring three others, the most dangerous gunman in the outlaw stable.

Johnny Ringo and Curly Bill Brocius were two of those three others. And they were out of it.

But the third was Frank McLowry.

Wyatt broke off the thought. He stood up. Moved around the desk. Reached his hat from its wall peg.

"What time is it?" he asked Morg, absent-like.

"Along about 1:30," offered the latter, digging out his German silver stem-winder to check the guess. "On the nose," he nodded, confirming it.

"Likely," was all Wyatt said, "we'll need to be careful."

"Likely," agreed his two brothers with one nod.

They went out into Toughnut, past their saddled horses, past the silent courthouse, past the suddenly empty intersection beyond it, walking three abreast and dead-march slow, tall and lonely and frock-coat-black against the bright October sun.

They held up at the corner of Fourth and Allen, making silent note of the fact that the main stem had not yet taken on the deserted look of Toughnut.

"Looks like we've beat Ike back from the couthouse by a couple of minutes," observed Morg laconically.

"We can likely use the time," nodded Virg. Then, to Wyatt, "How you figure to go in from here?"

"They'll be along the north side, somewheres," said the latter. "I'll drift in alone, up the south side. You two tail me. Keep back and out of sight as much as you can. All right?"

"What's the idea?" Morg was quick with it. "I don't see the call for you to go in by yourself. How come, Wyatt?"

"Just don't figure they've ganged up yet, that's all, boy. Still a good chance we can cut them out of the main herd one at a time. You know my way. Where I can, I'll always buffalo a man rather than shoot him."

"Well, it does raise more hell with their reputations," grinned Morg tightly. "They purely hate to be beat up and dragged off by their boot heels."

"I don't like it." It was Virg objecting. And not grinning.

Wyatt checked to him. Virg had been a peace officer longer than any of them, was the senior brother in years, knew his way around in a gunstalk as well as any man alive. When he talked, you listened.

"How so, Virg?" he asked quietly.

"Too many bets to cover. I'd say a better deal would be to box in Allen from here to Fifth. Morg stays here. I drift around by the alley, to Fifth. Then you go on in, like you say. That way, if you flush any of them, we've got them nailed either way they fly."

"You'd say right," nodded Wyatt at once. "Cut your stick."

They gave him two minutes to get into position. Then Wyatt turned to Morg. "Kid, watch yourself."

"All right. How long will you be?"

145

"Five minutes. Only want to see can I catch me a couple of them before Ike's had time to spook them."

"I'll follow you in five minutes, if you don't show meantime."

"Good enough. You feel all right, Morg?"

"Feel fine. How about you?"

"I'll do."

"Yeah, shouldn't wonder if you would. So long."

"So long, boy."

And that was the extent of the first part of it. Wyatt just chucked his head and sauntered off up Allen like he was on his way to his noon dinner.

The second part of it went off smooth as antelope tallow under a front-wheel brakeshoe.

Two minutes after leaving Morg, Wyatt jumped his first bird. And dropped him on the jump.

Tom McLowry had tailed Ike over to the courthouse, met him coming out, and hotfooted it across the vacant lots behind the southside buildings to spread the news ahead of him. Ducking in the back door of Becknell's Hardware, he came sprinting out the front. He bumped into a large, well-dressed citizen just passing by on his afternoon stroll. As said, this citizen was a fair-to-middling big man. He didn't bump worth a damn. Fact was, he resented Tom's rudeness. Took it so to heart he called him an awkward, discourteous son-of-a-bitch.

Tom was not the one you used such language on in vain. He came around from the bump reaching for the six-guns he'd somewhere come by since riding into town. When he did, he got belted alongside the head with the barrels of a .12 gauge Parker; then, quieted down with a little soft-spoken legal advice.

"Unhook them, Tom. Pass them over by the belt." Wyatt sighed the rest of it, as a man would who was burdened beyond suffrance with the weight of his official woes. "Some day you boys will learn you can't play with firearms inside the city limits."

Tom, not letting that weary shrug throw him for a minute, worked the buckle loose real careful and handed the heavy belt over. Once shut of the guns, though, he turned right brassy. "All right, Earp, go ahead and jug me. See how long the lock holds!"

146

Wyatt shook his head gently. "Wouldn't think of it. You run along and find your little friends. Only run that way." He motioned him north with the Parker. "I'm southbound and don't care to see you again."

Tom went the way he was told. And Wyatt went the way he said he was going. He hadn't taken six steps when he held up, frowning. Some thoughtless cowboy had left a nice bay mare standing on the sidewalk over on the north side. This was a misdemeanor and could not be tolerated, naturally. No matter that in Wyatt's business you knew a man's horse as quick as you did its rider, and that in this case you knew the bay mare belonged to Frank McLowry.

Frank was in the Crystal Palace sharing an afternoon cup with Sheriff Johnny Behan. He had two guns on and his coat off, but the sheriff apparently hadn't noticed these illegal items. He put it out later that he had spotted them and had in fact gone into the Palace to talk Frank out of sporting them around town.

Maybe so, maybe not.

He wasn't working very hard on his disarmament program when Wyatt stuck his head in through the cut-glass doors and advised whoever owned the sockfoot bay mare out front to get her off the sidewalk. She was blocking traffic and breaking the law.

Frank stood away from Behan, and away from the bar.

He shook out his arms, loosened his wrists, started on the slow walk for Wyatt and the doors.

Wyatt stepped back out into the street, letting him come out to him. Frank did just that, strutting right up to him and sticking his chin in his face.

"It's my mare, Marshal, but it's your move. I ain't touching her."

"I'll take your guns before we get to the mare," Wyatt told him quietly.

"You said that right!" growled Frank. "You'll have to take 'em!"

They still tell it around Tombstone that Frank came out of the Palace flashing his big draw back of his big talk. And that Wyatt stepped right in and buffaloed him anyways. Now, nobody buffaloes Frank McLowry's kind when he's got his guns out. Not Wyatt nor anybody else.

147

But there never was any buffaloing to it. The fact was that Wyatt had that stagged-off Parker pinned on Frank's belly all the way across the Palace barroom and right out into Allen Street. When Frank pulled his long swagger to wind up with his face in Wyatt's, he wasn't putting on a show for anybody but the early afternoon customers. He wasn't for one precious minute buying any of his own bull.

And Wyatt knew it.

He patted the twin tubes of the Parker, grinned, shrugged his big shoulders, let the muzzle bores steady down on Frank's middle shirt button. "I'll play these," he said. "Pair of twelves with a buckshot kicker. What you got?"

"You goddamn fourflusher!" snarled Frank. "You've bluffed your last hand with that scattergun. I'll catch up with you one of these days, by Christ!"

"You've already used up enough wind to blow that mare off the sidewalk," Wyatt told him. "Now, pass over your guns and get her out in the street where she belongs."

Frank folded. He was a gunfighter, not a goddamn fool. Wyatt took the gunbelt and draped it over his right shoulder to balance the hang of Tom's outfit across his left. He watched Frank move the mare, then stride, black-face mad, across the street and into Spangenberg's Gun Shop.

Wyatt spared another grin for that.

Good enough. Everything was working out fine. Old Gus Spangenberg was an honest Dutchman and could use the business. And a new gun never worked as slick as the old ones.

With the grin, he was easing on up Allen. The five minutes he had given Morg still had twenty seconds to run when he ambled up to Virg on the corner of Fifth and passed him the top of a very good afternoon.

So that was the way the second part of it went. From the office door of Toughnut Street, to Virg on the corner of Fifth and Allen, it had so far taken just twelve minutes. It was square on the dot of a quarter to two when Morg drifted up from his station on Fourth to join his big brothers.

Their subsequent stroll back down Allen to Hafford's

148

Saloon, where Wyatt thought it best to hole up and wait for the next waltz, took less than two minutes. This wasn't because the boys were in any hurry but only for the reason that Tombstone was shaking herself out of her noon-dinner siesta some fast now. And getting the general idea pretty well in mind that the main show was going on any minute.

The sidewalks were all at once as clear of obstruction, horse or human, as a Presbyterian front pew with Old Nick standing in for the regular preacher. From Fifth, clean down to Hafford's on the corner of Fourth, they met only two citizens.

One was a genial drunk who stumbled out of the Palace to ask for a light. He got it. Along with some timely instructions. Morg furnished the match; Virg, the pat on the shoulder and the fatherly counsel.

"Spread out, pardner. There's due to be a big dance down the street, shortly. Don't look to me like you're in any shape to dig a shin. Head south. The music will come from up north."

The other townsman was a Spanish-American gentleman of some dignity and bearing. But a little young for gunfights.

"*Hola, Chico,*" Wyatt greeted him pleasantly.

"*Buenas tardes, señores.*" Chico swept off his ragged straw, looked up and down the empty street, frowned soberly, "*¿Que pasa, Patron? Es muy tranquilo—*no?"

"*Es muy tranquilo—*yes!" grinned Wyatt.

"Beat it, kid!" growled Virg, restless with the delay and breaking in roughly. "There's going to be *mucho disturbio* around here, you *sabe*, boy?"

Chico looked at him, puzzled. "*¿Come se dice, señor?*" he asked him.

"Big trouble, Chico," Wyatt answered him in English. "Guns. Bullets. *¿Comprende, paisano?*"

The boy's eyes got saucer-big.

All of a sudden Ceferino Sebastiano Jimenez Paz y Gutierrez *comprende*-ed plenty.

And *muy pronto.*

"*Adios, señor! Hasta la vista!*"

"Hold up, little pardner." Wyatt caught him by an arm. He dug in his vest, brought out two silver dollars, pressed them quickly into the kid's free hand.

Chico held the hand out, unfolded it, popped his big brown eyes at what he saw there.

"*¿Porque dos, señor?*" he asked Wyatt, wonderingly.

"*Porque* you might not get another chance at me, *amigo mio!*" smiled Wyatt softly, and turned and went down the street with Virg and Morg.

26 ☆

They say his coat-tails were really flapping when Mayor Clum tore into Johnny Behan's office ten minutes after Ike Clanton was turned loose. His indignant demand for action from the Cochise County sheriff was answered by Behan's declaration that he had already disarmed "the boys" and that they were right then on their way to the O.K. Corral to pick up their horses and clear out.

This was news to Clum. He let Behan know it.

"Why, I just saw the lot of them coming out of Spangenberg's!" he protested. "Every man of them had a gun on him!"

The sheriff turned up his hands. "I did what I could, John. There's no law against buying a new gun."

"Then those hoodlums have no idea of leaving town and you know it!" snapped the little mayor angrily.

"I only know what they told me." For some reason or other Behan wasn't very worked up.

"Then you won't act to stop them? You refuse to arrest them?"

"Arrest them for what?" snapped Behan, showing his first irritation. "Getting their horses out of a public corral?"

"If you won't stop them, I know who will!" Clum said it like a threat. "You know what that will mean."

The sheriff shrugged. "I've no say over the Earps. But if you're bound to stop somebody you'd best stop them, not the Clantons and McLowrys."

"Sheriff Behan," said Clum, dropping his voice and letting it come formal and straight. "I'm asking you to do your duty, arrest those men. I will back you on it and the Committee posse will back me. I can have thirty men here inside of ten minutes."

"That won't cut it by half."

"Behan, I'm warning you . . . !"

"Warn the Earps, you're wasting your time on me. This ain't my mess, it's theirs. Let me tell you something, John Clum . . ." he ticked it off, laying a stubby forefinger at him with the charge. "There's more on my side in this thing than on theirs. Every thinking man in this town knows the Earps have been spoiling for a chance to ride outside the law. They've been six months trying to smear mud on me and to get something on those cowboys yonder. They haven't turned up ten cents' worth of real proof on any of them, nor hurt me in any way. I'm clean in this whole damn thing. Oh no, don't worry about me! Nor about the Clantons and McLowrys. Worry about your precious Earps, *Mister Mayor*. Worry plenty!"

It wasn't just loud talk. Clum knew that. At no time during their terms in Tombstone could Wyatt or either of his brothers have touched Johnny Behan in a popularity contest. The Earps were each and all of them proud, aloof, hard-to-know men, dedicated to their jobs and taking no time from them to make local friends.

But Clum knew something else.

He knew *Wyatt* Earp.

"You're forcing me to go to him," he told Behan. He said *him*, not *them*, and Johnny Behan knew what he meant. Still, he checked it out.

"Meaning exactly what?" he asked quickly.

"That I will back him and that the Committee will back him," rasped Clum, "and that we will all worry about it later. Good day, Sheriff!"

"Good day, Mayor," answered Johnny Behan, and waited only until he was out of sight before settling his own hat hard down over his face, and stepping swiftly out the door and across Frémont Street toward the O.K. Corral.

For the second time in twenty-four hours Wyatt turned Clum and his offer of Safety Committee backing flat down.

"John," he said, putting his big hand on the other's shoulder, "this is nobody's fight but mine and Virg's and Morg's. If you make us go into it with a thirty-man citizen posse behind us, winning it won't mean a thing. The

151

posse breaks up and goes home and next day forgets the whole thing. The gang lays low for a spell, gets back together, hits you again and you've got the same fight to make all over.

"Lawmen, men like me and my brothers that have been given badges and a regular job to do, are something else again. We do what we're paid to do and we do it without any help from anybody. You'll have just the one fight and that will be the end of it. They know we won't break up and go home. They know we'll be there after it's all over. Right where we were before it started. Back of our badges and meaning to stay back of them."

Clum saw the way it was.

He knew, too, that Wyatt was right.

He had had his Citizen's Safety Committee posse long before the Earps came to Tombstone. It had been helpless in its clumsy leaderless way even to slow the rustling and stage-robbing down, let alone stop them. Yet, in a few swift months, first all alone, then with Virgil and finally Morgan and Doc Holliday to help him, Wyatt had fought the outlaws to a dead draw. Now he had them backed into their last corral and was asking only that Tombstone stand back and give him and his brothers fighting room to finish it once and for all.

Clum was no hero worshipper. Still, he knew that what Wyatt in his slow way was asking, was the simple privilege of doing his duty without interference—and the privilege of getting killed in the line of that duty if need be. Hero worshipper or not, it made a man's heart swell just to stand and look at such a man and to know that he had been your friend and that you had stood hand-close to him in history.

Yet, in that moment before he put his last words to Wyatt Earp, the tough little Tombstone mayor was no fool, either.

He knew that above and beyond the law, or any duty to that law, the quiet head of the Earp clan was a killer.

And that he meant to kill *now*.

"You won't see it any other way, then?" he said at last and low-voiced.

"No, John. Me and Virgil and Morgan will go it alone. *We'll go right now*."

The stillness that followed was not without its dissent.

The objection came from a back table of the otherwise deserted saloon, and it came in a reedy, croaking voice that Tombstone had learned to know well those past months. And to listen to when it made its rare orations on the subject of gunplay.

"You may go right now," said Doc Holliday, moving out of the rear corner gloom into the sunlight of the front window, "but I reckon you won't go alone."

They watched him come across the room, a parchment-skinned scarecrow of a man, overcoated even in the October mildness against the raging chills of his disease, limping and hobbling forward on the cane he habitually used when the lung fever was high within him and its weakness draining away his frail strength.

"This is our fight, Doc," Wyatt told him gently. "There's no call for you to mix into it."

Doc stopped, leaning on his cane, the pasty sweat of the simple effort to walk plastering the lank thinness of his blond hair over the bones of his forehead and temples. He just looked back at him and then he said it, his voice no more than a hoarse whisper. "That's a hell of a thing for you to say to me, Wyatt."

For *you* to say to *me*. That was all. Yet, in those six words lay a lifetime of understanding between two lonely men. An all-night speech could not have twisted the knife of its reminder any sharper in Wyatt Earp.

"*It was,*" he said softly. "Let's go, Doc."

You know how it went then.

Wyatt first, flanked by Morg and Virg. Doc, hobbling off to one side and behind the three of them, using Wyatt's shotgun for a cane now.

The Earps—strange, implacable men, all better than six feet tall, all looking so much alike in their size and power and cat-easy ways of moving, no stranger could tell them apart.

And Doc Holliday—fence-rail thin but nearly as tall, a living ghost shadow to the terrible flesh and form of the others.

The four of them, coming down Frémont now. Walking the middle of the street. Not hurrying, not slowing. The O.K Corral not fifty steps away.

Only Doc Holliday with the shotgun this time. All the

Earps, and Wyatt in the lead of them, wearing only their beltguns, holding their hands slack and free and proud away from them. And Wyatt wanting it that way. The time for the Buntline Special and the old Parker double was long past. This time nobody was going to jail. This time it would be hand against hand, nerve against nerve. No special weapons, no walk-ups behind, no cold scatter-gun drops.

This time they would see him with *the Colts*.

There would be no room for any man to cry a foul or claim an unfairness.

This time they were going to get it where they had been begging for it.

In the belly.

Ahead, scarce forty feet now, were the open-swung gates of the corral yard.

In the yard itself, their sweating backs to the wall of the building which formed its north side, waited the five outlaws: young Billy Clanton, just turned seventeen, white in the face and silent now, but hard in mind and dangerous in gunhand as any of them; Ike, shivering uncontrollably, the fear coming up in his drying mouth, thick and dusty as boll-weeviled cotton; Tom McLowry, not afraid and not unafraid, not thinking, even, but watching Frank and drawing his strength from him; Frank, the oldest and most ready of them all, thirty-one the coming spring, a dark-skinned, high-trained, deadly man; last, the twenty-one-year-old William Claiborne, the boy not yet a man, for all his birthdays. He was an unbalanced, twisted boy, who had killed three men in the past four months. He had but one ambition and that the crazy one of being called and known as Billy the Kid, succeeding to the title left vacant by the gunfire following Pat Garrett's soft call of the real Billy in the darkness of Pete Maxwell's New Mexico ranchhouse.

There they were, two men, two boys, and a coward, all calling themselves cowboys. They were dressed to look the part and fit the call; all slender, well-set-up men; high-booted, silk-scarved, sleeveless of vest, gay and gaudy of striped shirt.

Ike and Billy Clanton and Frank McLowry, each had a single Colt in a belt holster. Tom McLowry's .45 was stuck handle-high in the waistband of his Levis. Billy

154

Claiborne had two guns worn low and laced down in double holsters.

Their cinch-tight horses stood hard to hand, the jut of the Winchester butts showing above each scarred saddle scabbard.

Still the Earps came on. It was thirty feet to the gates now, narrowing to twenty.

In the last, still seconds Johnny Behan made his lone play. Wyatt heard the bang of his office door as they came abreast of it. He never stopped walking.

Behan was up to them, waving them down.

"It's all right, boys!" he shouted. "I've disarmed them. You can let them be."

"Did you arrest them?" asked Wyatt, not altering the slowness of his stride.

"No, I didn't do that. No need for that. I . . ."

"Get out of the way, then!" said Wyatt flatly, and brushed him back with one sweep of his arm. It was ten feet to the gate then, and Behan was running for cover. Wyatt was turning left oblique and into the O.K. Corral.

With him, right and left, went Virg and Morg.

Behind them, Doc stopped square in the open gateway.

The Earps bore down upon the five men waiting along the building wall. Across from Virg were Billy Claiborne and Ike Clanton. Fronting Wyatt were Billy Clanton and Frank McLowry. Morg had Tom McLowry all to himself.

Wyatt stopped the dead march in the last half breath. They measured it later. It was only nine feet from his bootprints to the building wall.

Nobody moved. Nobody made to move. History handed Virg, not Wyatt, the opening words.

"You men are under arrest," said Tombstone's sometime town marshal. "Throw up your hands."

One set of hands went skywards—Ike's.

Four sets went the other way.

Frank and Billy Clanton took Wyatt. Billy was a little wild. His first shot clipped Wyatt's shirt. Frank's first shot didn't even touch him. With good professional reason. Wyatt's eyes had never left Frank. He was the number one gun, and had to go first. Frank's Colt barely cleared its leather when Wyatt's slug hit him three inches above the belt buckle. He grabbed his guts and went down. Wyatt's second shot nearly tore Billy Clanton's right arm

155

off, spinning him clear around and knocking him off his feet. Both his men were in the dirt, with the fight only three seconds old.

Tom McLowry dove behind one of the saddled horses, firing at Morg. Morg, in a cold way nobody ever forgot, just stood there and let him shoot, holding his own gun easy and careless, waiting for that one clear shot.

Virg was just as dead-calm about it. He let Billy Claiborne have three pegs, then threw down on him. But Arizona's "Billy the Kid" had already had all he wanted of it. He broke and ran, and Virg held up his fire. He saw the boy dive for the door of the north-wall building. He saw the door flash open to let him in. And he saw who flashed it open. It was Johnny Behan.

Now Wyatt leaped toward the horse behind which Tom McLowry was firing at Morg. He drove two bullets into the animal, having not time to move it any other way. It reared, screaming, and Tom slid out and away from it. Wyatt threw down on him but in the same instant Ike Clanton ran crazily up and grabbed his gunhand, slobbering, "Don't kill me! Don't kill me! I ain't shooting!"

It was all the time Tom McLowry needed. Morg had run over to help Wyatt with the hysterical Ike. As he did Tom dropped him with a bullet through the base of his neck. When he saw Morg hit, Wyatt went crazy.

He kicked Ike away from him, roaring like a hairedup silvertip. "Goddamn you, this fight's commenced. Get to fighting or get out!" Even in the full roll of a boiling mad, he couldn't shoot a man that wouldn't shoot back. The little second he took to spare Ike's miserable life nearly cost him his own. In its span, Tom had thrown down on him and was letting off with deliberate aim from not eight feet off.

It wasn't Wyatt's fault that aim got spoiled, nor Tom's. It was Doc Holliday's.

For the first time in the fight, Doc had a shot at a man with no Earp in his way. Tom screamed like a woman as both barrels of Doc's double went into him. He ran ten feet around the corner of the building, into Frémont and fell stone-dead.

With Morg down from Tom's bullet, Wyatt leaped to

shelter him, yelling, "Stay down, stay down! Make yourself small!" The leap turned his back to the wounded Billy Clanton. The youngster, still on the ground, made the border shift, throwing his gun to his left hand and leveling it on Wyatt's back. Morg, his mind a long ways off from making himself small, saw him in time. Billy had struggled to his knees to make his shot at Wyatt. Morg shot him through the belly. He staggered up to his feet and Virg, whirling from watching Claiborne vanish into the building, drove a .44 slug into the youth's chest, putting him back down into the dirt.

At this point, Doc dropped his empty shotgun, drew his Colt and ran in toward the Earps. He jumped over Frank McLowry, thinking him dead and done and safe out of it from Wyatt's first shot. He thought wrong. He heard Morg bellow, "Behind you, Doc!" Then Frank was coming up off the ground and snarling, "I've got you, by God!"

"Think so, do you?" Doc came around, throwing the question and his snapshot at Frank, together.

Frank fired with him and Morg threw one in from the sidelines to make it three. The outlaw's shot cut across the muscles of Doc's back. But it was his last shot. Doc's bullet drilled him heart-center and Morg's smashed the top of his head off.

Frank was dead. Tom was dead. Ike and Claiborne were clear out of it and still running. Only young Billy Clanton, the gut-tough seventeen-year-old, was yet in the fight. The Earps took him out of it, merciful short. But not before he took one of them.

He got as far as the north corner of the building wall, hunching his bullet-riddled body along it, trying to get around it and into Frémont as Tom McLowry had done. Virg, who had put the last shot into him, snapped two more at him, both misses. The boy fired back, needing both bloody hands to hold the gun up. The hold was good. Virgil Earp was down with a .45 ripping his left thigh to the bone.

Of the law, only Wyatt and Doc were still on their feet, and Doc was shot in the back and couldn't steady his hand for any real fine shooting.

Wyatt did it like a man had to, like to a poor dumb-brute animal that was dying but still dangerous. He put

157

the first, careful bullet through the boy's hips, anchoring him for the second one through the side of the head and into the brain.

Billy Clanton was dead and the Battle of the O.K. Corral was over.

27 ☆

Wyatt had no more than time to look at Morg's wound, and the handful of citizens who had seen the fight from Frémont Street to begin to crowd into the corral, when Johnny Behan came hurrying out of the building door he'd helped Ike Clanton and Billy Claiborne get away through. He braced Wyatt and the others, in a voice loud enough to be heard clear across Frémont Street. "All right, you men are under arrest!"

Wyatt just looked at him. He was too dumbfounded to do anything else. So were Doc and Virg. But one old mossyback in the crowd, a gray-beard billy goat of a hard-rock miner named Beatty Comstock, sure wasn't. Old Beatty horned in and spoke right up in Wyatt's behalf, and some hot about it, too. "By Tophet," yelled the old man, "you'd best be in no hurry to arrest the marshal! He done just right and the people hereabouts will uphold him!"

Wyatt gave him a grateful nod, stepped into Johnny Behan. "You bet we did just right. But you threw us. You told us they were disarmed."

"It was plain murder!" The sheriff was still talking loud. "They threw up their hands when you ordered them to. You're under arrest—the lot of you!"

"We won't be arrested," said Wyatt quietly. "We'll answer for what we've done when the time comes. But this isn't the time, *Johnny!*" He put a scathing softness to the name. "You'd best get out of our way, you understand?"

There's no doubt Johnny Behan understood. What he would have done about it past that point remains to be guessed at. For, coming down Frémont and turning in at the corral right on top of Wyatt's refusal to surrender, was the whole kit and kaboodle of the Citizen's Safety Comittee. Mayor J. P. Clum was in charge and not looking for any back talk from Sheriff Johnny Behan or anybody else.

"We'll be responsible for these men," was all he told Behan, and Johnny bought it and backed off.

With Clum directing them, the Committeemen picked up Morg and Virg and carried them off down Frémont, Wyatt and Doc Holliday walking rearguard and nobody arguing about it. They took the wounded men to Clum's house. There, they set up a rotating guard to see that no reprisals came off, and sat the clock around waiting for Johnny Behan to make his move.

He made it next morning in an unsigned article in *The Nugget*, the paper that all along backed him and the rustler bunch. The article covered the whole of the front page, charging the Earps, flat out, with wanton assault and premeditated murder, and claiming all the outlaws had raised their hands when asked and that only two of them, Frank McLowry and Billy Clanton, had guns on them, and that even they didn't use them until both had been shot by the Earps.

Clum and his *Epitaph* did what they could, printing a fine editorial that started off:

> "The feeling of the better class of citizens is that the marshal and his posse acted solely in the right in attempting to disarm the cowboys, and that it was a case of kill or get killed. . . ."

But it was a little late in the afternoon for editorials—fine or faked. Tombstone took the O.K. Corral killings to heart. Before forty-eight hours was up the town was split wide open. But not down the middle. Rather than that, considerable to the left of center, with Wyatt and his few eyewitness defenders bunched up over on the short side of the split.

It's a chaw of bully beef that's still going on down there in southeast Arizona. Fact is, some dull evening when you want to get cut down to size you just step into any general store from Tucson to Tombstone and let on that Wyatt was right and that Johnny Behan was a low-down bastard. What hits you in return will be plenty hot enough to give anybody a fair idea of the temperatures that were running down there fifty years ago.

Behan and *The Nugget* were off to a sprinting start. They never let up. The slop they printed about the dead rustlers would have turned a strong man's paunch inside out, but Tombstone had a big belly. It swallowed up such stuff as the following without a heave.

> "Little Billy Clanton, not yet eighteen and a boy known and liked all over the valley, had as his last thought a sacred promise he had made to his dear mother. He had sworn to this beloved lady that he would never die with his boots on. As he lay bleeding out his life, his last request was for his boots to be removed, that he might die with his pledge fulfilled . . ."

And even more:

> "Ike Clanton has been the victim of scurrilous lies. He did not rush up to beg for his own life as reported by the Earps, but to plead for the safety of his young brother, Billy. It was this brave motive, alone, which led him to dash so courageously, and unarmed, through the hail of the murderers' deadly fire . . ."

The wonder was that it took three days to get the warrants sworn out. But Johhny Behan knew just how long it took a public pot to come to the boil. He waited, keeping his nose in the wind. The third morning after the fight he thought he smelled steam. Within an hour he had a big posse of rustlers deputized and out looking for Wyatt and his brothers with their hip pockets full of murder warrants.

Fortunately, the wind was blowing Wyatt's way, too. He beat the posse to it, surrendering to Judge Wells Spicer and demanding a full court inquiry. That was the 29th. The hearting started next day with only Wyatt present, as Morg and Virg were still bedded with their wounds.

That was some inquiry. It lasted six weeks to the day

and what went on in it would be longer than the rest of the story put together. In the end, it all added up this simple: Behan and *The Nugget* could have most of Tombstone believing Wyatt and his brothers were murderers but they couldn't sell it to old Beatty Comstock and a tough dozen other eyewitnesses; nor to hardminded, stringstraight, Municipal Judge Wells Spicer. On December 12th Spicer closed the hearing by refusing to recommend an indictment to the grand jury then in session.

And the grand jury refused to make one on its own hook.

For a brief, uneasy twenty-four hours the Earps stood freed and clear of any charge.

Then the lightning struck.

On December 13th, a likely date for such unlucky doings, the rustlers met in executive session at the McLowry's Sulphur Springs ranch. They sat as their own grand jury, Judge William Brocius presiding. It took them three minutes to return an indictment for murder against the Earps, two minutes more to pass sentence under the indictment.

There's been plenty of fool talk about that meeting. It was actually told around Tombstone so Tom Sawyersilly as to claim the boys met in a "secret canyon at the dead of night and signed the verdict in blood."

They did no such thing, naturally.

What they did do was to scrawl out a list of lawmen and others that weren't going to be allowed to leave town alive. The original masterpiece was worked out on the back of a tomato can label by Curly Bill. He used the stub of a tally pencil and printed it the best way he knew how. Which was with all the N's backwards and the big and little letters mixed up something scandalous.

But not so scandalous that that "educated gentleman," Mr. John Ringo, couldn't read it well enough to make six legible copies, one for each of the condemned men: Wyatt, Virg, Morg, Doc Holliday, Beatty Comstock and Mayor J. P. Clum.

Delivery of the lists, through contacts inside the town, was carried out that same night. Clum got his first. The way he told about it, years later, set the stage about right. "As for myself," the old mayor recalled, "I felt that if another fight should occur within the city, the rustler clan would not overlook an opportunity to rub me out, but I did not believe—desperate as I knew them to be—that they would deliberately plan to murder me. I was mistaken."

That, as the fellow says, was the understatement of the year.

But let old Clum wait. Wyatt is our man. It's when he got his copy of the death list that the fur really began to fly. Which same was not long after the mayor got his. Say about twenty minutes. Say about eleven-thirty the night of December 13th.

He was alone in his office on Toughnut Street, burning the midnight gas jet and chewing a cold cigar; trying his damnedest to make headstall or tailcrupper of the whole mess—and getting no place.

Virg and Morg were up and around but still stiff with their wounds. The worst of the outlaws, Ringo and Curly Bill, were yet at large. Johnny Behan had taken a setback but would never let up until he had got out a warrant he could serve and make stick. Doc was a very sick man, likely to go out with the lung fever before spring. The town, taken by and large, was still in sympathy with Johnny Behan and his "poor cowboys." Crowds of gullible citizens continued every day to visit boothill, read off those three heroic headboards put up over Frank, Tom and Billy by the sheriff and his sad friends: MURDERED ON THE STREETS OF TOMBSTONES and to come away wiping their damnfool eyes and weeping out loud that Wyatt and his brothers were a no-good bunch of bloodthirsty killers.

Cleared by Judge Spicer or not, it looked bad for the Earps. And bid fair to look a hell of a lot worse before the new grass came again.

About now, a man in Wyatt's boots could give serious thought to getting out of Tombstone and far out of it. He and Virg and Morg had done all any three men could. There came a time when a man got sudden sick of fighting *inlaws*. Outlaws were one thing. You knew how to handle them. But when the good people turned against you, as sooner or later they always seemed to do, you were licked. You had small choice. It was either get out and move on, or stay and get indicted. As the old wall clock behind his desk ticked away toward twelve that night, Wyatt was moving hand-close to reaching for his hat.

But it's the little things that forever trip a man up.

Little things with big brown eyes and ragged straw sombreros.

Wyatt heard the hesitant knock. He straightened in his chair, let his voice go soft, his eyes show the quick back-light of the old smile. Here, anyways, no matter from what direction the wind blew, was a friend.

"Entre usted, amigo," he called, low-voiced. *"¿Que pasa? ¿Que es este vez?"*

What it was this time, Chico told him, following the usual bow and hatsweep, was that the Señorita Belloit had urgent need to see the Marshal. This was a matter of the supremest importance and could not wait for daybreak.

"A man can see that," Wyatt told him soberly in English. Then, warmly, *"Mil gracias, hombre."*

Chico took his dollar and departed, head light, heart big as a Spanish bull's within him. It wasn't the money. Bah! What was *dinero* when such a one as *El Mariscal* had called you *hombre*—a man!

There was no light showing in the shack when Wyatt came up to it. Lilly let him in, in the dark, shut the door hurriedly, then lit the single candle back of the bath curtain. He could smell the wick smoke of it lingering in the close air of the little room, knew from that she had blown it out when she heard him coming.

"You're scared, girl." He frowned it, sensing the fear in the very look of her. "What's all the hush about?"

"Wyatt, I *am* scared!" she whispered. "This time I'm *really* scared. Look at this!" She held out the crumpled piece of ruled notepaper to him.

He didn't take it right off. She was not the kind to spook at shadows. He knew that. Or to jump sideways off the trail at just any piece of scrap paper. A man could know before he looked at it that he wasn't going to like what he saw on that soiled sheet.

He took it then, and went to the light of the candle with it. He studied it a full minute. Not that it took him that long to read its three lines. That was done in the first glance. And easy done. It wasn't addressed to anybody and it wasn't signed. All it said was:

"Don't bother to try leaving for you'll not make it now. You've killed your last cowboy. . . ."

"Where'd you get it?" said Wyatt at last.

He said it so quiet and unruffled you'd have thought it was an invite to a house-raising or a baby-baptising. But Lilly knew him by now. She could read that strange backlight in his pale eyes for what it was and for what it meant. What it was, was naked fury, and what it meant was murder.

"Ringo," she said, and watched the heatless fire leap higher behind his empty stare. "He said it was for you."

Ringo again! God in Heaven, must it forever be Ringo? Must it always be him? Hounding and pushing and snapping at a man's heels until he got his crazy brains kicked out? Would he never let up on you? Did he have to keep at a man until there was nothing left but to take him over the hill? To grab up the loose end of his rope and drag him off into the night and leave him there like you'd had to leave Old Shep?

Even as the questions rose wearily in his mind, Wyatt knew their answer.

The kid would never quit until he had killed his sheep and been caught doing it. Once he had done that, he knew you would come for him. And when you did, he meant to show you what you'd known he must from clear back in the trail days out of San Angelo: that nobody named Wyatt Earp could beat him to a gun in a fair-called draw.

In the cold end, Johnny Ringo could no more keep away from Wyatt Earp than a moth-miller from an open-wick gas flare.

"What else did he say, Lilly?"

He broke the long silence to put the slow question. She felt the tiredness and the emptiness of it. "Only that you wouldn't lack for company in hell," she said. "You know Ringo. Once he's got his mouth open, he's got to empty it."

"Such as what company?" he asked heavily. "Outside of Morg and Virg."

164

"Yes, them," she told him. "And Doc and Mayor Clum and poor old Beatty Comstock."

"Six of us, eh? They should have made it seven. It's a luckier number."

"Do you think they meant it, Wyatt?" She put it tensely, slant eyes holding on the slab granite of his face.

"They mean it, Lilly," he said. "Curly Bill's too old to play games."

She took it like you'd expect her kind to. Not flinching any, nor whimpering. Just laying the big one to him straight and quiet. "What will you do now, Wyatt?"

"Well, first off," he shrugged it, trying to lighten it with the grin, "I'll see that old Beatty clears out safe. He can go tonight. He's been dodging Apaches in the Whetstones and Dragoons since '71. He can evaporate like a puff of war smoke. Then I'll try and get Clum out on tomorrow night's stage. I'll have him go on down the road a piece and board it where they won't spot him. After that, I can tackle Virg and Morg and Doc. They won't want to go but I allow they . . ."

She broke in on him, shaking her head.

"I said what will *you* do, Wyatt."

"Me," he said at once, "I'll stay."

He said it that easy and natural you knew nothing else had entered his mind since reading Ringo's note. It was the way of him, Lilly thought, and the pride and the thrill and the worship of him that was in her put the blood to pounding wild in her veins. *This was a man.* No other could touch him. Should they try, they would be warned once in that slow, quiet voice of his not to try again. But should they *threaten* to try, there would be no warning.

To threaten a man like Wyatt Earp was to shout into the thunderhead, calling for the lightning to come forth. And expecting, when it did, to catch it in your bare hands.

She had not answered his quick statement, but now she did. Her voice was fierce and sharp, crying out to him there in the candlelight with all the longing and the love that was in her.

"And so will I, Wyatt! I'll stay with you, boy! As long as there's a breath in my body. As long as you will have me. *As close as you will hold me!*"

He took her in his great arms then. Lifting and carrying her light and gentle as a little child. Toward the

165

flicker of the candle. Leaning swiftly to blow it out. Moving, then, back through the darkness, across the tiny room and to the welcoming, remembered fragrance of the clean-frayed sheets. And to the waiting, dreamless rest and the long, slow, blessed peace of the old wrought-iron bedstead.

"Close enough, Lilly girl?"

His wide lips, strangely soft with the whisper, found hers in the close-wrapped darkness of the silent cabin. Not demanding, not rough, nor animal-eager, nor body-anxious. But only asking with a gentleness that held no coarseness. And taking with a strength that knew no brutality.

She answered him with her lips. And with the perfumed closeness of her small breasts and slender body. And with the one, long, wordless sigh that said it all, a million times over, in the last second before their mouths met.

After that, there was just the blue wick-smoke of the blown-out candle, and a long time of stillness and contentment in the little shack behind the brassy blare and gaslit bedlam of Tombstone's Bird Cage Theatre.

28 ☆

Old Beatty Comstock disappeared sometime before dawn of the 14th, fading out like the cloud of Apache war smoke Wyatt had likened him to. He was seen no more in Tombstone. Mayor John Clum, stiff-backed about it but still limber enough in the head to buy Wyatt's warning, boarded that night's Benson stage eight miles out of Tombstone.

Virgil and Morgan would have no part of any retreat which Wyatt wasn't a party to. It isn't known what Doc Holliday said but it's a safe stack of blues that it was mighty close to his previous, "that's a hell of a thing for you to say to me," position. It's a known fact that midnight of the 14th saw him sitting square in the middle of a tablestakes game at the Crystal Palace, betting his cards high and waiting with his pistol in his lap for any of the Sulphur Springs boys to put their bullets where their billy-doos were.

But the gang had a cushier spot for their lead. At 11 A.M. of the 14th, five hours out of Tombstone, the Benson stage ran into a crossbuck of blasting Winchesters. There was no command to halt. The bandits just opened up and poured it in.

"Whistling Dick" Winters, the driver, was hit in the leg and his off-side lead horse shot through the throat. A dozen slugs ripped through the body of the coach itself, making it look like whatever the attackers were after was *in* the stage, not on top of it. Which it sure as hell was.

That run carried no mail sack, no express box, no payroll pouch, no bullion shipment. All it carried was Mayor J. P. Clum. And twelve of the fourteen shots fired went through the tonneau where he was sitting.

The outlaws had dismounted, apparently to make their aims surer. They didn't make them quite sure enough. Leg wound and injured lead horse, no matter, Whistling Dick kept his teams on the flat gallop. A mile up the road he pulled them in, cut the staggering leader out of the traces, shot him through the head, sprang back to the box and got the stage safe away before the bushwhackers could remount and come up to it.

It was not until he made his regular stop in Contention City that driver Winters found he'd lost his passenger— Mayor Clum was gone.

Dick put that report on the wire from Contention City. Before morning Tombstone was hashing over the news that its mayor had been kidnapped out of the Benson stage, was still mising and had to be presumed dead.

But though little John Clum was a long ways from getting measured for his pine tuxedo. Not trusting Whistling Dick to get his horses back under way before the ambushers could catch up to the halted coach, he had slipped out of it and into the brush, made his way, afoot, to the Grand Central Mine's stamp mill, borrowed a horse from the mill's super, ridden a long circle on the remaining twenty miles to the railhead at Benson. He was there by daylight and didn't miss his train.

Before news of his escape reached Tombstone the Safety Committee had pressured Johnny Behan into making up a posse and riding out to the site of the ambush. That's all he did, though, just rode out. Except to ride right back in. He never tracked the would-be killers one solitary foot, though there was blood all over the place and pony prints leading away from it clear enough for a blind squaw to trail walking backwards.

Since there was no mail on the run, Wyatt was helpless to interfere. His lack of movement was purely physical. His mind was going five miles a minute.

When it came to the time that the highest official of the biggest city in Arizona Territory could be shot at and run through the brush like a damn rabbit, with the sheriff of Cochise County taking no more action than to amble out and sniff at the blood on the sagebrush, and with the soft-bellied lawmakers up to Prescott setting on their legislative behinds and letting him get away with it, it was time and more than time for a man to know his own number was higher up than a gas bag balloon at the county fair.

He and Virg and Morg redoubled their *que vives*, but you can't watch all the doorways, all the time.

Short weeks later, just after 11 P.M., December 28th, Virg was nailed coming out of the Oriental Saloon. He was rushed to Doc Goodfellow's office where it was found his left arm had been shredded with a charge of No. 2 gooseshot fired from no more than thirty feet. Doc Goodfellow's report said it as good as anything: "Longitudinal fracture left elbow necessitating removal entire joint. Flesh wound, minor, left thigh." Tombstone's town marshal would never use his left arm again. Incapacitated for his job with elections but days away, Virg was all through as a peace officer in Arizona. He was replaced at once by Dave Neagle, one of Johnny Behan's longtime deputies.

Wyatt now moved his wounded brother from Doc Goodfellow's office into a room at the Cosmopolitan Hotel. Him and Morg each took a room that flanked Virg's. A twenty-four hour guard was run. A flophouse cockroach couldn't have got up that hotel corridor without he was stopped and gone over for a gun by the Safety Committee vigilantes who swarmed outside the injured lawman's quarters.

Wyatt Earp's war was on, and the seige of it shut down tighter around him than the gee-string of a Chiricahua's front-cloth. In his mind that January night there was no doubt where it would all end. They had run Clum out of

168

town, shot Virg, had him and Morg holed up. It was only a matter of time.

But time—and telegrams—are sometime things; things which had shown a previous habit of horning in on Wyatt's fate. Mayor Clum had stayed with that Benson train, clean to Washington, D.C. Him and his Safety Committee had had about all they aimed to take off of the rustlers and were stirred up as a stick-poked yellow-jacket's nest. Some thirty days had passed since Virg had got winged and Clum and the Committee hadn't been standing around with their thumbs hooked in their galluses the whole of that time.

Wyatt found this out through his usual source—Chico Gutierrez. It was ten o'clock the night of the 25th when the corridor guards passed the little Mexican into Virg's room. Wyatt took the wire, read it twice through to make sure, handed it without comment to Virg, as Morg moved in to read over his wounded brother's shoulder. It was addressed to Wyatt, said what it had to say, point-short.

> FRÉMONT RESIGNED. J. J. GOSPER ACTING
> GOVERNOR. HAVE ADVISED HIM YOU BE
> GIVEN SPECIAL AUTHORITY COCHISE COUNTY.
> AUTHORITY GRANTED. GOOD LUCK.
>
> > C. P. DAKE, U. S. MARSHAL,
> > ARIZONA TERRITORY

It never was shown, that during his term as Governor of Arizona Territory General Frémont was in any sort of cahoots with the crooked bunch in Prescott or, through them, with Behan's gang in Tombstone. But one thing that was shown, time and again, was that the old soldier never was quite up to controlling the political shenanigans which went on down in Cochise County while he was in office. By that token his removal and replacement by tough old J. J. Gosper should have marked the beginning of the end for the Behan boys. That it marked, instead, the end for another of the Earps is short, hard history.

Through early February Wyatt, with Morg and Doc Holliday as special federal deputies backing him, made arrests among the Sulphur Springs crowd right and left; arrests which, as always before, fell apart in Behan's locally controlled courts.

But to frustrate Wyatt's arrests was not enough for Johnny Behan with the cards coming his way like they were now. When no judge in Tombstone would issue warrants for the Earps on account of their legal status as federal officers, he quick enough found a justice of the peace in Contention City who would—and did. Trial was set for February 14th. The warrants were made out for Wyatt, Virgil and Morgan Earp, and Doc Holliday. The charge was the tired old one of having murdered Billy Clanton and Frank and Tom McLowry.

Wyatt had known that Behan meant eventually to get him on that charge. He knew as well that he, Wyatt, would never have a better chance than right then to beat that charge. He obeyed the summons quiet and peaceful as a suckling lamb.

It was five minutes of ten the morning of the 14th when him and Morg and Doc walked into the Contention City courtroom. Each of them was wearing his federal mashal's star pinned full out in the open, and each of them was wearing something else, likewise in the full open—a well-oiled brace of .44 Colts.

It was four minutes of ten when Johnny Behan and six armed deputies followed them in.

At three minutes of ten the Contention judge began reading off the charge. Sixty seconds later he ran out of gas and started to sputter, for thirty good reasons.

It was just two minutes before ten when Colonel William Herring, heading the Tombstone Citizens Safety Committee in Clum's absence, marched into His Honor's hearing room with the full membership of the Citizens Committee vigilantes behind him.

At 9:59 Herring began stating his legal position for the judge's benefit.

It took him fifteen seconds.

"We're here," he announced in a loud steady voice, "for justice or a fight, and ready for either. You haven't any more jurisdiction over this case than a jack rabbit. If there's any hearing, it'll be in Tombstone. Have I made myself clear to all parties?"

In the little stillness that followed, there was no doubt he had. Behan never opened his mouth and the Contention justice only opened his far enough and fast enough to agree in complete legal detail with Colonel Herring.

It was straight-up ten o'clock when Wyatt and Morg and Doc stalked out past Johnny Behan and boarded their horses without a backward look.

One month later, the night of March 18th, it happened. There would be longer ways to tell it but none better than the way George W. Parsons put it down in his diary. That's the diary that old G. W. kept of the daily goings-on in Tombstone at the time. The one that everybody knows is just about the only real record that was kept, saving for editor Clum's *Epitaph* pieces.

Parson set it down like this, and you can lay your last thin dime he had it straight.

"... Another assassination last night, about eleven o'clock. I heard the shots, two in number. Poor Morgan Earp was shot through by an unknown party. Probably two or three in number in Campbell & Hatch's while playing pool with Hatch. Wyatt was there, sitting along the wall watching the game. The shots came from the ground window leading into alley running to Frémont Street. The second shot was fired apparently at Wyatt Earp. Murderers got away, of course, but it was and is quite evident who committed the deed. The man was Frank Stilwell in all probability. Morg lived about forty minutes after being shot, and died without a murmur. Bad times ahead now. . . ."

Bad times ahead *now?*

Well, you've got to hand it to those old boys like George Parsons on one thing.

Nobody could ever touch them for stating a situation six miles short of somewhat.

You could hit them in the nose with a sackful of steer manure and they wouldn't smell anything in it but the grass seeds.

29

The killers of Morg didn't get away into the night as fast as had the wounders of Virg.

In addition to the testimony of George Parsons, and that of pool-hall owner Hatch and the other eye witnesses, the coroner's jury produced a surprise witness—Pete Spence's wife.

This was a very civic-minded lady. It would only be small to point out that her sudden interest in impartial justice was maybe brought on by the fact Pete had busted her jaw in a family argument just ahead of doing Morg in. Point was, she showed up and testified under proper oath that the killers were Pete, Frank Stilwell, an Indian called Charlie, another Indian she didn't know, and a John Doe white man she'd never seen before. She thought there were two, three others in on the action but they hadn't been to her house with Stilwell and the others. She also stated that Pete had told her Curly Bill was running the show and that Ringo was in town along with Curly.

On the evidence submitted, the six coroner's jurymen returned a verdict, in important part as follows:

> ". . . it is the finding of said jury that the deceased came by his death from the effect of a gun shot or pistol wound on the night of March 18th, 1882, by Peter Spence, Frank Stilwell, one Joe Doe white man, an Indian called Charlie and another Indian, name unknown. . . ."

On the same evidence Wyatt made his own decision.

He let it be known openly throughout Tombstone that he was going after the killers and any of their accomplices their trails might lead him to. He was still Deputy U.S. Marshal for Cochise County and he would arrest them if they didn't resist. Just as openly, he advertised his hope that they would resist. He didn't say, nor did he need to at this point, what he meant to do in case they favored his wish.

Offhand, this open threat might not appear typical of

Wyatt. To understand it, though, you have only to keep in mind where he was standing that March night in 1882 when the coroner's jury brought in its findings on Morg's death.

In keeping with his promise to Clum and the Committee that he would not take the law into his own hands, he had so far kept to the legal letter in his war with the rustlers. In doing so, he had given the outlaws the first two shots, free. Those shots had done for Virgil and Morgan. By declaring that the last of the Earps didn't intend to wait for the third shot, he was only paying the hard price of his own conscience. Even in the depths of his black grief over the death of young Morg, Wyatt could not bring himself to hunt from the shadows as did his enemies. The hyena and the pariah dog might stalk forever through the outer brush. When the lion set out to hunt he padded full into the middle of the clearing, put his great head to the ground and rumbled out a warning that shook the rocks for miles around.

But blind rage and born courage to the contrary, once Wyatt had roared he fell as silent as any of the coyote shadows he was tracking. It was this same cold common sense and straight-line thinking which made him the most dangerous man of his time, and that now came into noise-less play after that first thunderous warning.

The next thing to do was get Virg out of town. With Wyatt away on the trail, his half-paralyzed older brother would become crippled prey to the waiting wolf pack. When Wyatt put it to him that way Virg couldn't argue. Nor did he. The only limit to his courage was the same icy sanity that marked the outer edge of Wyatt's. He only looked once at his brother, nodded slowly, told him he would get ready.

The plan called for Wyatt to accompany Virg as far as Tucson, where Crawley Dake was swearing in a special U.S. Marshal's posse to accompany Wyatt back to Tombstone. The first part of it went off slick as the seat of a horsehair couch. Or so they thought. They boarded the train in Benson at 2 in the afternoon, Wyatt scouting the platform and depot while Virg superintended the loading of Morg's corpse into the baggage car. The destination of the dead youth and his maimed brother was the Colton, California home of the senior Earps, sometime lately removed from the Missouri homestead birthplace of the boys.

The train left Benson on time, was rolling down on Tucson about dusk and on schedule.

That was as far as the slick part of it went.

Five miles east of the Pima County town, the emergency bellcords jangled, the brake-sand hit the rails ahead of the locked drivers, the four-coach train ground to a sudden, steaming standstill.

Wyatt had no more than time to duck swiftly away from his window and head for the car vestibule when the door curtains parted and Deputy Marshal Joe Evans, of Crawley Dake's office, stepped through them.

What he had to say to Wyatt took the shine off the horsehair settee, right now.

Frank Stilwell and Pete Spence were in Tucson. They had an unknown halfbreed with them and had been joined not an hour before by an old friend of Wyatt's—Ike Clanton. And more. The rustlers had received three telegrams from Tombstone during the day. Had sent two of their own in reply. That was all, Evans declared, that he had to report. Wyatt, he added, could take it from there.

It turned out Joe Evans was dead right. Wyatt not only *could* take it from there. *He did.*

In those days they didn't know what a dining car was. On the S. P.'s run west out of Benson your last chance to eat short of daylight was Tucson, where the train held up for a full hour while passengers and crew alike piled off and stocked up on vittles to carry them through the night.

Wyatt and Joe Evans stood guard outside the depot hash house while Virg ate. Soon as he had finished, they herded him back aboard his coach, Wyatt and the Tucson deputy then splitting up, the former to take his post on the car platform ahead of the coach, Evans watching from the one to its rear.

Nothing happened.

The few passengers stretched their legs up and down the depot platform in the gathering twilight, bought their Indian country trinkets from the stony-faced Pima and Papago women, finished their after-supper cigars, climbed back on the train and took their seats.

Presently, the engineer and the fireman walked across the switch siding and crawled up into the cab. Two short toots of the whistle broke the growing quiet. The S.P.'s Number Nine, westbound for Yuma, the Arizona line and Los Angeles, was ready to roll.

Preparing to swing down to the depot platform, Wyatt took a last look around. It was full dark now, the smoky yellow of the cars' oil lamps marking the squares of the coach windows against the unpainted wood of the station walls.

Suddenly, he saw something.

Or thought he did.

A man couldn't be sure in the flickering, uncertain light.

But over along the siding, yonder. Back of that little string of flatcars on the switch. Deep in the shadow of the trackside water tank.

Yes, there it was.

The dull bounce of lamplight off of worn metal. Smoke-blued, slender, scabbard-worn metal. Gun barrels! Two, three—no, by God—four of them!

The old Parker started for his shoulder, automatic as the jump of cheekflesh to a slap in the face. But in the dark he had forgotten the pipe of the car platform's guard rail. The Parker's barrels glanced off the rusted metal, ringing the night with the sound of steel on iron—and the four shadows melted away from the flatcars and were gone.

He leaped over the handrail, hitting the depot platform on the crouching run. A figure loomed in the darkness. The Parker snapped onto it. Dropped back away. It was only a halfbreed peon, scuttling around the corner of the station. He let him go, plunged on down the siding toward the end of the string of flatcars.

It was later discovered this "peon" was the fourth member of the rustler bunch that was in Tucson to get Wyatt and his wounded brother. He was dressed as an Indian laborer though he was a white man, and was for sure the "unknown halfbreed" reported seen with Spence, Stilwell and Ike Clanton.

But if Wyatt had missed the minnow, he landed the lunker.

He jumped him halfway down toward Number Nine's chuffing engine, ran him toward the head of the train,

175

shouting at him to halt. He was not ten feet behind him when he cut across the tracks, full into the beam of the engine's headlamp. "One more step and you get it in the back!" he yelled at him, and grounded the Parker's butt on his hip with the warning. The fugitive stopped dead, whirled defiantly, stood at bay and blinking in the glare of the oily light. It was Frank Stilwell.

He could see Wyatt only as a black shape against the engine's beam. He stepped back toward him, moving slow, peering into the glare, both hands low and brushing the Colt handles in his twin holsters.

When he was four feet from Wyatt, still squinting to see who it was, he lunged for the Parker's barrels, catching them by the muzzle ends, jumping his whole strength into forcing them upwards. The movement brought him face-close to Wyatt.

It had been many times remarked how singular-alike was Wyatt to his dead younger brother. It must have been that, coupled with the bad, smoky light of the headlamp, for there is no other explanation for the strange, last word that Frank Stilwell spoke.

Eyes wide, desperate grip tightening on the Parker's barrels, he gasped it out, face a sudden fishbelly white even in the yellow stain of the engine's light.

"Morg . . .!"

His only answer was the twisting heave of Wyatt's shoulders, forcing the shotgun's muzzle down and into his belly, just under the heart. The first barrel tore his chest away, driving him two steps back and halfway around. In the time it took him to fall halfway out of the headlamp's narrow arc, Wyatt gave him the second barrel. He was dead before his slack body bounced off the gravel of the roadbed.

Wyatt stood over him, looking down, his own dark thoughts drifting upward into the winter night along with the slow curl of the black-powder gun smoke from the Parker's barrels. He had caught and killed the first of Morgan's murderers. But he had stepped beyond the limits of his, or any man's law, in doing it.

Vengeance is mine sayeth the Lord—*and Wyatt Earp!*

From this moment forward, he could expect no mercy from friend or foe.

176

30

Wyatt's dark forecast flowered the same way it had been seeded—in violence.

No town likes to have another's gang-killings carried out in front of its Union Depot. Tucson was not Tombstone. It took immediate steps to let the western world know it.

Neither was the Tucson *Star* the Tombstone *Epitaph*. Pima County's leading paper plastered the story of the Stilwell slaying across page one. It named it murder and demanded instant apprehension of the guilty party. This, however, was on the morning after the killing. Long before that time, Wyatt was far gone from Pima County.

For the better part of the first hour following the departure of Virg's train, he hunted the vicinity of the depot and its spur trackage with Joe Evans. They flushed no further birds from the rustler covey and when, at the end of the time, Crawley Dake's three special deputies showed up to report the growing temper of the town and to advise him to clear out, Wyatt gave up the hunt. With Crawley's men, Texas Jack Vermilion, Sherman McMasters and Turkey Creek Jack Johnson, he flagged down the eastbound, eight o'clock freight, boarded its caboose and was across the Pima County line before Tucson had identified the body of the outlaw celebrity sprawled in the gravel of its main line right-of-way.

Wyatt had always said that he held three good friends to be easy worth a hundred enemies. As he holed up in the Cosmopolitan on his return from killing Stilwell, he knew that now, if ever, a man was going to find out who those three friends might be.

Search his mind as he would, however, he could think of but two of them, Lilly Belloit always excepted: Mayor John Clum, who was three thousand miles away in Washington, D. C., and Marshal Crawley P. Dake, who was at hand but had already stretched the limits of his office in furnishing Wyatt the special U. S. deputies and the warrants they held for Morg's murderers.

But there *was* a third friend—one he had long forgotten —ex-Fargo shotgun rider, Bob Paul.

He got the reminder from one of the handful of lesser Tombstone lights that had never wavered in their backing of him: Jake Shagrew, night operator for Western Union and longtime Safety Committee vigilante. He knew, the minute he opened the hotel room door and saw Jake standing there in the hall, that all hell was due to barrel out of Chute Four. And likely bust its cinch on the way. Any message of less than life and death delivery weight would have been brought by Chico Gutierrez.

"Thought you'd ought to see it first, Marshal," shrugged Jake, and handed him the telegram.

Jake Shagrew had never thought righter. Wyatt's eyes narrowed.

> J. C. BEHAN
> TOMBSTONE, COCHISE COUNTY:
> GOT WARRANT FOR MURDER HERE.
> ARREST ANY TIME. DON'T LET
> HIM GET BY YOU NOW.
>
> C

He handed the yellow paper back to Jake.

"Ike?" he asked, watching him.

"Could be." Jake watched him back.

"Well?" rasped Wyatt.

"Well," said the night operator slowly, "seems I did take a little company time asking the Tucson operator how was his wife—and a few other things over there."

"Such as?" snapped Wyatt.

Shagrew gave it to him then. All of it.

The Pima County Sheriff had been out of town when Wyatt downed Frank Stilwell. During his absence, nobody came forward to identify the outlaw's killer. But when he'd returned the following noon, a citizen who knew Wyatt well enough to call him even in the pitch-dark had stepped up to put the finger on "poor Frank's murderer." He had named Wyatt Earp, leaving the Pima sheriff no choice but to issue a warrant for the latter's arrest. The sender of the telegram announcing that warrant to Behan might sign himself "C" till Old Nick froze his nose—he was still Ike Clanton.

Oh, and one little thing more.

The Pima sheriff had dropped around to the Tucson

178

telegraph office and suggested to the operator that any messages going through to Johnny Behan be also shown to the deputy U. S. marshal in Tombstone, as a matter of routine law enforcement co-operation. He hadn't said to show it to Wyatt first. Nor had he needed to. He knew who was night operator in Tombstone.

Wyatt took the information with his usual slow nod. All that remained was for a man to recall who had got to be Pima County Sheriff since riding shotgun for Wyatt and Wells Fargo back in '81. When he'd done that he knew where his third friend was, and *who* he was.

He was in Tucson and his name was Bob Paul.

Wyatt also knew that he was in real trouble, three friends or no three friends. While Jake Shagrew stood quietly by, his mind twisted and turned with every pull of the big hand on the straw-yellow mustache. When hand and mind had made their last turn and final twist, he knew what he had to do.

This was the warrant Behan had been waiting for.

There would be no beating this one.

Wyatt could not refuse to answer it, for any peace officer who kills a man in the line of his job has got, legally, to answer for that killing. But to this killing there was no legal answer. At the same time, to surrender would mean a long trial in Pima County and when it was over, win, lose or draw for Wyatt, Morg's killers would have gotten clean away.

One thing a man didn't have to guess about.

He had to get out of Tombstone and stay out of it. Every hour he now remained was only raising the local odds on a bullet in the back for the last of the Earps. And raising them to the point where no man, not Wyatt nor any other, could beat them. Bob Paul's grudging warrant was a gilt-edge hunting license for Johnny Behan and his rustler posse. It opened the season on deputy U. S. marshals in Tombstone and at last put the law behind the deadly guns of such as Curly Bill Brocius and John Ringo.

Wyatt had no idea of hiding in the city brush until they got ahold of that warrant from Bob Paul and walked him out and blasted him down like they had Virg and Morg. But the wide open country of Cochise County was something else again. Out there, a man could see a long ways. Out there, they would have to come to him. And, out there, a man might meet them a little better than halfways when they did come.

But even that deep-ditch last stand depended on one thing—the friendship of Bob Paul.

Gambler that he always was, Wyatt now put his last dollar on the Pima County Sheriff.

"Jake!" he growled suddenly. "Here's what you do. You wire Bob that I'll surrender to *him,* any time. Tell him I reckon we both understand he won't just exactly kill his horse rushing that Tucson warrant over here. You got that?"

"I got it," said Jake. "How about this wire for Johnny Behan? I got to deliver it."

The grin Wyatt gave him took all the heat sudden out of that stuffy hotel room. "Sure, Jake, you deliver it. Only don't sprint about it, see? A man your age shouldn't be running around town these cold nights. She's a late spring and you might take a bad chill. Just walk, Jake, just walk."

"By damn, you're right, Marshal. Way I've bin feeling of late, I reckon it'll take me all of twenty minutes to totter over to the Frémont jail."

"That ought to cut it about right," nodded Wyatt. "I'm beholden to you, old horse."

"Sure, Marshal," said Jake Shagrew, and backed awkwardly out the door. When he had closed it and turned away down the dim-lit hall, he had had his last look at the lion of Tombstone. He never saw Wyatt Earp again.

It was twenty minutes of ten when Jake Shagrew left the Cosmopolitan Hotel that night of March 21st. It was nearly a quarter after ten before Wyatt's three deputies rounded up the fifth member of their little posse and got him back to Wyatt's room.

Doc was drunk as usual. Which just suited Wyatt.

"Sober," he always used to say of Holliday, "Doc was a poor sight. His hands shook, he coughed all the time, and was sicker and grouchier and of less use than a potted Apache buck. Properly drunk, he was steady as an old cutting horse, pleasant and gracious as a Confederate colonel, dangerous as a stepped-on diamondback. Taken with just the right amount of bourbon in him," he never failed to add, with that dry grin of his, "Doc would go bear-hunting with a buggy whip."

His pleasure at seeing Doc Holliday satisfactorily primed was short-spanned. Colonel Herring broke into the room right on the Georgia gunman's boot heels.

"Wyatt, you're trapped. Johnny Behan and Dave Neagle are down in the lobby. Outside in the street they've got at least ten deputies."

"They bother our horses yet?" asked Wyatt quickly.

"No," said Herring, "the horses are at the rail, out front. They're all saddled and set to go like you ordered."

Wyatt looked around at his deputies.

"Well, boys?"

Vermilion, McMasters and Johnson were not just old federal officers; they were, each in his own professional right, gunmen of reputation. None of them opened his mouth. Each, in turn, just bobbed his head a little. Wyatt never even looked at Doc. There was no need to.

"Colonel," he said to Herring, "you'd best wait up here until this is over."

"Not much!" the Safety Committee leader exclaimed. "I mean to see this, by thunder!"

Whatever it was Colonel Herring had hoped to see, it was for sure not what he did see.

Wyatt and his men came down the lobby stairs, descending slow and watchful, Wyatt in front, the four others flanking him. All of them had on two beltguns and all of them, save Doc, who never favored the weapon by choice, carried double-barreled shotguns.

It went so quick and simple it was all over before the regular guests in the lobby had time to look up from their *Nuggets* or *Epitaphs*.

As Wyatt hit the lobby floor, Behan moved nervously up to him and said, "Wyatt, I want to see you."

Wyatt, about as nervous as a rattlesnake in a gopher hole, stopped moving. He looked at Behan a long three seconds, nodded easily. "Johnny, someday you'll see me *once too often*."

The Cochise sheriff got a mite pale. He stepped back out of the way, deciding right then his warrant could wait.

Outside, Wyatt halted his little posse and stared at the sheriff's deputies. "If you gentlemen are waiting to see me," he announced politely, "you can quit waiting. *I'm here*."

Like master, like men. Not a deputy moved. Not a one of them but what felt, like Johnny Behan before him, that he could well afford to go right on waiting. Wyatt turned away form them, Doc and the others following him. They climbed on their horses, Wyatt reining Big Red back toward Behan's patient boys.

"Don't look over my shoulder," he advised. "It makes me nervous."

Wyatt went only far enough into the Dragoons to be reasonably safe from immediate pursuit. There, he called a halt until daylight. This was not going to be any rush job like the first visit to the Sulphur Springs ranch. He was going to take his time, start with the rustler hideout, work south from there, combing every inch of Cochise County in his last search for Morg's killers.

With dawn they rode on, reaching the ranch about noon. Again, the only bird remaining in the bush was Indian Charlie Cruz. This time, however, the halfbreed "flushed," making for his ready-saddled horse on the run. McMasters creased him with a snapshot of his Winchester, knocking him sprawling in the ranch yard. He wasn't bad hurt and Wyatt soon had him talking.

Cruz added some big names to the list already in Wyatt's mind. In addition to Spence, Stilwell and himself, Morg's ambush party had included Ike Clanton, Billy Claiborne, Curly Bill and John Ringo. Of the seven, though, only five had been in on the actual kill, Claiborne and Ike having acted as floating spotters along the front side of Allen Street, hence had not been close enough to the shooting to be considered any real part of it. As to the rest, the "big five," Curly and Stilwell had been the trigger men. Cruz and Pete Spence had been posted as lookouts back and front of Campbell & Hatch's. Ringo had held the horses in the Frémont Street alley.

As of right then, Cruz didn't know where any of the others were but thought they had all gone back into Tombstone the night before. There had been some talk between Ringo and Curly about posseing up for Johnny Behan to help hunt down Wyatt. Whether that was just big talk, or if they had actually meant it, the halfbreed couldn't, or wouldn't, say.

Satisfied the Indian cowboy didn't know much more and near satisfied he'd held only a dumb hand in the whole deal, Wyatt was about to turn him loose when a last dark thought struck him. It's the sort of thing a man doesn't like to put down but when you're telling about somebody like Wyatt and mean to be straight about it, you don't hold any of the bad cards back.

"Hold on a minute," Wyatt now said, stepping again toward the breed. "Neither of my brothers nor me ever harmed *you,* did we?"

"No," muttered the Indian, suddenly and unaccountably afraid, "you never did."

"Then what made you want to help kill my brother?"

Wyatt asked it very softly. The breed, sensing he was about to be let go, shook off his fear and opened up a little. "Well," he shrugged quickly, "Curly Bill, Frank Stilwell, Spence and Ringo and them boys, they're my friends. They said we'd all make money if you Earps was out of the way, and Curly—he give me twenty-five dollars right then."

"Twenty-five dollars?" said Wyatt, softer still. "What for?"

"Well, for shooting anybody that made a pass to cut in while him and Frank killed you Earps. That was the way Curly put it, near as I can recollect."

Twenty-five lousy dollars! The cold shock of it leaped through Wyatt's mind. The miserable price of a man's life. A priceless man like Morgan Earp.

Something happened to Wyatt then. The look that came into his eyes was frightening to see. He turned slowly to his posse, his back to Cruz, his voice whisper-hard.

"I'm going to kill him," he said to Sherm McMasters. "He's got two guns on. You tell him you'll count to three, and that I won't draw until after *tres.* He's to go ahead and pull any time he's a mind to. If he beats me, he's to go scot-free. Tell him in Spanish so there'll be no mistake."

Wyatt spoke some gutter Spanish, like most south-westerners, but McMasters rattled the tongue off like a native. He nodded and turned to the anxious halfbreed, repeating Wyatt's offer.

Cruz cried out as though he'd been struck in the face with a bull whip. "Wait, wait!" he pleaded, starting toward Wyatt. "I didn't do nothing. I only . . ."

"Uno!" said McMasters.

"No, no!" yelled Cruz. *"Por Dios!"*

"You mean *dos*!" nodded Sherm McMasters.

183

The halfbreed made a sound in his throat, a squealing, high sound like a terrified mongrel dog. He lunged toward Wyatt, pawing wildly for both his guns at once.

"Tres!" hissed MacMasters. And Wyatt drew and shot.

Cruz's guns were out of their holsters and up and leveled, when the single .44 smashed through his forehead.

They left him where he went down, crumpled in the churned-up dirt under the hoofs of his saddled pony. It was significant of a time when the law rode on a peace officer's hip and not in the fuzzy minds of twelve good men and true, that none of the deputies looked back nor thought Indian Charlie Cruz had got anything less than a fair trial by a jury of his certain peers.

The results of that trial, if not its methods, were beyond legal argument.

The second of Morgan Earp's murderers was dead.

And his executioner was riding only hours behind the remaining three of the original five.

31 ☆

Before leaving for the outlaw ranch, Wyatt had set up a rendezvous with Colonel Herring. This was the abandoned No. 1 shaft of the old Lucky Cuss strike. They reached the hideout about dusk, unsaddled and had a cold supper of the beef and tortillas they'd thrown in their saddlebags on starting out. Along about nine o'clock, Herring's contact man showed up. He was Jack Craker, an undercover Wells Fargo agent, little known in Tombstone and a safe man to use as a go-between.

Craker had some news that didn't settle that cold beef in their bellies worth a hoot.

Cruz had been right. Curly Bill, Ringo and the lot of the Sulphur Springs bunch had indeed come to town. And, to the bad surprise of even Behan's stoutest friends, had been at once deputized by the Cochise sheriff to make up the posse that was to hunt Wyatt down. They had split into two outfits; one under Curly Bill, to comb the west side of the San Pedro; the other under John Ringo, to search the east flank of the valley. Both posses had left town late that same afternoon, with Behan, after his crafty way, finding some last-minute important business to keep him from accompanying either bunch.

"What about that warrant?" snapped Wyatt impatiently. "Did Bob Paul bring it over from Tucson yet?"

"No," said Craker, "Paul ain't come over, so far. But Colonel Herring's been in touch with him and he told the Colonel to let you know he couldn't stall it much longer."

"Good," grunted Wyatt. "It sort of makes it interesting."

"You mean it's been dull up to now?" drawled Sherm McMasters, the cynic of Wyatt's little posse.

"I mean Johnny Behan's bit off a pretty big chunk, even for him. Without Bob Paul shows up with that warrant, or without he wires Behan permission to push it, it amounts to Johnny ordering a man he's got no legal jurisdiction over shot on sight. That's me, boys, and I say that makes it interesting."

"I allow you're right," agreed Texas Jack Vermilion. "Especially when you consider that we've got legitimate federal warrants for five of those sons-of-bitches who are posse-ed up on our tails this minute."

"Yeah," added Turkey Creek Johnson dourly, "and more so, when you figure they ain't got no legal paper to serve on us past the powder wads in their Winchesters."

"Of those five warrants," said Wyatt, thinking aloud, and back to what Vermilion had said, "there's three I'll serve if I have to stay in the brush the rest of my natural life."

Doc Holliday knew the five names Wyatt had marked in his mind way back at the time of Spence's wife testifying at Morg's inquest. He also knew that two of those five were already crossed off for keeps. "Well," he croaked, frog's voice made reedier still by the raw spring night, "who gets the short straw this time, Wyatt? Curly? Spence? The kid?"

"We'll take them in order," answered Wyatt thoughtfully.

"Which is . . . ?" asked Sherm McMasters.

Wyatt stood up. He settled his Colts in their holsters, and picked up the Parker from its leaning place against a pile of shoring timbers.

"Curly Bill," was what he said. And went off through the dark toward Big Red.

Craker had said that Brocius's posse had set out for the

Babocomari section of the Whetstones, meaning to make its field camp at Iron Springs. That's Mescal Springs on today's maps but it was Iron Springs when Wyatt and his U. S. deputies rode down on them the late afternoon of that March 23rd in '82.

The day had turned off a scorcher. They had ridden thirty-five miles since sunup. Their horses were sweat-caked and heads down with the daylong heat. They, themselves, were nerve-weary and dangerously off their ordinary sharpness. They hadn't seen a pony track all day and a preliminary look at the grove around the springs from up on a spur of the Whetstones to the north, had shown not so much as a horsefly moving down there. Vermilion, McMasters and Johnson were practically asleep in their saddles. Even Doc, that usually peerless watchdog, was half-drowsed-off with the sunblaze monotony of the long ride.

Only Wyatt was awake.

Two hundred yards from the grove, he waved his followers to a halt, again studying the silent trees and naked rocks of the spring. It was too quiet up there. A man didn't like things that still. Yet they had no choice. The horses had been ten hours without a drink and the next water was twenty miles north.

"Get down and watch the back trail, Doc," he said at last. "The rest of us will go on up."

"She's watched," nodded Doc. "See you watch yourselves."

They went on then, another hundred yards. Still the silence held. At fifty yards Wyatt got off Big Red, motioned the others to slow down and hang back.

He looped Red's reins over his left forearm, leaving both hands free with the Parker. He took a last look at the grove and at the brushy gully flanking it on the Whetstone side. He could not get the smell of trouble out of his nose. Yet he went on, hunting-cat-slow now, feeling for each advancing foot placement, not looking down and never taking his pale blue eyes off the grove or the gully brush.

He was into the trees, then, close enough to see the splash and shimmer of the spring water in its shallow granite basin. Still, nothing. He paused uncertainly. Started another careful step forward.

That was it.

The man on his right, farthest away from him, came up

186

from back of a belly-high boulder, winging away with his Winchester. It was Pete Spence.

The one on his left, no more than six long strides away, rose up out of the gully brush with a double-barreled shotgun at his shoulder and blasting. This one was Curly Bill Brocius!

Pete Spence was forgotten. The sudden rush and stumble of other rustler forms springing up through the trees behind Curly was ignored. Wyatt stood like a rock, feeling the whistle and stab of Curly's charges cut through his coat and vest, bringing their murderous pellets within the last inch of tearing him apart—and yet, miraculously, missing him!

He took his time, then. The calculating, short, impossibly tiny segment of time that only the master gunman understands, or can comprehend, as any least part of a piece of time at all.

Both of the Parker's buckloads, nine chilled shot to the charge, took Curly Bill in the chest. He flopped and went down like a rag doll, the whole left side of his rib-cage, with half the heart and lung beneath it, pulverized and blown away.

Spence had fired three times, all wild misses. Now, with Curly Bill dead before he was down, and Wyatt swinging on him with his Colts, Pete broke and ran.

Wyatt flashed three snap shots from the hip. He heard him yell, knew he had hit him. At the same time, he emptied the rest of the loads in both revolvers at the other rustlers, now dodging for better cover throughout the grove. He heard one more agonized yell, figured he'd winged another of them by pure chance.

The whole thing, so far, had taken less than thirty seconds. The unexpected, bloody end of their leader had been the shock that stampeded Spence and the others, making Wyatt's momentary survival possible. But there were seven men back in those trees, not counting Pete, and none of them were green hands. They got over their initial jolt as Wyatt, all guns empty and knowing he was a fine, fat target caught in the wide open, wheeled and ran for Big Red. By the time he grabbed and boarded the nervous gelding, the Colt and Winchester fire was coming out of that grove thick as sleet in a late spring snowstorm.

Wyatt was nicked once; his horse twice. His deputies,

mounted when the fight started, and too old a bunch of ambushers to try and fire back at dismounted men from horseback, had scattered for the rocks. Doc, strictly a poker-table-range pistol man, had seen no chance to snap a shot from his position, and was now fighting his excited horse, trying to board him and come up to Wyatt's aid.

It was high time to break off the Battle of Iron Springs.

Sliding Big Red in among the rocks, Wyatt shouted the order to "crawl horse and get the hell out!" Doc and the others objected immediately, wanting to "stay and smoke the sons-of-bitches out!" But Wyatt knew a bad thing when it was looking him straight in the face.

There was no way in the world to get at the rustlers now. They held the only water hole for miles around, and they held it under eight hidden Winchesters. "Nothing doing!" he barked at Doc. "We're all alone here. They'll have reinforcements coming along any time. Get aboard your horses."

"Wyatt's right!" yelled Sherm McMasters, ducking free of his granite pile and running for his grazing pony. "Quit when you're ahead, Doc!"

"Yeah, pile out while the piling's good!" voted Texas Jack, and legged it for his own mount.

So pile out they did, Wyatt leading the full gallop retreat, the others pounding hard on Big Red's digging heels, the rustlers lobbing a few long rifle shots to sign and seal it, official.

In that they had been driven off from the spring and had to leave the field without serving a one of their warrants, at least on a live rustler, you could call it a defeat for the federal posse.

Wyatt knew better.

He had lost a battle, only. And damn near won his war doing it.

Curly Bill Brocius was dead.

It was like breaking the back of a snake.

The gang might still thrash around and strike out blind for a short spell. But without Curly it would crawl off and die, come sunset. Riding now, eat across the long shadows of the San Pedro, his strange light eyes hard-set and colorless as the bleached granite spine of the Whetstones, Wyatt Earp could see that last sunset coming swiftly down.

32

Wyatt's look into that sunset of the 23rd had been a good one. The end came so quick now, and with such a sudden flood of outside forces, that none of the local bunch got a good idea of what had really hit them until the dust cleared away weeks later.

It began by looking bad for Wyatt.

Pima sheriff, Bob Paul, having delayed as long as the safety of his job would let him, climbed down off the Benson stage in Tombstone just after seven o'clock the evening of the 23rd. By 7:30 Johnny Behan had the last thing he thought he needed to nail Wyatt, the long-awaited Pima County warrant for the murder of Frank Stilwell. At 7:45, Ringo and his posse rode in to report a blank on their sweep of the east valley. Worn down and heat-wilted as him and his men were, the news of that Pima County warrant put the starch back into them, stiff as a cemetery headboard. "We've got him!" crowed Ringo. "By God, this time we've got the bastard!"

"Yes," said Johnny Behan, "we sure have. When Brocius and his boys get back, we'll make up one big posse and take out soon as there's light tomorrow."

"He can't get away!" grinned Ringo, dark face flushing excitedly. "Sooner or later he's got to come in for food and fresh horses!"

Sheriff Bob Paul, forgotten in the rush, had been standing quietly watching them. His terse question now broke over Ringo's head, to reach Behan. *"Brocius?"* he asked softly. "You mean *Curly Bill* Brocius?"

Johnny Behan was riding his optimism hard and heavy. "You know any other Brocius?" he demanded belligerently.

"You mean to say you deputized that outlaw?" continued Paul quietly. "That he's legal part and parcel of your regular posse?"

"Certainly. Not only him but John Ringo, here, as well!"

"Ringo! Are you crazy, Behan?"

"Lookit here, Bob Paul! I'm running a law office, not a lonely hearts club. When I've got to go out after killers like Wyatt, I don't mean to do it with any of these run-down Citizen's Safety Committee outfits from around here. You understand?"

"And you're actually expecting me to ride with a posse like *that?*"

"Ride, or don't ride!" triumphed Behan. "We don't need you. We got all we need, or want, right here!" Defiantly, he slapped his vest pocket and the Pima County warrant Paul had given him.

Bob Paul looked around the room, first at Johnny Behan and his big scowl, then at Johnny Ringo and his wild grin. Last, he looked at the hard-eyed riders ranked around the office walls behind them.

"Likely I'll be going then," he nodded softly. "For any fool can plainly see you've caught and killed your man already."

It was five minutes to eight, as he said it and turned away.

He had just reached the door, when it burst open to admit Pete Spence. Pete was white-faced, showing the yellows of his eyes, half-staggering with exhaustion. He didn't see Bob Paul, who stepped quickly behind the door, and didn't heed Behan's warning wave to look behind him.

"They got Curly!" he blurted. "Goddamn near tore him in two. Phin Clanton's got a slug in his leg and I got this one in my arm, here. I rode my hoss dead getting back. Oh Jesus, boys, you never seen . . ."

"Shut your idiot mouth!" snarled Ringo. "Slow down, make sense. *Who* got Curly?"

"Wyatt, fer Christ's sake! Him and that son-of-a-bitching shotgun of his. Both barrels. So mortal close the shot-wads are still sticking in him. Oh Jesus, it was bad, kid. Terrible bad!"

"Curly's dead . . ."

Johnny Behan barely breathed it. The shock of it was too much to soak up. It stunned him, making him forget Bob Paul was there, or anything else.

"Dead!" Pete was still seeing it, six hours and forty miles after. "God! I never see a man get it so messy. Listen, Johnny!" His voice rose near as high as a woman's with the naked fear in it. "You've got to protect me! I'm done with hunting him. I ain't going out no more, you

190

hear? Gimme a cell, anything, fer Christ's sake! Just so's he can't get at me like he done Curly!"

"All right, all right!" snapped Behan. "I'll lock you up for the time, or whatever you say. Only just leave off your infernal bellowing for five seconds. We've got to think, man! We've a hell of a site more to worry about than you, Pete."

"All I want is protection!" Pete began his desperate plea again, but this time it wasn't Ringo or Johnny Behan that cut him off. It was Sheriff Bob Paul of Pima County.

"It's what you want, my friend," he said, stepping quietly up behind him, "it's what you'll get. You're under arrest, Pete."

"Wait a minute!" Behan was on his feet with the challenge. Putting Spence safe away in the Frémont jail where he could be turned loose next day, and letting Bob Paul have him to tote off to Tucson, were two mighty different colored cayuses. Pete knew way too much, and was way too scared of what he knew. "Just hold up now, Bob. He's already give himself up to me. What's the idea?"

"The idea," said Bob Paul, "is protection. The boy wants it, he's going to get it. About three years of it. In the territorial pen at Yuma!"

"*Yuma!*" gasped Behan, unbelievingly.

"As long as we're playing warrants," nodded Paul, "try this one on for size." He threw the document on Behan's desk, eyeing him flatly.

"What is it?" said the Cochise sheriff weakly, not offering to reach for it.

"It's *federal issue*," answered the other officer. "For the murder of Morgan Earp. Good in any county in Arizona. And good," he added, quoting softly, "'for not more than three nor less than two years,' in Yuma or any other federal penitentiary."

Jerking his head at Spence, he finished abruptly.

"Lock him up, Johnny. And see that he's still here when I come after him." Turning to go, he had one last word. It was for Ringo.

"Sorry I've got no warrant for you, kid. But I reckon the one Wyatt's got will do."

"What the hell you mean?" snapped Ringo excitedly. "He ain't got no warrant for me!"

"No?" said Bob Paul quietly. "I think he has. The same one he served on Curly Bill."

Old-hand lawman that he was, the Pima sheriff didn't go too far too fast. Fact is, he went only across Frémont Street to where the shadows were good and thick inside the O.K. Corral fence. He stayed there for half an hour watching the jail office. Well before the time was up, things began to happen.

Not ten minutes after he'd left Behan and the others, a rider came tearing down Frémont from the south. He piled off his horse and ran inside.

It was a frost-clear night, letting a man see and hear perfect. First, Bob Paul saw and heard that the newcomer's horse had been used up. The flank steam clouded up off him into the March moonlight. His blowing heaves to get his wind back carried across to the corral loud and heavy.

Then it was Ringo and his posse men coming out into Frémont. And Behan following them, to stand in the jail doorway. There was a lot of commotion while the men scrambled for their horses. The Cochise sheriff had to raise his voice to be heard over that commotion, and Ringo had to do the same to be heard back.

"I still say you'd ought to wait for daylight." It was Behan, worrying out loud. "Providing they *are* holed up out there where Judd says, they'll not leave before first light. Ike and Phin and the others of Curly's bunch will be along shortly. You'll need every man."

"I'm running this show now!" Ringo was defiant, his quick, crazy laugh ringing the night air. "This time we do it my way. Like I told you, we'll hole up out at Kennedy's ranch till midnight. You can send Ike or Phin, or any of the others that come in, out there to join us. But we go on in, whether they show or not."

"Damn it, kid, he can't get away. Take it easy. Why not wait up, like I say?"

"You bet he can't get away, brother! By God, I know that Lucky Cuss diggin's. It's a perfect trap and I ain't waiting around to spring it. All *you* got to do is see nobody leaves town after we do, to tip him off."

"All right." Behan's decision was made, you could tell that by the way he said it. "You and the boys go along. I'll guarantee nobody from here will beat you out there.

192

Now, for God's sake, kid, clean it up for keeps this time!"

Ringo's only answer was another of the cracked, quick laughs. As he galloped his posse off up Frémont Bob Paul let go the breath he'd been holding the better part of a full minute.

Damn the last-end luck!

A man knew that Behan had the men to make good his promise to seal off the town. In the past twenty-four hours he'd arrested five different Earp supporters trying to get out of Tombstone and into touch with Wyatt in the field. In a final-hour drive like this one, where they evidently knew exactly where Wyatt was hiding, the Cochise sheriff would stop at nothing to make sure Ringo and his deputized rustlers got the marshal. And, once they had him, he would never live to share that Frémont Street cell block with Pete Spence.

Worse than that, only Bob Paul knew how "final" was the hour for Behan and his outlaw bunch that late March night. Before leaving Tucson, he had gotten new territorial Governor, F. A. Tritle, just appointed by President Chester A. Arthur to take over from acting Governor Gosper, to agree to come to Tombstone secretly, so that he could see for himself how things went there. Tritle was due to arrive the 27th, only three days away, and Paul had his promise that should local conditions in his opinion warrant it, he would appeal to President Arthur to clamp down martial law in Cochise County. Now, damn the lousy luck, all that careful arranging was apt to be out the window.

But Bob Paul was not the one to sit in the shadows, crying over his luck, lousy or otherwise. Maybe a man couldn't leave Tombstone but there was no law against his getting the hell shut of the O.K. Corral in a tall hurry.

Ten minutes later, he was telling the whole story to Colonel William Herring.

Herring figured, as did he, that Johnny Behan could make good on his word to keep any man from leaving town to warn Wyatt. But the colonel was a lawyer by profession and had a devious mind. If a man couldn't do the job, how about a woman? Well, sir, yes, it so happened he did have a particular woman in mind. A real one, by the Lord Harry!

He caught up to Lilly in the wings of the Bird Cage,

193

just leaving the stage after her final turn. "Got to see you at once," he nodded. "Make it my shack. Five minutes," she nodded back.

She was there in five minutes, too, but what she had to say stopped the clock, right then. "I can't go!" she pleaded. "Good God, Colonel, Johnny Behan will have me watched harder than any *man* in town. It would be the worst thing we could do for Wyatt, to have me try to get through to him."

"Well," said Herring wearily, "I guess that licks us. If a man can't get through and a woman can't get through, who in the Lord's name can?"

When he said that, Lilly's mind brought up to a dead halt. She swung on him, her slant eyes blazing. *"A kid!"* she cried. "That's it, don't you see, Colonel!"

"See what, damn it all, ma'am!"

"Chico—Chico Gutierrez!"

"The Mexican lad? The little urchin who runs telegrams for Jake Shagrew?"

"Yes, oh yes! Listen, Colonel, it's the only way we can get through to Wyatt. The only way they'd never tumble to!"

"By the Lord, girl!" muttered Herring. "I *do* see. You've hit it square on! I'd better handle it, though. They'd likely spot you. You wait here."

"Better yet," said Lilly Belloit quickly, "I'll wait over at the Bird Cage. That'll cool them off on me. And, Colonel!" He held up his stride as she called after him. "Be sure Chico understands the message is for *El Mariscal*!"

Chico understood, all right. He also understood some other things, such as the spider web of back-country sheep trails old Joe Ruiz, his maternal grandfather, had taught him. It was one of these trails, faint and twisty and climbing up back of Goose Flats to follow the base of the Dragoons down toward the Lucky Cuss's shaft No. 1, along which his bare feet pattered now. As he ran, he wasn't fretting any about Sheriff Behan or his hard-boiled guards. Even a Mexican boy knew some things, such as that proud *gringo* deputies would never stoop to watch a despised *paisano* sheep trail.

It's too bad that last telegram to Wyatt wasn't saved. It would have been one for the book-writers. It covered three yellow sheets of Western Union message paper, top to bottom. It gave Wyatt every last detail he needed to know, from the make-up of Ringo's posse, and its time-table at Judd Kennedy's ranch, to the fact of Governor Tritle's coming visit and what that visit might likely mean to Johnny Behan's long rule of unlawfulness and disorder.

But, in raising that sudden hope, it also struck it dead. Tritle wasn't due until the 27th. Behan and his crew of rustler killers had seventy-two hours to run out their last hunt for Wyatt Earp.

The saving part of the whole bad mess was the time of night it happened to be when Sherm McMasters, on picket down the slope from the Lucky Cuss, threw down his Winchester on little Chico Gutierrez and advised him to try another sheep trail.

It was only a shade after eleven.

And it wasn't minutes past that shade before Wyatt had read his last message from Western Union's night office in Tombstone, had passed it on to Sherm and the others and turned to old Joe Ruiz's grandson.

He picked the boy up in his arms, held him there for a minute, close against him, patting him proud and awkward as a mother grizzly with a learning cub that had just done something the proper way. Then he set him back down, quick and stiff about it, and they both just stood there, the man no less embarrassed than the kid.

The others had finished the telegram, and Wyatt was suddenly conscious of them watching him and the boy.

He took him roughly by the hand, pulling him away and out of their sight and earshot, back of the pile of shoring timbers. There, he dug out his buckskin coin bag, made him take the whole of it.

"But, señor . . . !" the youngster started to protest in his broken English. Wyatt cut him off, sharp and quick.

"But nothing!" he growled back at him. "You're a good boy, Chico, and will make a good man. You take it and get out of here. Right now. The way you came. And fast! ¡Vaya!" he concluded in rasping Spanish. "Pronto. Ahora. ¿Comprende, amigo?"

Again, Chico understood. He stepped back, sweeping him the old, ragged-hat bow. "Hasta la proxima, señor." Then, softly, his small form fading into the darkness with it, "Vaya con Dios, Mariscal. . . ."

"Hasta la proxima, hombre," Wyatt called after him, and knew as he called it there would never be another "next time" for him and Chico Gutierrez.

33 ☆

It kept coming fast. When Ringo and his posse closed in on the Lucky Cuss next morning, all they got for their trouble was Doc Holliday's croaking advice that "Wyatt's not around. He said to tell you he's gone off to see a man about shooting a dog." Since it had only the one warrant for Wyatt, and none for his followers, the posse could only kick its horses out of there, cussing Johnny Behan for somehow letting word leak through of Ringo's approach.

For the next three days the kid and his gun-belted pack of outlaw bloodhounds ranged the Sulphur Springs and San Pedro valleys around the clock. All they had flushed out when they rode back into Tombstone on the 27th was half a dozen surprised coyotes and two or three indignant chaparral birds. But when they walked their blown horses down Allen Street, they gave Governor Tritle a first-hand good chance to observe for himself what kind of deputies Johnny Behan was using to run down a U. S. marshal whose main crime appeared to be that his own hip pocket was full of legal warrants for some of the same rustlers and stage-robbers the Cochise sheriff had sworn in to shoot him on sight.

Back in Prescott once more, Tritle wired President Arthur for permission to raise a company of territorial militia to invade Cochise County and hand it a dose of law and order that would settle it down for keeps. The President went him one better. He declared a state of revolt in southwest Arizona and asked Congress to clamp Cochise County under full martial law, using Colonel Biddle's federal troops from nearby Fort Grant to apply the clamp.

That did it.

But it didn't do it that day. Nor the next.

The simple announcement that Tritle had gone clean up to the President of the U. S. for help was enough to shake Johnny Behan into calling off his rustler posse and breaking it up overnight. But swift weeks passed before

Congress got around to making Tritle's threat official. Meantime, Wyatt still had to stay in the brush, neither him nor his friends inside town considering it anyways safe for him to show in Tombstone until the troops moved in, for the hard and good reason that Behan's outlaw posse, though officially scattered, was still hanging around town, waiting to see what would happen. And Behan himself, while crafty enough to act like he sudden didn't know any of his former pals, was still sheriff and still just praying and laying for the chance to grab Wyatt on that cussed Stilwell warrant.

March ran out, April went by, the uneasy spring started on into May. Wyatt was still in the brush. Behan and his warrant were still waiting for him to show in Tombstone.

It was Bob Paul, finally, who found the way out.

He contacted Wyatt early in May with the information he had arranged, through Tritle, for him to take sanctuary in Colorado. Governor Pitkin of that state had agreed to refuse extradition, should Behan seek it. It was the one, legal way Wyatt could beat the Cochise sheriff and the Stilwell murder warrant. There just wasn't any other.

Wyatt thought about it long and hard.

He paced the little prospector's shack over in the Chiricahuas where he was holed up, pulling and tugging at his drooping mustache for the better part of an hour. And all the while, Bob Paul kept putting the quiet pressure on him to go on and get out while he could.

In the end, he had to see it the Pima sheriff's way. No matter which slant of the Tombstone compass you took your bearing from, you had to see the whole sweep of the past months, not just your little personal part in them.

Curly Bill Brocius, the brains and body of the rustler gang, was dead. Johnny Behan was all through in Cochise County, could never hope to stay in office past the upcoming elections. Ike and Phin Clanton, Billy Claiborne, Frank Patterson and Pony Deal, the last remaining of the name-outlaw guns, had lately left Tombstone to cross into Old Sonora and seek the benefits of Mother Mexico's gentler climate. Pete Spence was on his way to Yuma Prison, was as sure out of the way as ever one of Wyatt's bullets could have put him. Of the original five of Morg's killers, only Johnny Ringo was yet at large.

That last is what did it, or at least it was the story Wyatt himself put forward long years after.

According to Paul, the kid was not only still at large, he was still actually in Tombstone. What more reason did a man need for taking Bob Paul's friendly advice to clear out while the clearing was good?

Well, maybe there was one more little reason. But it was one that would never be known by anybody but Wyatt Earp, and one he never admitted to, to a living soul, not even to himself. Before bringing up the fact that the kid was still around town, Bob Paul had mentioned the fact that somebody else *wasn't*. He had dropped it, casual-like, along with the general news of what had been going on in Tombstone since Wyatt had been in the brush. And he'd not noticed the quiet way Wyatt had winced when he'd dropped it.

Evvie Cushman had sold the Miner's Rest and left Tombstone for good. Nobody knew where she was bound nor why she had pulled out. Johnny Behan had spread it around that she'd told him she couldn't stomach any more of the senseless killings and brutal bloodshed brought on by the Earps, and was moving on to some more civilized camp where her kind might still be of use to decent men and where the law meant something more than first degree murder. But everybody figured Johnny was only trying to make some last-minute amends in his own busted-down fence and nobody rightly believed she'd told him any such thing.

As a matter of fact, she had, and as a matter of mining-camp history she went on and lived out her life pretty much as Behan told it around that she meant to, helping out the "decent" men and hating the ones like Wyatt in a dozen camps from Arizona to Alaska, and winding up, as everybody knows, a famous part of the big Klondike rush sixteen years later. But as of the hard-eyed minutes of Bob Paul's last talk with Wyatt, no man then alive could know these things, and all Wyatt could do was fight down the way his heart sank when Bob mentioned Evvie's leaving on account of him, and then to go ahead and use Ringo as a trumped-up reason for getting out himself.

There had been some long and bad-silent seconds while he turned all this in his mind, but now Wyatt wheeled abruptly on the Pima sheriff and threw in his cards.

"All right, old pardner, I'll do it. I'll go on up to Colorado like you say. I got one little matter to clear up before I do, however. That's no concern of anybody's but mine, though. Meanwhile, you can do me a last favor if you're a mind to."

"You got only to name it, Wyatt, you know that."

"I know it, Bob. And thanks . . ."

It was all he ever said of gratitude to Bob Paul. Or ever needed to. It was a day and time when six words from certain men were worth a lawbookful of windy depositions from others.

"You tell Lilly Belloit I'll be by to see her on my way out, tonight, soon as the town's quiet. Say, along after midnight sometime."

"I wouldn't do that, Wyatt." Paul shook his head with the quick, honest frown. "It's like to mean your life, man. Remember Ringo."

Wyatt shook his own head, looking past him, his pale eyes seeing through and beyond him and far away.

"I'm remembering him," he said. Then, nodding softly, "You tell Lilly like I said, Bob. I'll be there. . . ."

And he was there.

The late moon was in its one o'clock cradle over the Whetstones when Lilly heard the quick, familiar sound of his step outside. She listened breathlessly as he led Big Red into the empty lean-to behind the shack, eased its creaking door shut, came sliding along the cabin's east side and around its corner to the swiftly opened door.

"Wyatt, oh Wyatt . . . !"

He held her there in the darkness a long time, neither of them trying to say what didn't need any saying. He kissed her hair, her tear-wet cheek, and, finally, the desperate, clinging softness of her lips.

He stood back then, and Lilly knew as he did what that kiss had meant to him. And what it had to mean to her. It was the way his kind said good-bye to hers. Not with cold words or hot promises. But in the only simple, honest way they knew. With a soft, tender kiss, and making all the vows they ever would make, just with the way that kiss was given and with the way it was taken.

"Boy," she whispered huskily, "be good to yourself. It's all I ask. Believe that—for always!"

"I'll believe it, Lilly," he said awkwardly. "And I'll believe it for always. Maybe some day, Lilly girl—somehow —some place—I don't know . . ."

"Sure, Wyatt," she murmured. "Someday, boy. Someday . . ." She broke on it, the quick catch of the sob tearing at his heart. But when she spoke again, her voice was steady, almost calm-like.

"Good-bye, Wyatt."

He stepped through the darkness, taking her frail form once more in his great, clumsy arms. The silence again. Long and tense and without words. But this time when he broke away, there was no kiss. No soft good-bye. No tears.

The tears came only after the last sound of him and of his sorrel gelding had faded away from the little shack behind the Bird Cage Theatre. The hours and the bitterness and the heartbreak of those tears were still there when daylight came creeping gray and dirty along the deserted wheel ruts of Toughnut Street.

Lilly Belloit never saw Wyatt Earp again.

Nor did Tombstone.

When the murk of that early May night closed behind the remembered, ramrod straightness of his tall figure, the last of the great lawmen was gone.

He came no more to Cochise County.

Nor again to Allen Street.

They found Johnny Ringo, or the man they said was him, sitting at the base of a scrub cedar near Turkey Creek in the foothills of the Chiricahuas. He was sitting very quiet, like a man will with a bullet hole in his temple and the back of his head blown off.

Apparently he had been carried to the spot and propped carefully up the way they found him.

That way can still be read in the records of the Cochise County Coroner's office:

> ". . . He was dressed in a light hat, blue shirt, vest, pants and drawers. His boots were missing but evidently he had traveled no great distance without them. His revolver he grasped in his right hand; his rifle rested against the tree close to him. He had on two cartridge belts. The undernoted property was found with him and on his person:

"1 Colt's revolver Cal. .45 No. 222, containing 5 cartridges.

"1 Winchester rifle, octagon barrel Cal. .45, model 1876 No. 21-896, containing a cartridge in the breech and 10 in the magazine.

"1 cartridge belt containing 9 rifle cartridges.

"1 cartridge belt containing 2 revolver cartridges.

"6 pistol cartridges in pocket . . ."

So, that was it, and the coroner's inquest had nothing to do but issue the old reliable, "came to his death by party or parties unknown," to write the last word on John Ringgold. Even as they did, fate had to have her last, crooked grin with Johnny Ringo. For the words the coroner actually used were, "Cause of death unknown but *supposed* gunshot wound!"

To this day they don't know who shot the man they found by that cedar tree. At the time, there was only one clue—a clean set of shod-horse prints coming to the tree and going away from it—and that clue faded fast. An hour after the body was found, a late spring thundershower broke and washed the hoofprints clean away into Turkey Creek. All the coroner's jury could do was listen to Old Man Yost, who'd found the body, tell them those prints were from "a hoss that went clean in front saving for a calk inside the front right shoe, and traveled tolerable wide behind, with a left rear shoe that twisted a mite, leaving a sort of a smudge." After that, all they could do was shake their heads, puzzled-like, and allow it was too bad the deceased wasn't able to speak up for himself.

Which you might say it was, providing you agreed it was Ringo by the tree yonder.

For there's one thing you can take for true, call the rest of this story any way you want. It will be the last word on the subject and after it's been set down and you've thought it over, you can make it out any way you see fit.

Johnny Ringo would have known that twisting set of pony prints.

And in the ending

That was all there was to the old man's story. When I pressed him for closer details on the obviously unsatisfactory ending of Johnny Ringo—how he had come by the kid's story in the first place, and so on—his only answer was to shake his craggy white head, stare off into the twilight sky over the mountains to the south of Prescott and the Pioneer's home, and mutter, "That's the end of it, youngster. It's all done and over long ago now, and far best forgot. The kid was bad. He didn't have no good in him. Nobody could know that better than me."

That was as close as I ever got.

I left him there in the growing dark, a tall, straight-backed old man, still singularly handsome. One who, in the proud days of his youth, must have stood some inches over six feet. And who, fifty-one years later, could still startle you with that wild, flashing, light-quick smile.

As I said in the beginning, he never told me his real name and I never asked him.

Somehow, I never felt I had to.

ABOUT THE AUTHOR

WILL HENRY was born and grew up in Missouri, where he attended Kansas City Junior College. Upon leaving school, he lived and worked throughout the Western states, acquiring the background of personal experience reflected later in the realism of his books. Currently residing in California, he writes for motion pictures, as well as continuing his research into frontier lore and legend, which are the basis for his unique blend of history and fiction. Ten of his novels have been purchased for motion picture production, and several have won top literary awards, including the Wrangler trophy of the National Cowboy Hall of Fame, the first Levi Strauss Golden Saddleman and five Western Writers of America Spurs. Mr. Henry is a recognized authority on America's frontier past, particularly that relating to the American horseback Indian of the High Plains. His recent books include *Chiricahua, The Bear Paw Horses, Summer of the Gun* and *I, Tom Horn,* the latter is now a TV movie.